Readers' comments fc

'I found The Limner's Art entertaining, page turning and can't wait for the next book in what must be the first of a series - so many well-rounded characters have been introduced I want to know how they are faring, and relieved there were no dead bodies popping up. Well done to author Kathy Morgan - a ripping yarn'
- Denise J.

'I have just finished the book - desperately wanted a few more chapters to tie up loose ends... From reading your posts on facebook it sounds as though my wish will be granted in the next book(s)!
Really enjoyed it - well done - very impressed'
- Frances H.

'My Mum has finished your book and I quote "I thoroughly enjoyed it, and couldn't put it down". She is an avid reader so that is a major victory'
- Jean H.

'I loved this, great first book.'
- Nova R.

'So enjoyed the read, getting to know the characters very quickly, the plot was brilliant and kept me hooked and on the line to the very end! Looking forward to your next book'
- Frances J.

Kathy Morgan lives on the Dorset/ Wiltshire border, where she runs an antiques business with her partner. They have a variety of animals, and Kathy enjoys exploring the local countryside with her horses and dogs.

The Limner's Art is Kathy's debut novel.

The Limner's Art

by
Kathy Morgan

Copyright December 2015 Stormybracken Publishing Kathy Morgan.
Printed by KDP.

4th edition September 2021

A CIP catalogue record for this title is available from the British Library.

For Bob, who has tried to share his love for antiques with me, and has the patience of a saint.

Acknowledgements

Thank you to all my wonderfully supportive friends and family who have had nothing but encouraging words to say about my first step into the world of fiction writing.

My mum and dad for having faith in me; your encouragement boosted my confidence and gave me the chance to take this next step, thank you.

Special thanks to Clare, Lesley, Fiona, Ali, Elsa, Zaria and Nova who all came up with practical help when I needed it.
And thank you Martin for taking a chance on an author with no track record.
All errors of plot and typos are my own!

Thank you to Linda for allowing me to use the photograph of beautiful Hope on the cover, a Fresian mare xxx

Thank you Charlton Chilcott-Legg for the wonderful image of a portrait miniature on the front cover, and a map of Woodford!

The Limner's Art

There are a variety of ways to access the written word in the twenty first century, and you may have read this in a hardback book or a paperback book, on an e-book, or even listening to it on a CD. Before researching for The Limner's Art I had never realised how fascinating the history of writing was. According to the information available to us, we believe it probably developed in a number of places in the world simultaneously. The earliest records of written words were discovered in Egypt and in China, most likely evolving from numerical signs and ideograms or logograms as a way of recording oral communication. Isn't it amazing to think that some of you will be listening to this story I originally typed into a computer, the evolution of writing travelling in a full circle. The technology for recording and retrieving information has surely developed in ways our ancestors could not possibly have imagined.

If you are reading this in a physical book then the paper we use today has its origins from more than two thousand years ago when manuscripts were written on papyrus and parchment, and over time these formats were replaced with the more durable and practical vellum. A Limner was a person who 'illuminated' these manuscripts with gold and silver, the word limner originating from the Latin word *luminare* which means 'to give light'. As the years passed luminare developed into a general term given to everyone who added any colour or medium of illustration and decoration to the manuscripts.

By the sixteenth century, during King Henry VIII's reign, wealthy book-buyers of the French and English Courts were looking for more luxurious items to buy and show off their riches, and so the illuminations, which by then had evolved into illustrations, were offered independently of the manuscripts as 'Portrait Miniatures'. At the time the word 'miniature' in the title did not mean small; the capital letters in the illuminated manuscripts were coloured with red lead which in Latin is *minium* and the Latin for illumination is *miniatura*, and so it was only by association that the description within 'portrait miniature' came to the present day meaning of a miniature portrait painting.

A limner's art was a portrait miniature, and was a prized possession which only the wealthy could afford. These paintings were delicate and would fade or be damaged easily, and so were usually encased in wood or metal, be integrated into jewellery or snuff boxes, or be displayed as a Work of Art in its own right. Painting miniature portraits quickly became a fashionable hobby for the rich and the upper classes, and in 1612 'Graphice' by Henry Peacham in which he gave advice on 'gentlemanly pastimes', included miniature painting as a suitable leisure activity for his audience.

The artists would use paint brushes made from squirrel hair, and developed their own paints, all neatly protected and stored in wooden work boxes. These boxes were also designed to be used as an easel onto which the artist could position and fix the material on which they were creating their work of art. The portrait miniature artist could then easily carry their work and tools from house to house as necessary.

Although the early portrait miniatures were painted in watercolour onto vellum, artists also drew plumbagos using lead or graphite, but over time these mediums would fade. Enamel painted onto metal became fashionable, and then in the early eighteenth century the artists started to paint their watercolours onto ivory instead of vellum. Trade in ivory had been going on for thousands of years by this time, and although I personally think that ivory looks best on the live elephant or walrus, in those days it was an exciting new material which was more durable than vellum, and gave the artists an opportunity to develop their skills while giving clients a longer lasting keepsake of a loved one.

During Elizabeth I's reign people would wear a portrait miniature of the Queen as a sign of their loyalty to her, and Queen Victoria wore jewellery bearing portrait miniatures of her children.

The discovery and development of photography in the early nineteenth century provided a cheaper way of producing portraits than painting. In 1839 the first commercially available photographic form was the daguerreotype, and this process quickly became popular, the Royal Society of Miniature Painters was established in 1896, but by that time the art was no longer the thriving and lucrative business it had been in the previous centuries, although the art form still continues today. Taking a selfie must surely qualify!

The modern-day commercial value of portrait miniatures varies greatly, depending on the quality of the frame, who the artist was, and who the subject is, if known. If this story spikes your interest then the Victoria and Albert Museum in London (free entry!) houses the national collection of British portrait miniatures in a small, darkened room on Level 3, with a far more in depth explanation of their history and development than I have shared here. There are also several books on the subject including one the V&A have published to support their display titled 'The Portrait Miniatures in England' by Katherine Coombs. The Wallace Collection, another museum with free admission, also has many portrait miniatures at Hertford House in London. These mostly French portrait miniatures were donated by Lady Wallace at the end of the nineteenth century.

If you hadn't been aware of the existence of portrait miniatures before, I bet you will be now!

Character list in alphabetical order:

Alison Isaac – equestrian coach, sister of Jennifer, daughter of Peter

Andrew Dover – antiques dealer

Barry – works at Williamson Antiques

Caroline Bartlett – daughter of Lisa Bartlett

Charlotte Williamson – daughter of Cliff and Rebecca, sister of Nicholas and Michael

Chris Moses – antiques dealer

Christine Black – ex-wife of Paul

Cliff Williamson – owner of Williamson Antiques, husband of Rebecca Williamson

Daniel Bartlett – Black's Auction House employee, cousin of Caroline Bartlett, son of Gemma

Darren Marshall – burglar

Dave Truckell – school mathematics teacher

David Barker – owner of Swanwick Manor, husband of Margaret, father of Frederick

Des – works at Williamson Antiques

Frederick Barker – son of Margaret Barker

Gemma Bartlett – co-owner of The Woodford Tearooms, sister of Lisa, mother of Daniel and Nathan

Hazel Wilkinson – antiques dealer

Hannah McClure – fitness instructor, wife of Ian McClure

Heather Stanwick – daughter of Kim and Robin

Ian McClure – policeman

Jackie Martin – equine vet and mother of Rebecca Williamson

James Wilde – solicitor, husband of Joanna Wilde

Jennifer Isaac – equine vet, girlfriend of Paul Black, sister of Alison, daughter of Peter

Joanna Wilde – antiques dealer, wife of James

Kim Stanwick – wife of Robin, mother of Heather

13

Lisa Bartlett – co-owner of The Woodford Tearooms, mother of Caroline, aunt of Daniel Bartlett

Margaret Barker -

Mark Kenyon – antiques dealer

Michael Williamson – son of Cliff and Rebecca, brother of Nicholas and Charlotte

Mike Handley – landlord of The Ship Inn, and husband of Sarah

Mrs Maxwell-Lewis – farmer

Nathan Bartlett – son of Gemma, brother of Daniel

Nicholas Williamson – son of Cliff and Rebecca, brother of Charlotte and Michael

Nicola Stacey – works at Williamson Antiques

Patty Coxon – Detective Sergeant

Paul Black – owner of Black's Auction House

Peter Isaac – equine vet, father of Jennifer and Alison Isaac

Rebecca Williamson –wife of Cliff Williamson

Robin Stanwick – married to Kim, father to Heather

Sarah Handley – owner of The Ship Inn, and wife of Mike

Simon Maxwell-Lewis – antiques dealer

Tom Higston – barman at The Ship Inn

Tony Cookson – antiques dealer

Also featured:

Ernie – Alison Isaac's horse

Flo – Alison Isaac's horse

Florence – Lisa Bartlett's Staffordshire bull terrier, and sister to Gemma's dog Suzy

Lucy – Jennifer Isaac's greyhound

Maggie – Kim and Robin Stanwick's horse

Mollie – Kim and Robin Stanwick's horse

Suzy – Gemma Bartlett's Staffordshire bull terrier and sister to Lisa's dog Florence

WOODFORD
By Charlton Chilcott-Legg

Chapter One

Monday 9th March 2015, 8.20am

Nicola Stacey hurried down Woodford High Street, her right hand clamped to her head in an attempt to prevent her hat from flying off as the strong wind tugged at it in fierce wet gusts, her stance enabling the bitterly icy rain to run down her arm inside her open sleeve. She wished she had remembered to wear her gloves. She had several pairs but was always leaving them inside coat pockets or hand bags, and unfortunately none were in this coat or the bag currently safely and dryly secured across her body inside the coat. She was relieved to reach the big solid front door of her workplace, Williamson Antiques, but struggled with the stubborn lock and the unwieldy key as the rain poured in a river off the peak of her hat onto her freezing hands when she looked down to check the key's angle. She took a deep breath, muttered something her mother wouldn't want to hear, and tried again; letting out a little 'Yay!' when this time the key went in smoothly and turned easily.

Nicola quickly stepped through the door and into the lobby, grateful to have finally escaped the torrential conditions outside. She had started working at Williamson Antiques when it first opened eighteen years ago, and had been having a similar 'discussion' with the front door lock and key for all those years. Some days she got it right first time, other days, like today, it took two or three goes to unlock the door and although she knew it depended entirely on how careful she was, on days like this March Monday when the weather was foul and she was in a hurry to get in, it always took longer.

Nicola entered the alarm code which hadn't changed in eighteen years either and her fingers pressed the keys in the correct order without her consciously thinking about the sequence or the numbers. Next in the Opening Up routine came the two locks on the inner door, which unlike the front door always opened easily and Nicola's hands and fingers worked automatically. She was through the door, from blustery wet High Street to warm dry antiques centre in less than thirty seconds, despite the delay at the front door, and her still soaking right hand reached up to the six light switches, and they were flicked on 1,2,3………

The scene of devastation in front of her made her gasp, and stop the sequence of the last eighteen years as she stood frozen to the spot.

Slowly her hand moved from the light switches to cover her mouth, her eyes wide with shock as she tried to take in the chaos in front of her. When she had closed the antiques centre the evening before, as always she had taken one last look over her shoulder and smiled at the beautiful tableau filling the enormous room: there had been brightly lit glass cabinets proudly displaying their contents of fine and expensive jewellery and precious china ornaments, and imaginative displays of antique furniture and other home decorations. Now she struggled to comprehend the grotesque sight which had replaced beauty overnight. Instead of neat and ordered displays safely and securely behind glass, there stood chaotic ugly spaces, the cabinets' only contents now jagged shards of glass hideously replacing walls and shelves to the structures, the antiques scattered all across the floor, unrecognisable at first glance, shattered into thousands of pieces. As far as she could see without moving - Nicola's feet felt as though they were glued to the floor, onto which she was becoming aware her soaked but thankfully rainproof coat was dripping – every item had been destroyed. The carefully designed display stands exhibiting all the fine-looking Georgian, Victorian and Edwardian furniture, the stunning crystal and cut glass decanters and drinking glasses, Oriental vases and pictures ornately painted in strong vivid colours, and contrasting delicate English porcelain tea sets, all smashed together into one big mass of distorted wreckage.

Nicola could not take her eyes off the once beautifully crafted furniture which was now in ruins, her brain very slowly starting to take in the details of the wood broken and splintered, the upholstery ripped and the stuffing bursting through the wounds. And in amongst the devastation apparently unbreakable items like the bronze statue of a rearing horse and several sets of fire dogs and fire irons lay like guilty criminals having clearly been used by the vandals to cause most of the damage.

Nicola became aware she had stopped breathing as she tried to gather her thoughts and comprehend what her eyes were seeing. She forced herself to relax her shoulders and let out a shuddering breath, the action seeming to bring on a violent shaking to her whole body, and she started to breathe in short bursts, aware she was whimpering but unable to stop. It was all so shocking, everything apparently destroyed, all the tiny Chinese cups and saucers she had carefully cleaned and re-arranged the day before while the antiques centre was quiet and empty of customers, all the Staffordshire figures which had been gathering dust along the top shelves for the last few months, everything, everything within eyesight was broken.

As her body started to come back to life, Nicola's thoughts began to form some sort of order and she suddenly realised she may not be alone, that the vandals could still be here and watching her, ready to do to her what they had done to hundreds of thousands of pounds worth of antiques. Her feet went from frozen to flight mode in a split second as self-preservation finally kicked in, and she hurriedly backed out of the door and turned and ran out into the street, pulling her phone out of her bag as she went, the thought to lock-up and re-set the alarms not even entering her head for the first time in eighteen years as she burst into the relative safety of the café next door to phone the police.

Chapter Two

Monday 9th March 2015, 9.45am

The Woodford Tearooms was one of many local businesses which had thrived in part because of the commercial success of Williamson Antiques. Antiques dealers live on cups of tea and coffee, and love nothing better than to sit around a table on comfortable chairs discussing deals and gossiping, so on a daily basis, either on their way to or from the antiques centre, or in some cases both, any number of dealers would pop in to the tearooms and spend a few pounds on food and drink whilst loudly discussing the silver price, or for many more pounds quietly complete a deal or two.

The Woodford Tearooms had changed hands three years ago and was now run by a pair of sisters in their forties, Lisa and Gemma Bartlett, both of whom had been married and had their children young, and were now older, wiser, single, and thoroughly enjoying running their own business together. Also because they had four children aged 17-21 years old between them, they had plenty of help in the evenings after school or college, at weekends, and during university holidays.

Since the sisters had taken over the business they had made a few alterations to the internal appearance of the Edwardian building. The first change had been to the décor, warming up the stark white walls with light paint colours and decorated with pretty landscape paintings of the area by a local artist who was only too pleased to use the sisters' tearooms as a gallery in exchange for a small percentage for the sales of her artwork. They replaced the red gingham table cloths and curtains and the ancient dusty artificial flowers in the windows with single coloured table cloths and chair cushions, and added fresh flowers to the tables collected from their own gardens or during their early morning walks with their Staffordshire Bull Terrier sisters Florence and Suzy.

They had also installed a large cabinet along one wall displaying ceramics and hand-made jewellery, all by local artists, with the dual purpose of promoting local business with attractive art and craft work adding to the ambience of the tearooms.

The heavy brown chipped pottery teapots which poured their hot brown liquid contents everywhere but into the practical white pottery cups had been replaced by a variety of pretty lightweight fit-for-purpose teapots with clean spouts. The sisters had scoured the local Drayton Flea Market, Black's Auctions and next door's antiques centre for the mismatched flowery china trios on which to serve tea plus something delicious for those who wanted to indulge; the something delicious also presented on silver plate tiered cake stands.

A High Street business cannot survive on tea and cake alone, so the sisters had also built up a popular breakfast and lunch menu, which was supplied in chunky mugs and substantial bowls and plates, perfect for feeding hungry walkers, cyclists, horse riders, and antiques dealers.

It was through the front door of The Woodford Tearooms that a highly distressed and soaking Nicola had rushed an hour earlier, her mobile phone clamped to her ear as she gave precise details of where the police urgently needed to come to and why. Gemma and the only two other customers, a couple of mums grabbing a quick cup of coffee after dropping their children off at the local school, had instantly sprung into action to help her. Within minutes they had re-organised tables and chairs and retrieved her soaked outerwear so that Nicola could continue to make the necessary phone calls in relative comfort.

Now her wet hat and coat, which was still dripping, hung on the stand by the front door, but she was comfortably seated next to the wood burner which was still warm and glowing from the day before, slowly sipping her second hot drink since she had arrived. The first had been a Hot Chocolate which Gemma had decided was the best thing she could offer Nicola considering the circumstances. This second mug was full of tea, and Nicola sat holding onto its warmth with both hands as though she would never let go, shivering even though she had long since dried out from the rain outside.

The local police had turned up within a few minutes of her call, and had quickly ascertained there was no one still in the antiques centre. PC Ian McClure and PCSO Sophie Boston had already briefly interviewed Nicola where she now sat, in what she felt was a rather unsatisfactory information-gathering session for everyone present. There really was nothing more she could tell them than they could see for themselves, other than the doors were locked as they should be, the alarm was on until she turned it off, the lights were off until she turned them on, and she didn't see anything out of the ordinary until that awful scene of devastation once she was inside the room.

Sarah Handley, the landlady of the local pub, The Ship Inn, and her best friend, was with her now.

After first phoning the police, and then Cliff Williamson her boss and the antiques centre's owner, Sarah was the next person she called. Sarah had left the drinks delivery for her husband to deal with and rushed straight down the High Street to the tearooms to be with her friend, passing Williamson Antiques as she went. She had slowed down to peek in as she drew level with the entrance, but her view was blocked by the closed solid oak front door, so Nicola's description of the scene was the only one she had, but that was vivid enough for her to have a good idea of the thorough job the vandals had completed on destroying all those antique items.

Although most of the stock in the antiques centre left her cold, Sarah did have a weakness for portrait miniatures and had been eyeing a pair housed in an intricately and ornately carved wooden folding frame, dated around 1770, of a newly married couple. She loved family history, and as well as continually researching both her family tree and her husband Mike's, she had started to test her skills by trying to build a picture of the families around the portrait miniatures she collected. Anyone who has ever dipped their toe into the Family History pool will know what an all-consuming passion it is, and Sarah had found that her recent menopausal night-time awakenings could be put to very good use. She was currently following an intriguing story about a great great third cousin and his various medical complaints, all of which, it seemed, had been reported in the newspapers at the time. Running a public house is a full-time job, with unsociable hours, which means that spare time for personal leisure activities is valuable. Sarah and Mike were careful to manage the rota of staff so that they could both have time off together and individually

24

during every month, and she spent her personal non-pub time engrossed in genealogy.

Sarah had been considering whether to buy the portrait miniatures from the antiques centre, and had made a quick search on the family name to see if it would be an interesting study, but hadn't made up her mind whether to go ahead. Well, she thought to herself, the thieves have made that decision for me then! Judging by Nicola's vivid description everything breakable was destroyed, so a couple of delicate watercolour paintings on a thin sheet of ivory behind glass in wooden frames, however skilfully crafted and ornate, were not going to survive being stamped on by a few heavy pairs of boots.

Her heart went out to Cliff and Rebecca Williamson and all the stallholders. What an awful thing to happen. She didn't even own the portrait miniatures and she felt their loss keenly. What on earth must it be like for them?

Sarah turned her attention back to her friend, who had finally run out of phone calls and hysterical adrenalin and looked exhausted. Nicola's skin was drained of all colour, the pallor accentuated by her dark eyes and hair, her normally sleek and perfect bob awry from nervously running her hands through her hair while she was with the police in an effort to remember in the exact order details of her shocking discovery only an hour before.

Sarah put her hand on her friend's arm. 'Come on pet, no point staying here any longer, why don't we go back to yours and put the kettle on? I'll buy us a couple of slices of that delicious apricot flapjack, and we can relax in the comfort of your sitting room for a while.'

Nicola smiled at her, grateful to her friend for taking charge, and followed her out of the tearooms, past

Williamson Antiques and back up the High Street to her cottage.

Chapter Three

Monday 9ᵗʰ March 2015, 10.30am

A Monday morning in March is a quiet time in the tearooms so Gemma would usually be working there on her own, but on that particular Monday she was run off her feet with customers, including an almost constant demand for takeaway teas and coffees, not something she would usually supply but the police presence and distressed antiques dealers next door needed sustenance. By mid-morning Woodford Tearooms was filled with local people and antiques dealers, including some of the distraught stallholders whose stock had been, at the very least, badly damaged in the antiques centre, all concerned to find out what had happened.

Very little goes on in the antiques trade without someone knowing something, or foreseeing it would happen, but in this case there really wasn't any information coming up as a possible cause for such a devastating attack on one of their local businesses. It still wasn't known at that point what was missing, so theft was where the main focus of speculation was concentrated, with quite a number of stallholders beginning to generate lists of likely people and places where their precious stock could end up. Suspicion and mistrust was thick in the air.

Gemma called her sister for help and more supplies, so once Lisa had made a quick stop at the local shop for more provisions then she and Gemma were kept busy in the tearooms for the next few hours.

'Four more bacon sandwiches, two coffees, one tea, and one hot chocolate please Lisa!' called Gemma through the serving window.

When the sisters had bought the business from the previous owners they had spent some of their money redesigning the layout so that the kitchen was not closed off from the tearooms, and one person could easily supervise the customers and prepare food during the quiet times. The large serving window made it much easier to keep an eye on the customers while also preventing them from wandering into the cooking area.

Gemma leaned over the wide shelf into the kitchen and added in a whisper 'look who's here, do you want to serve him?' she said, with a cheeky grin and wink.

'Him' was Andrew Dover, and Lisa had a huge crush on him. Gemma was pleased that her sister was finally starting to show an interest in the opposite sex after a really horrible time when Lisa had discovered seven years before that her husband had been cheating on her with two other women at the same time, and had a son with one of them. The divorce had been ugly, her two children had been devastated, and the three of them had clung together in a desperate way for a number of years until finally Lisa began to realise there was life after such a ghastly experience and had begun to allow her children to start to have lives of their own too.

It had been Lisa's idea to start the tearooms, and Gemma was only too pleased to join her as she had reached a crossroads in her life. Gemma had come to realise that the joint catering business she had with her own husband wasn't 'joint' so much as 'his', and she was getting frustrated with the situation while he was perfectly comfortable with their status and was not

28

prepared to change to accommodate her. Despite their differences her husband had fully supported her decision to leave and start up a new commercial venture with Lisa. Once they had agreed to dissolve their business partnership it wasn't long before Gemma and her husband admitted to themselves and to each other that it had only been the catering business which was keeping them together, and so they separated with relief, few bad feelings on either side.

Gemma hadn't seriously contemplated starting a new relationship with anyone, she was far too absorbed in her business and with trying to keep track of her own two children, although 'children' was a familial term these days she supposed as they were 19 and 21 years old. Nathan was away at agricultural college and rarely came home except with a car load of washing and requests for money, while Daniel had moved out two years ago to live in a rented flat with a friend, and worked at Black's Auctions in the town. But seeing Lisa's reaction over the last few months every time Andrew Dover walked into the tearooms, the way she blushed and couldn't look him in the eye and forgot whatever order she had just taken or whether or not she was holding the jar of cinnamon in her hand because she was about to or had already put some into the cake she was making, was awakening something long forgotten in Gemma.

The sisters had discussed Andrew Dover at length, and both decided that he didn't have a clue about Lisa's feelings for him. Lisa was certain he didn't feel the same about her, but Gemma wasn't so sure about that. She had noticed that he only ever came in on the days Lisa was working so it was unusual to see him on a Monday, and she wanted to observe his reaction when he realised Lisa was there too.

'Go on, I'll carry on making those sarnies, you come out here and take his table's order, he is here with Tony Cookson and some man I've never seen before.'

Lisa grinned, checking that her long blond curly hair was securely fixed into the French plait she routinely wore for work, identical to her sister's.

'OK, here goes, give me the pad Gem 'cos I'll need to write this down or I'll forget something simple in the order like a cup of tea!'

Once the women had swapped places and Gemma was sure the bacon wasn't going to burn she peered around the corner of the serving window from where she had a good view of the table Andrew and his friends were sitting at. As Lisa walked towards them, self-consciously holding her tummy in and determined not to stutter and blush as she always seemed to when he was in the room, Gemma smiled with delight. Andrew's face was a picture! He was in mid-sentence and stopped when he noticed Lisa, seemingly unable to tear his eyes away from hers as she carefully manoeuvred between the chairs and tables which filled the space in between them.

'Lisa!' he exclaimed, 'I didn't know you worked here on a Monday morning?'

Lisa's spirits plummeted like a whole heap of stones. Instead of the delighted welcome she was expecting Andrew sounded peeved rather than pleased to see her.

'Oh, er, I don't, well I am today, obviously, but no, no, I'm not usually here on a Monday morning, sorry, er…'

Gemma groaned and turned back to the bacon, which was now on the Quite Well Done side of the bacon cooking spectrum. Short of running out and taking Andrew's order herself she couldn't help her younger sister out of the enormous pit of embarrassment she seemed to have stepped into. Even from the kitchen Gemma could see how red her face was.

'Come on Lisa,' Gemma muttered under her breath. 'Just take their orders and come back in here to safety.'

She was feeling guilty for encouraging Lisa to go out there and speak to him, so she busied herself with making the sandwiches and drinks rather than carry on watching the disastrous scene unfolding in the tearooms.

'Three teas please Gemma' sang a voice through the hatch.

Gemma whirled round, and there was Lisa, still bright red but smiling and able to talk properly. 'Oh Lisa are you OK? That looked excruciating!'

By now Lisa had come into the kitchen, which meant they could talk relatively privately.

'Oh wasn't it awful' laughed Lisa. 'I thought he was cross that I was here, and all my confidence deserted me in one massive swoosh, I couldn't even take their order properly, Tony had to repeat his request for tea four times. But guess what! Andrew has just asked me if we can make a birthday cake for his Mum's 70th next month. Isn't that wonderful!'

'Oh, yes, wonderful!' said Gemma brightly, before allowing a slight frown to pass across her face. She wasn't too sure why it was 'wonderful', but if her sister was happy then so was she.

Chapter Four

Monday 9th March 2015, 10.45am

Andrew Dover suddenly realised Chris Moses, the third man at their table who specialised in Treen items, had asked him a question.

'Sorry, Chris, what did you say?'

Tony and Chris exchanged looks. 'I asked you if you had lost much stock in the burglary next door? But perhaps you would like to tell us more about the waitress who just took our orders!' said Chris, with a grin and wink.

'Oh, what? You mean Lisa? Oh, yes, she and her sister are the owners here, they both work really hard and this place is a real success because of them. Have you tried their Shepherd's Pie? Lisa makes it using lamb from the Higston's farm over in Brackendon. Delicious. And their Victoria sponge, she makes that too. Lisa makes the most delicious cakes so one of hers would be perfect for Mum's 70th birthday party next month. Mum hasn't been well recently, so Rachael, my sister, thought it would be a good idea to give her something to look forward to. Mum and Rachael are planning a party with as many members of the family as possible. Rachael reckons there will be over one hundred and sixty of us, so we're going to have it at The Ship Inn, in their function room at the back. Sarah and Mike have been really good about helping us out, given us a big discount because we are local, and because of the number of people we have invited. My sister reckons you should count on at least ten percent of invites being declined, but so far everyone has accepted, plus four more members of the family have been added. It's going to be huge! People are coming from all over the world to celebrate Mum's birthday, I think the furthest will be coming from Australia, with another five coming over from Canada. Mum is absolutely thrilled; it definitely gave her an incentive to get up and about again after her knee operation. She doesn't want to be using crutches on The Day. Actually could you chaps excuse me, I'd better ring Rachael and tell her I have ordered a cake.' And with that Andrew drew breath before hurriedly pulling his phone out of his pocket and turned away from them, only too aware that he had been gabbling, so pleased to be talking about Lisa he couldn't stop himself.

'Love' mouthed Tony to Chris, with a nod towards the kitchen.

'Yup!' mouthed back Chris, with a grin.

Chapter Five

Monday 9th March 2015, 4.00pm

Sarah was absolutely right, thought Nicola. She had been revived after a few hours of rest surrounded by her home comforts, although her boss Cliff, and work colleagues Barry and Des, had been in phone contact with her all day. Now that she had recovered from the shock of the morning's events she felt ready to head back to the antiques centre and begin to coordinate the mass clear-up operation, even though she knew they wouldn't be starting today.

Nicola was a practical person, she liked order and logic, so wanted to have an idea of what they would all need to do to restore the antiques centre to its former glory. The few seconds she had spent in the doorway that morning had not been enough to properly set out an action plan for the immediate future.

Nicola walked in through the open doors of Williamson Antiques to find that Cliff Williamson was still in shock, standing staring at the total and utter devastation which now filled the space that had previously been his beautiful antiques centre.

He was a big man, both in personality and in stature, with auburn hair he kept close cropped or it would erupt in curls all over his head, which he hated, his normally playful hazel-coloured eyes now fixed in an unnatural-looking wide-eyed stare, hardly blinking at all, his tanned skin now a ghostly greenish-white. He was usually a positive force wherever he went, easily sensed and heard before he was seen, his energy and enthusiasm for living infectious on those around him. But today Nicola thought he looked shrunken, and a good deal older than his forty two years, so much so that she almost hadn't recognised him.

When she had phoned Cliff that morning with the terrible news, she was starting to suffer from the shock of it all and struggled to string two words together, but he had gently and firmly told her to stop and catch her breath, and then calmly asked her: a) had she phoned the police and b) was anyone hurt. After that he had told her to stay where she was and he would join her in the short time it took to drive from his home to the antiques centre, which on that day was seven minutes instead of the usual quarter of an hour.

Although initially he had gone straight to the antiques centre, he only walked through the lobby, saw the scene of devastation, turned on his heel and out the doors to find Nicola in The Woodford Tearooms. Once he was sure she was alright and safe in the capable hands of Gemma and Sarah, and that she hadn't seen any of the intruders, he went back to the antiques centre to wait for the police.

But now as she stood quietly and observed him she could see that his intrinsic calm and the no-nonsense practical approach with which he had tackled everything the day had hurled at him seemed to have drained away, to be replaced by turmoil, despair, uncertainty and a strong sense of defeat.

Nicola had worked for Cliff for eighteen years, and had enjoyed every moment. He was a fair boss, clear about the direction he wanted his business to move in, a hard worker, loyal to his staff, and they were loyal to him in return.

She had realised before she left her home they wouldn't be doing any clearing up that day. The police and scene of crimes officers hadn't finished their investigations, and more photographs would need to be taken by police officers from a different department. Nicola, Cliff, Barry and Des all felt the same about seeing the hard work that went into sustaining and constantly developing Williamson Antiques eradicated so violently in one night, for reasons they were all still apparently in the dark about, and all four of them needed some time to gather their thoughts and revive their energy and enthusiasm for the project. Des and Barry had gone home earlier that day, back to their wives and comfortable clean and ordered homes, away from the mess that was their workplace. But Nicola felt the enormity of the task ahead of them was overwhelming, as she stood with her employer, silently contemplating the undertaking they would soon be attempting.

'I don't think there is any more you can do today Cliff,' she said, quietly, putting her hand gently on his shoulder. 'Why don't you go home now? I'll lock up for you.'

It took a while for him to respond, and she almost repeated her suggestion, but then he slowly shook his head, still staring out over the mess of his broken business and said: 'Thank you, but no, you go, I'll lock up in a minute.' And then as she prepared to leave he took a deep breath, straightened up and pulled back his shoulders, turned to look directly into her eyes and said in a much stronger voice, throwing his arms about to illustrate his point, 'although I'm not sure there is much point is there? There isn't much left to steal, and the thieves can get in undetected anyway, despite all the alarms and cameras and locks!'

Taking another deep breath, he stopped what had rapidly been turning into a loud angry rant, gathered his thoughts and said more quietly 'I am so sorry Nicola, you have been fantastic today, I know it has been a shock for you too. Well, for all of us. Obviously don't come back into work until I've been in touch, I'll give you a ring when I have an idea of where we go from here. Thank you for all you have done today.' And with that his body seemed to shrink down again as he turned away from her, back to face the nightmare that had been his dream.

After Nicola had left, Cliff closed the doors behind her and went over to lean on the counter where he laid his head on his arms, and sobbed.

A few minutes passed before he stood upright, wiped his eyes and nose with a handful of tissues from the box under the counter, and went upstairs to wash his face.

The police hadn't been able to tell him much other than the vandals had gained access through an upstairs window, which was more than he had been able to tell them, he didn't know anything useful for their investigation. Nothing appeared to have been stolen - there were enough undamaged valuable bronzes and items of jewellery mixed in amongst the broken, smashed and dented stock to suggest that theft had not been the motive, and this amount of damage didn't justify nicking a few glass decanters or pottery meat plates, plus the safe didn't appear to have been touched, nor anything upstairs to do with the running of the business.

There had been far too many people through the antiques centre over the previous days and weeks for any meaningful forensic evidence to be gathered; the alarms hadn't been activated, nothing was on the surveillance tapes, both the ladder used to reach the window and the doorstop used to break the window were kept in the yard at the back of the building, and the vandals had not left any useful drops of blood, fingerprints, boot treads, or hair to identify them. No other businesses had been affected, and nobody had come forward to say they had heard or seen anything. The police were not very optimistic that there would be a quick result, and neither was he.

As he walked back down the stairs Cliff gasped out loud when he felt a sharp physical pain in his gut as memories came pouring into his brain of all the hard work which had gone into developing this successful and thriving business, his mind replacing the horrors of the day with images of the past. All those years of carefully building up the reputation of Williamson Antiques, one stage at a time. Cautious planning and project management ensuring each tranche of stallholders were firmly established before expanding the numbers again, so that each new stage of development could be paid for by the previous one until eventually the whole of the ground floor of the nineteenth century building was filled with (mostly) quality antiques, all individually displayed in thirty-six different stands and cabinets according to the dealers' preferences and stock. The time and skill he had put into weeding out the ones who put little or no effort into maintaining their stands, booting out the ones who stamped all over everyone else's hard work. The fun he had coaxing, enticing and supporting dealers whose track record and stock suited his vision for his very own Antiques Centre.

Cliff sat halfway down the white painted wooden staircase as he closed his eyes, his face contorted in misery while he thought about all the effort he had put into saving the money needed to spend up front in the early days, to buy and then develop the building in the way he wanted it, the big gamble he had taken a few years later with his family's future by obtaining a rather large bank loan so he could shell out as-yet unearned cash for the shop's fixtures and fittings, for the lighting system and display stands and cabinets, for the advertisements on the local radio and in the local papers. This enormous cash outlay had enabled Cliff to compete with other antiques centres in Brackenshire for the best dealers, promoting his business so they would want to take a stand or a cabinet in Williamson Antiques, and to ensure that every item of their stock could be displayed to its best advantage and justify their faith in his business.

It had taken several years before the business had not only paid off its debts but also started to pay for itself, and even more before he could earn a decent wage.

By that time he had a wife and children to support, and he chose they live a lifestyle which he felt truly reflected his status as a successful business man in Woodford: they lived in a big six bedroom detached house on an exclusive estate at the edge of the town with fantastic views across the fields to the sea a few miles away; he and his wife, Rebecca, both drove expensive cars, always turning them in for a newer model after a couple of years. Admittedly that was probably as far as their family expenses went. They didn't take big family holidays, the children went to the local state schools so no eye-watering school fees to pay x 3, and their annual food and clothes bills were probably on the low side for a family of five.

Cliff's contorted expression of pain changed to a frown as he sat up a bit straighter and wondered where he could save money on expenses, because he was going to need a lot of money in the next few months and maybe even years if he was going to get this business back up and running. There was nothing of use in any savings account to help now, or even cash hidden away under the mattress or in a biscuit tin as his grandmother used to do. When he had first started out he was fortunate that in those days the banks were only too pleased to lend people like him money; you knew your Bank Manager and he knew you, and in Woodford the local bank manager had been a Regular in The Ship Inn so Cliff had often shared a pint or two with him, but the man had long since been moved onwards and upwards away from the area. Cliff grimaced; he didn't imagine the faceless teenagers who now made the decisions at his bank would support him if he went with those original business proposals and financial forecasts, or even updated ones to suit the developments in the antiques world since then. Both the financial world and the antiques world had seen a lot of changes since those days, and none of them were for the better as far as he was concerned.

He just didn't know how, or if, he was going to start again. His whole world had collapsed in one destructive orgy of violence by persons and for reasons unknown.

Cliff had moved to the town of Woodford about twenty years ago from London to work for the previous owner, Emily Grant. In those days it was called 'Woodford Antiques and Collectables' but was really a bric-a-brac shop. Emily and her husband Shaun had needed somewhere to store, sort and hopefully sell all the stuff they acquired from house clearances, so they had bought the former haberdasher's shop when it came up for sale in the 1960s, mainly because it had a useful yard at the back which was accessible from the lane behind and meant they could drive their van straight in and unload without holding up the High Street traffic. It also had a flat above where they could live. When Shaun died suddenly after a short illness Emily had realised she needed help if she was to continue in business, and so she advertised for an assistant and Cliff had applied and been given the job. She had wanted someone with experience of selling at car boots and flea markets, who wasn't afraid to work for a living, so she could finally clear out years and years of accumulated junk and fulfil her long-held dream of running a second-hand bookshop.

Although Cliff had lived upto Emily's expectations and made a good start on bringing some form of order to the jam-packed shop, he only succeeded in clearing about half of the accumulated junk before, tragically, Emily died of a heart attack whilst on a cruise ship in the Mediterranean. In the end she only survived her husband by a few months, and it was the first holiday she had ever been on. When Emily and Shaun were married they had two nights 'honeymoon' in his aunt's Guest House in Southsea, Portsmouth, before he had to return to work in his father's rag & bone business.

Cliff grew very fond of Emily in the short time he had worked for her, and knew that her life had been a lesson to live for today, not wait until tomorrow. But now, as he sat on the stairs of his once thriving and successful very own Antiques Centre, surrounded by his broken dreams, he wondered if living for today for the last twenty years had all been worth it. What did he have to show for it now?

Emily and Shaun had no children, and there were no living relatives that anyone could find, or a Will, so the shop and its contents, including their personal belongings in the flat overhead, were sold quickly and quietly through probate by the local firm Francis & Sharpe, to Cliff. Meeting Rebecca a few weeks before completion of the sale, in the local pub The Ship Inn, was perfect timing as far as Cliff was concerned. He felt he was ready to settle down with a wife and family, both of which he was sure would suit his expanding business image.

Rebecca was nineteen years old, very attractive, tall with a curvy figure and long curly black hair, and for her it was love at first sight. She was instantly and absolutely head-over-heels in love with this confident young man who had already achieved so much at only twenty four years old, and had big plans to achieve even more. They were engaged within a month, married within five months, and their first baby was born seven months later.

Cliff emptied and gutted the Victorian building, completely re-designed the layout so that the flat became the office and workroom with a vast open plan retail space downstairs, whilst keeping the yard at the back as a car park area for dealers who had stands and cabinets in the antiques centre.

He started with just twelve dealers and a waiting list of eight more, and jubilantly held the Grand Opening in September 1997 of Williamson Antiques. All the local shop keepers and other Woodford business owners came, glad to support a new enterprise on their High Street, and specifically one which looked so clean and up-market after the state of the previous business on those premises.

As he sat on the stairs eighteen years later it seemed so long ago, as though someone else had put all that time and energy into building up the business. Now he had a family to support, a place in the community to uphold, and a reputation in the antiques world to maintain. Cliff doubted he would have the ability to do it all again, and at that moment he didn't want to find out if he had been comprehensively defeated.

Chapter Six

Monday 9th March 2015, 6.00pm

While he was working hard, establishing and developing Williamson Antiques into the successful business it had become, Cliff had made several very good friends and allies in the antiques industry, and one of those friends was Paul Black. Paul was a good looking man, a similar age and size to Cliff, but with slightly-too-long (in his mother's opinion) brown straight hair, and both men liked to keep fit by running several miles together along the local country lanes most mornings, occasionally competing in local triathlons and marathons.

Paul owned Black's Auctions, a well established busy provincial independent auction house in Woodford, with regular weekly general sales of household items and bi-monthly specialist sales including Oriental, Railwayana, Automobilia, and Vintage Clothing.

Black's Auctions was originally started by Paul's father in the 1980s, and it had successfully evolved over the years as the demands of the trade changed, so was still going strong unlike many other antiques auction houses. When the Grant's house clearance business had ended with Shaun's death, Paul's father had quickly stepped into the gap in the market, and now there was a four-man team and two liveried vans answering calls for help over a wide geographical area, collecting and delivering a variety of shapes and sizes and valued goods to private houses, shops and warehouses.

Paul had mainly learned his trade by going out to the private house calls and discovering how to sort the collectable and saleable from the stuff destined for the dump, and although he had made some very costly mistakes in the past, usually by believing something to be more valuable than it actually was, he was far more knowledgeable now and rarely made an error, or when he did they weren't such large ones.

Paul would often come into Williamson Antiques in the weeks before a Specialist Sale looking for suitable items he could add to the catalogue to make sure there were a decent number and quality of items to draw the good paying buyers in.

Both he and Cliff had been flirting with the whole Selling Antiques Online game, and neither were particularly keen on the process, whether by auction, as a shop, or in Paul's case putting his auction catalogues online and even allowing his auctions to be viewed over the internet in real time, but they both knew they would have to bite that bullet sooner rather than later and make it work for them. Neither could grasp the concept of buying an antique you haven't touched, peered at intently for several minutes, even smelled and in some cases tested with your teeth!

They ran the only antiques businesses in the immediate Woodford area, and the two men worked with each other well, although there were several other antiques centres and shops in the rest of the County of Brackenshire, and three other auction houses, including one an hour away in the County town of Swanwick.

Paul was the first person Cliff telephoned, even before he rang his two other employees Des and Barry and before contacting any of the stallholders, when Nicola had called him with the news of the break-in. Cliff wanted to know if the auction house had been similarly attacked, but he also badly needed some moral support when he went to go and see for himself the damage Nicola had tried to describe over the phone to him. It had been a good decision to involve Paul, his friend brought just the right amount of balance to the day by being slightly removed, unlike everyone else in the vicinity who was directly involved, and if anyone was going to lighten the atmosphere with a few well-placed jokes and derogatory comments it was Paul, whilst still having a deep understanding of the seriousness of the situation. Paul had been backwards and forwards between the antiques centre and his own business, and was now knocking on the front door Nicola had been wrestling with a few hours earlier. Cliff roused himself from the miserable pit he was dwelling in and let him in.

And so it was with Paul that Cliff finally left the scene of devastation, and instead of turning left to go to the tearooms, they turned right to go to the pub. The Regulars at The Ship Inn were eager to buy Cliff a drink, as much as a chance to find out any news as to show solidarity for one of their own who was in bad shape.

'Whisky, Cliff?' called out James Wilde, the local solicitor, a small white-haired man with a sharp face carefully outlined by a sculpted beard.

'Thanks James, that is just what I need,' replied Cliff, gratefully, smiling for the first time that day as the warmth of his fellow Regulars' sympathy started to unknot, just a little, the tension in his neck and shoulders.

The three men took their drinks to the snug, where the fire in the small Victorian grate had been lit earlier in the day, and sat on the old stained velvet covered benches which ran around the walls of the small room. James winced as he bent down to move one of the chairs closer to the table.

'You OK? How are the ribs?' asked Paul.

James had been mugged a fortnight earlier, when he and his wife had been away for the weekend for a Valentine's romantic getaway which had ended in a hospital visit and police involvement. The mugger had not been caught so far, and James did not have much expectation that he ever would be. James had not been able to give the police any description of his attacker, and although his phone and wallet had been stolen in the attack, both were found just a few metres away, the wallet still containing all the cards and cash for their evening out.

'Fine, fine, so long as I remember not to do things like that!' grinned James, as he carefully sat down on the chair.

Soon they were joined by Tony Cookson, another of Cliff and Paul's close friends, a postcard dealer, who came in with his wife Lesley who ran a local publishing business, and also by James' wife Joanna who was a jewellery dealer and a stall holder in Williamson Antiques. Joanna was very quiet, like all the other stallholders she had been feeling a range of strong emotions all day, and now she just felt extremely tired. Obviously the destruction of the stock she had for sale in the antiques centre was going to hurt her financially, although she was one of the lucky ones whose stock was harder to damage than others so there were some surviving and saleable pieces. She would feel the loss of the antiques centre, however temporarily, as a vehicle to sell her stock, but Joanna was also a good business woman and the jewellery she sold through Williamson Antiques was not her only source of income. She was keen to know what Cliff's plans might be, whether he had any idea of who the vandals were and why they had done it, and when he was planning to re-open.

It seemed that every stall holder was in the pub that night, and that every stall holder wanted answers to the same questions they had been asking Cliff all day, but he still didn't have the answers. Eventually he just sat back and let the noise wash over him so that people finally got the message and left him alone.

The drinks kept coming though, while the events of the day were chewed over and over as more people arrived, and soon the snug lived up to its name. The noise levels would reach a crescendo with everyone talking at once, offering up theories, re-telling events of the day as they knew them, and recalling old arguments and disagreements Cliff had had over the years with various 'characters' in the antiques trade.

Chapter Seven

Monday 9th March 2015, 7.30pm

Rebecca Williamson frowned as she looked at the kitchen clock; Cliff was usually home by seven o'clock in the evening on a Monday, after he'd had his usual post-work pint and/or whisky at The Ship Inn, although it wasn't unusual for him not to phone to tell her he was going to be late. She had given up waiting to eat with him years ago, instead preferring to sit down with their children at six o'clock for their evening meal, and leaving Cliff's on the warming plate. She finished stacking the dishwasher and turned it on, before going upstairs to check that all three children really were sitting at their computers working and not playing games or on social media.

Once she was satisfied everyone was hard at work she went back downstairs to phone her mother, Jackie Martin, from whom Rebecca had inherited her stunning looks, and whose favourite pastimes were Zumba and holidaying in Portugal when she could get away from her veterinary practice in Woodford. Rebecca was looking forward to sharing with her mother the weekend's activities of her own daughter Charlotte, the youngest of the three Williamson children, who had been competing in a swimming gala the day before.

'Oh my goodness Rebecca, I've been waiting for you to call, I didn't know whether to phone you or if you'd be busy helping the police. How are you? How is Cliff? Is there any news?'

Rebecca's mind went blank as panic set in. She felt a wave of ice cold take hold of her body and bile rise up her throat into her mouth, as she started to shake. She had no idea what her mother was talking about but it sounded bad.

'What, what's happened to Cliff? Where is he? Is he alright?'

'Cliff? He is fine as far as I know; it's just the stock which has been damaged. Rebecca, haven't you been with him? At the antiques centre?' she asked curiously. Jackie realised something wasn't quite right about her daughter's responses to her, and changed her tone to a gentler one. 'You do know what's happened Rebecca, don't you?'

By this time panic was rapidly being replaced by anger, the chill she had been feeling morphed into heat, relief making Rebecca uncharacteristically lash out at her mother.

'Well clearly no, Mum, I don't know what has happened, just tell me please!'

'Your antiques centre was broken into last night and everything has been ruined!' Jackie exclaimed. 'You must know, everyone knows!'

'Well I don't know, you are the first adult I have spoken to all day, I've been cleaning out the utility room since half past nine this morning until the children came home from school, and they didn't say anything about it,' said Rebecca, a sulky note entering her voice. 'So no one has been hurt? Nicola, Barry, Des, everyone is safe?' she asked, pulling herself together.

'No one hurt that I have heard,' said her mother. 'Has Cliff really not told you?' she asked, exasperation creeping into her voice although she was trying hard not to upset her daughter any further.

'No, he hasn't,' said Rebecca. 'It's not like him,' she said, clearly puzzled by the information her mother was giving her.

Her mother wisely kept her thoughts on that subject to herself.

'Oh where is he? He is usually home by now. Why hasn't he told me what is going on? Oh, what is going on! I'd better hang up now mum and give him a call, he may be trying to get through. Bye, thanks for letting me know, I'll ring you when I know something. Love you!'

Jackie carefully replaced the receiver of her home telephone and sat back in her chair, a thoughtful expression on her face.

Chapter Eight

Monday 9th March 2015, 9.00pm

'Oooh I've just had a thought, I bet it was Tom the Clock, do you remember when he beat you to an Edwardian longcase clock at that auction in Sussex a few years ago, and he went round telling everyone that general dealers like you shouldn't even bother turning up to bid on a clock like that because you didn't understand the value of them, and he ended up with egg on his face when it turned out to be a 1950s fake? I bet it was him!' exclaimed Paul Black.

Everyone in the room instantly fell about with laughter, all the tension of the day finally finding a release at the thought of poor old Tom the Clock being the perpetrator of the extensive damage caused at the antiques centre. The man was over six foot tall and weighed at least 125kgs. He struggled to get in and out of his car so the idea that he could even climb a ladder, let alone manoeuvre his great body through the first floor toilet window of Williamson Antiques, struck everyone as hysterically funny, tears pouring down faces of men and women alike as everyone elsewhere in the pub looked in surprise towards the snug, wondering what had caused such a loud outburst of hilarity.

Suddenly, as if a switch had been pulled, the noise levels plummeted into silence, and everyone sat gazing at their drinks, surreptitiously wiping away the tears which had only a few seconds earlier been joyfully running down their cheeks. No one had been injured that anyone in the pub were aware of, but this was still a violent attack committed by persons unknown who may even be in the room with them, and it was not a laughing matter. People started to glance uneasily at each other, quickly looking away when they made eye contact, shifting in their seats as they tried not to look guilty of suspecting their neighbour. The evening continued in a far more subdued and muted way until eventually everyone made their excuses and left, eager to get away from the oppressive atmosphere which had descended on the gathering, until the only people remaining were Cliff, Paul, James Wilde and Tony Cookson. The questions of Who and Why were no nearer to being answered by the time Mike Handley, the landlord, called Time.

The three men were standing up, unsteadily, putting on their coats, checking their pockets for keys and phones, Mike had called a taxi for Cliff; Paul, James and Tony all lived close enough to walk home. They were the last ones to leave the pub, sombrely making their way through the pub's front door out into the shockingly cold night when suddenly 'Rebecca! Has anyone told Rebecca?' exclaimed Tony.

Chapter Nine

Wednesday 11th March 2015, 11.00am

Rebecca and her best friend Christine Black, a shapely blond woman with perfectly straight blond hair cut in a precise horizontal line below her shoulder blades and always with a meticulously combed side parting, were in The Woodford Tearooms having a catch-up over a couple of cappuccinos and a slice of carrot cake each. They had been friends since school, and Christine and Paul had started going out together as boyfriend and girlfriend at around the same time Rebecca and Cliff had met. The Black's two children had been born in the same school years as Rebecca and Cliff's youngest two, so they had stayed friends as their lives followed similar paths, sharing the ups and downs of motherhood together.

The two couples used to regularly meet up when baby-sitters allowed, and the Williamson and Black families holidayed together at an adventure park two or three times a year. Everything came to an abrupt end when, nine years earlier, Paul had an affair with a woman who looked the complete opposite to Christine in that she was stick thin with a mass of unruly brown curls. Rebecca had sided with Christine, while Cliff had sided with Paul – it is hard not to take sides in those situations – and so their comfortable social life of the first few years of married and family life had suddenly come to an end.

For Christine that was probably the worst time in her life, when she hit rock bottom and felt she had lost all her confidence and self-respect. Paul's affair had come as a total shock to her. She had no idea there was anything wrong with their marriage, and his choice of woman who was, physically at least, so completely opposite to Christine was utterly demoralising for her, and his betrayal had been devastating.

After several years of extreme animosity from the time Christine had first become aware of the affair, sustained through a very unpleasant divorce, and then exacerbated by the – in her view and those of several people who knew them – indecent haste within which Paul and Monica were married, Christine had gradually been able to re-build her life, even to the extent that she and Paul could at least be civil with each other. The fact that Paul also cheated on Monica and they were divorced three years ago had contributed a tiny bit, but by that time Christine was able to rationalise their life together and so was able to feel sorry for Monica who, if she was honest with herself, had never really trusted Paul because of the way their own relationship had started, and had lived in fear of the day she would find out he was having an affair.

For the last six years Christine had been really happy and enjoying life again. Her hair and skin had suffered during those initial dark years, her hair was coming out in clumps at one point, and it had taken its toll on her self-confidence. She had lost a number of 'friends' who could no longer put up with her one-track conversation about Paul and Monica, obsessing about what they were doing, how they were paying for it, who they were with. There weren't many people who chose to be around such a miserable and depressing person, but Rebecca had stayed by her side, regularly trying to steer her friend's focus onto something more positive, but rarely succeeding.

It was only when Christine realised that she was in a chicken-and-egg situation and was the only one who could stop the downward spiral and bring happiness back into her life that things started to improve for her and she was able to find some joy in her life again. Yes Paul's behaviour, and Monica's too, was despicable and cruel, but she was not going to be able to change her own life for the better if she kept allowing their behaviour and actions to infest her thoughts all day every day.

One of her few remaining friends had been on one of those Journeys of Self-Discovery which Christine had always scoffed at, and her friend's new-found self-belief and obvious love of life had regularly pissed Christine off because she saw her friend's confidence as conceit, and her ability to look on the bright side and take something positive from a poor situation as naivety, or worse, deceiving herself.

The nights were the worst times during that period, when Christine rarely if ever slept through the night, and would wake up from horrible nightmares, or just be unable to switch her mind off from obsessing about Paul.

It wasn't until she was sitting hunched in a chair in the kitchen, nursing a camomile tea which her friend had recommended to bring peace and relaxation so she could finally go to sleep, but instead found herself thinking evil thoughts about her friend who probably was gently snoring at this very moment, that Christine understood what she had to do.

From that time onwards she made a huge effort to alter her attitude, to try to view things differently, to put more effort into looking after herself and moving forwards with her own life, rather than stagnating, worrying about what everyone else was doing. Immediately she felt better and had her first solid night's sleep in three years.

Christine made a big effort to turn her life around by trying new things like Zumba classes and volunteering one morning a month at the local Riding for the Disabled centre. She also made time every day to read, something she hadn't done since she was a teenager, and had discovered how much she enjoyed historical non-fiction books, losing herself in the romance of the architecture or marvelling at how luxurious modern life is now compared to the hardships and suffering of past times.

Her transformation from under her dark cloud still took a long time to emerge, as those old negative habits had been ingrained in her daily routines for many years, but Christine suddenly realised one day that she was no longer having to make an effort to think and act in her 'new' way, it had become her normal attitude. Her self-confidence started to return, then her hair started to bloom and shine, her skin cleared up, she looked years younger, and as Rebecca looked at her that morning she smiled just because her friend really did look radiant.

Now as they sat together on one of the cushioned window seats Christine looked at her friend sympathetically. 'And you had no idea until your mother phoned you?'

'No, I told you, I was up to my eyes in muck from moving all the appliances in the utility room!' Rebecca said, slightly defensively, her voice rising. She didn't want Christine voicing what she was trying to ignore. 'Anyway,' she said, shaking her long black hair back and attempting to change the focus of the conversation which was moving dangerously close to something she wasn't ready to think about, 'the whole thing is a bit of a mystery. Nothing seems to have been stolen, nobody seems to have a motive, no one knows anything, it is all a bit weird. Poor poor Cliff is really upset, he has worked so hard on that antiques centre.'

'Is he going to re-open it?' asked Christine, recognising what Rebecca was trying to do and kindly going along with her friend's wishes.

There was a pause.

'Oh I expect so!' said Rebecca, breezily, realising she didn't have a clue what Cliff's plans were, she hadn't asked him and he hadn't shared them with her. This was turning into a minefield. 'Shall we have another pot of tea, or is it time for lunch. I see Lisa has made her delicious spicy butternut squash soup for today's menu.'

Christine accepted her friend's need to change the subject, but was worried for her. This obvious lack of communication between her two friends was unhealthy, but for several years it had been the case and Rebecca had either deliberately or genuinely been unaware there was a deep problem in her marriage. Christine knew it wasn't her place to pursue the subject, and that her dear friend was clearly not open to discussing it, so as they were waiting for their lunch to be served she started to tell Rebecca all about the new man in her life.

'Oh he is just so sweet, and kind, and lovely,' she enthused. 'His name is Dave Truckell.'

'Not Mr Truckell, head of maths at Woodford School!' gasped Rebecca.

'Yes! My kids don't know yet, so you must not say anything until I am ready to introduce him.'

'OK, I won't breathe a word. How exciting! He is rather gorgeous, but I thought he was married?'

'Oh he was, but he and his wife split up last year.'

'How many times have you seen him?' asked Rebecca.

'Um, oooh, I think about five times now? Let me see, we met socially at my cousin's wedding so that's one, then we went for lunch at the Italian on the seafront, that's two, then we…' Christine ground to a halt as she remembered what they had done after the Italian lunch, and looked guiltily at her friend.

'Go on,' said Rebecca, her face lighting up at last. 'You went to bed with him didn't you! After only *one* date! You can't count your cousin's wedding because you were both already there!'

'What? Yes I can!' said Christine, laughing as she desperately tried to defend herself and not making a very good job of it. 'I waited five days before I slept with him, it's not like I just jumped into bed without knowing anything about him! We have been texting and emailing each other,' she said triumphantly, and then feeling that success was coming her way, 'plus I have had to sit through a few parents' evenings over the years you know, when he taught my boys.' She laughed. 'Anyway, this one is different, he is so lovely. I can't wait for you to meet him properly, without a teacher's desk between you. And it was well worth waiting for five days, we were like rampant teenagers! It's been two years since Phil.'

'Stop!' laughed Rebecca, 'I haven't had sex in I don't know how long, probably longer than two years, so I really don't want to hear the gory details about your successful love life. Well, seriously Christine, I do hope this one turns out to be better than the last two.'

'Yes, I was a bit unlucky there,' Christine said ruefully, rubbing her chin. 'What are the odds of the first men I sleep with since Paul both being married! Their poor wives. Cheating bastards like them ought to have a big sign branded on their foreheads which reads 'DO NOT TOUCH WITH A BARGE POLE.''

'That's a bit long to go on their foreheads isn't it?' said Rebecca, very seriously. 'I think it should read 'WARNING, NOT TO BE TRUSTED''

'That's almost as long!' exclaimed Christine. 'I think they should have 'BEST SERVED COLD' tattooed on their manhood. Or what about just the word 'CHEAT'!'

Other diners looked over at their table wondering what the joke was as both women giggled and laughed their way through several other versions of the warning sign, coming up with more and more humiliating ways to get their message across, until they were forced to use the paper table napkins to dab their eyes as their make-up threatened to streak down their faces.

Chapter Ten

Wednesday 18th March 2015, 6.30am

'Happy Birthday darling!' Rebecca drew open the curtains in her eldest son's bedroom and turned to look at him as he reluctantly emerged from under his duvet. 'Seventeen years ago today you made me the happiest mother in the world,' she swooped down and gave him a big hug. 'My little baby boy.'

'9lbs 2oz, four days late, eighteen hours labour' recited Nicholas with a grin, having heard it all before.

'And perfect,' his mother finished for him. She smiled as she ruffled his hair, just like his father's. 'Look how tall and handsome you have grown up to be. Hurry up and shower, your Birthday Breakfast will be ready in half an hour.'

It was a tradition in the Williamson household to celebrate their birthdays with the opening of cards and presents from the family over breakfast, and meant everyone had to get up earlier than normal. This hadn't been a problem when they were younger, indeed Rebecca had made a rule that no one was to leave their bedrooms before six o'clock in the morning on a Birthday Morning, but now the children were all teenagers it was a struggle to get the boys up in time for school, let alone even earlier for a birthday celebration. Charlotte had usually been to swimming training and home again by the time the boys emerged from their bedrooms, but Wednesdays weren't training days so she too could sit down with the rest of them and enjoy Nicholas's seventeenth birthday breakfast. The only member of the family missing was Cliff, who was away overnight at an antiques fair in Birmingham, and the rest of the family weren't expecting him home in time for dinner either. Nicholas had chosen a meal at The Ship Inn to celebrate with his family, and then his friends had something else planned for the weekend.

By the time Nicholas was washed and dressed his mum, brother and sister were already downstairs in the kitchen, all three of them eagerly awaiting his arrival.

'Come on Nick!' yelled Michael up the stairs to him. 'If you don't hurry up I'll open your cards and presents for you.'

There was a thundering of footsteps down the stairs.

'Oh no you don't you little ratbag,' yelled back Nicholas, affectionately. 'Keep your hands away from my presents.' He pulled up short at the kitchen door, a look of crushing disappointment on his face because instead of the usual pile of cards and brightly wrapped presents on the table, in front of his chair was one single white envelope.

'What's going on, has everyone forgotten me?' he asked, looking around at their faces, as every member of his family kept their eyes fixed on the floor in front of them. He slowly made his way over to the envelope, taking in his sister's barely disguised giggling and his brother's furtive glances out of the kitchen window. Nicholas picked up the envelope, felt it, shook it gently, and then opened it. Out fell a key.

'Oh my god oh my god oh my god' he started to shout. 'It's a car isn't it, you've bought me a car! You are the best Mum in the world! Where is it? Is it outside?' and with that he rushed out of the kitchen, fumbled with the front door handle before flinging it open, and there on the driveway was his very own vehicle. Charlotte and Michael had followed him out, almost as excited as he was, they had both been sworn to secrecy since Rebecca had collected the car two days before, and had helped to hide it in their huge four car garage at the side of the house.

He could see there was something on the front seat, and when he opened the door he saw it was another envelope. Inside was a voucher for ten driving lessons with a local driving instructor.

'Yes!' Nicholas shouted, holding the voucher up high, before jumping into the driver's seat and putting the key in the ignition.

'Oh no you don't,' laughed Rebecca, as she gently removed the key from the car's ignition. 'There is a little matter of applying for your provisional licence and passing your theory test before I'm letting you turn that key darling.'

'Oh Mum!'

'Everyone has contributed to this car, your Nana, both your Grandparents, Uncle and Aunty Williamson, Uncle and Aunty Parker, and Charlotte and Michael, so you have a few Thank You letters to write. Once you have sorted out the paperwork and passed your theory test you can get going with the driving part. You'd better get out of there and go and log on to the DVSA site.'

Before she had finished speaking Nicholas was already out and running back into the house. She turned to her two younger children and the three of them stood in the driveway having a big group hug, laughing about how excited Nicholas was, pleased their secret plan had been such a success.

Chapter Eleven

Tuesday 7th April 2015, 10.00am

Cliff stood in the large empty space which only a month ago had been a thriving business stocked with valuable and not-so-valuable antiques, one of The Places in the area the antiques trade would make an effort to visit regularly, his pride and joy. Today it was a source of despair and misery for him.

 Although the police arrived on the scene very quickly after Nicola's call, and had questioned all twenty seven stallholders plus Cliff and his family, Nicola, and Des and Barry, there was still no information available, no one seemed to know anything. There were no clues, no leads, nothing had been stolen, there had been no threats or suspicious-looking people in the days and weeks leading up to the attack.

The mystery of how the place had been entered and exited, apparently leaving the locks and alarm intact, had been easily answered, and Cliff had a very useful afternoon with a Crime Prevention Officer who had some excellent advice for the future. The vandals had entered the premises by smashing the upstairs toilet window at the back of the antiques centre, thus avoiding the window and door alarms which would only be activated when a window or door was opened. Then they had cleverly evaded the security cameras which covered the front of the antiques centre including the lobby and the counter area, but not the upstairs office and storage areas, and covered only a small area along the back of the salesroom where there were windows and a door. This was also where the architectural and garden stock were displayed so the easy access to the yard outside could be utilised for collection and delivery purposes of these usually heavy items.

All of this meant that the majority of the vast antiques sales area was unprotected. Cliff had believed no one could get to it without triggering the alarms so hadn't spent the extra money on total surveillance, and instead had put up dummy cameras, something he rather regretted doing now, and which all of the stallholders had been cross about as they had believed the place was totally covered by security cameras.

The fact that whoever had done all the damage must have known about this big hole in Cliff's security system was almost the only thing the police had in the form of a clue for their investigation, but as the existence and positioning of the dummy cameras was only known to the security company, Cliff and his staff Nicola, Barry and Des, all of whom had strong alibis and no apparent motives, it wasn't a great start to solving the mystery. Cliff knew it wasn't him, and couldn't believe it of the other three as they would certainly be out of a job if he couldn't get things back up and running, plus their salary was worked out as a basic low rate with the addition of a percentage of the overall takings, so it didn't make sense for any of them to have effectively destroyed their own income. The security company were quick to deny any involvement, and neither Cliff nor the police could suspect this local reputable firm who had a one hundred percent track record.

In the final post mortem there was very little salvageable from what had become the waste ground on his once-beloved shop floor, either in terms of the shop's fixtures and fittings or of the stallholders' stock, other than a few robust items of jewellery and the bronzes and iron items, and the main counter area which had been untouched presumably because it was covered by security cameras.

Fortunately whoever had broken in hadn't trashed the office area upstairs, so details of stockists and suppliers, as well as client information, were all still available and usable. In the end it had only taken a morning to clear up the wreckage. Cliff hired three skips, and he, Rebecca, Nicola, Barry, Des and all the stallholders had carefully sifted and sorted as best they could, everybody coming together in this time of crisis and working very effectively as a team, forming a human chain to pass the remnants of their livelihoods out of the building. They were united, sharing each other's despair at the loss of their stock, their earnings, their investments, but also having it in their hearts to feel genuine pleasure for the owner when something entire and therefore saleable was uncovered and retrieved.

Once they had finished, and everybody had left, Cliff was left alone with his silent bare building and his thoughts. He had never felt so lonely in his life.

Chapter Twelve

Saturday 18th April 2015, 10.30am

Lisa stepped back to admire her handiwork. She was very pleased with how Andrew's mother's birthday cake had turned out. Originally Andrew had asked for a Victoria sponge with some icing and the numbers 70 spelt out in candles, but when his sister Rachael came into the tearooms to, as Lisa quickly realised, check up on her brother's uncharacteristic burst of effort in the organisation of their mother's party, she recognised Lisa's talent for birthday cakes stretched much further than sponge, icing and candles, and between them they designed a far more extravagant cake.

'Oh Mum, that is spectacular!' exclaimed Lisa's daughter, Caroline, who had just bounced into the room after her morning run. 'Who's the lucky birthday girl?'

'Oh, just the mother of one of the antiques dealers who comes into the tearooms,' said Lisa casually, desperately hoping her daughter couldn't see her heart thumping at least ten times its normal rate as she thought of Andrew Dover, who would be coming to her house, *her house*, to collect the cake in half an hour.

'Do not touch it please!' she called out over her shoulder as she rushed upstairs to have a quick shower and change before he arrived. Cake making was dirty business and she wanted to look at the very least reasonable.

'Oh Mum!' cried Caroline again, although this time she was complaining not complimenting. 'I need a shower now!'

'I'll only be a minute,' Lisa yelled down the stairs, as she stripped in seconds and leapt into the shower before her daughter could beat her to it.

By the time Andrew rang the doorbell Lisa had showered in record time, even washing her hair, and was dressed in jeans and a frilly white shirt, although her plan of having an immaculately made-up face and gorgeous blond curls falling down her back had been replaced with no make-up and her wet hair dripping down her shirt. Checking herself in the mirror she grimaced at what she saw. When she had run through this scene over and over again she had imagined herself looking casual yet elegant, entirely different from her familiar tearooms' uniform of green polo shirt and jeans, plus green and white stripy apron when she was cooking, her hair tied back from her face in a neat plait, and if she was lucky a dab of foundation and mascara which usually didn't make any difference to the redness of her complexion from cooking and rushing about with food and drink orders. When she opened the door to Andrew she could already feel the familiar heat rise up her neck and infuse her cheeks, although fortunately by this time Caroline was safely locked away in the shower so wasn't there to observe her mother's obvious feelings for the man standing on her doorstep.

Lisa smiled and said 'Good morning Andrew, your mother's cake is all finished for you.' Exactly as she had practised. Phew, she thought to herself, at least I managed to get that part right.

However Andrew's reaction didn't go as she had planned when she had rehearsed their meeting several times in the preceding days. Instead of looking as though he couldn't resist her, and then leaning in to sweep her off her feet, he just stood on the doorstep staring rather oddly at her.

Andrew started coming into the tearooms because he had taken a cabinet in Williamson Antiques a few months ago, and the tearooms were conveniently situated for a quick cuppa or bite to eat after he had been in to re-stock his cabinet and check how everything was going. But a few weeks before the break-in at the antiques centre he was finding himself coming into Woodford just to go to the tearooms and using the antiques centre as an excuse for the trip, in the hope Lisa would also be there, and once he knew her work schedule he was able to guarantee to see her.

Andrew had been trying to pluck up the courage to ask her out on a date, and decided that the next time she was working he would ask her, but on the 9th March he had been taken aback by her emergence from the kitchen because he knew she didn't usually work on a Monday morning, and all his carefully planned speech flew out of his mind. When he asked her to make the cake for his mum's birthday his mouth was working entirely independently of his brain, and he had been kicking himself ever since as he didn't want to ask her out after that in case it complicated things with their business arrangement about the cake. But this morning he was very glad he had asked her to make his mum's birthday cake because it gave him the opportunity so see Lisa in her home environment.

However, as he stood rooted to the spot on her doorstep, he was struggling to concentrate on anything because she looked incredibly sexy having clearly just stepped out of the shower, and her wet hair was making her white shirt see-through, sending inappropriate thoughts racing through Andrew's brain. He was incapable of saying anything, let alone the smooth invitation to dinner he had been planning.

'Come in, come in' she smiled, and stepped back to allow him through the door.

Andrew shook himself back to the present, took a deep breath and prepared to ask her out there and then.

'Hi Mum! Hello,' said a young man as he breezed past Andrew, enveloped Lisa in a bear hug, and headed off into the house.

'Hello darling,' said Lisa, who hadn't been expecting her son to come home this weekend. Damn, she was sure Andrew was going to say something before Robert had appeared. Recovering her composure she yelled 'Don't Touch Anything!!!!' as she realised Robert was heading for the kitchen. 'And don't let Florence into the kitchen! Florence is the dog,' she explained. 'Come on Andrew, you had better rescue your mother's cake before my son eats the whole thing in one mouthful.'

Andrew grinned and followed her into the kitchen, where he stood in the doorway, this time gazing in awe at the creation on the work bench.

'Oh my goodness Lisa, this is amazing, Mum is going to love it!' he exclaimed, and then added nervously 'I'm going to be worried about moving it.'

'Don't worry,' she said. 'The cake is made up of four separate sections, and they will be perfectly safe in these boxes on your passenger seats with the seat belts around them. You can fit them all back together when you get to The Ship Inn, see?' she demonstrated how each section was independent of its neighbour. 'Come on, as Robert is here he can help you.'

Once the cake was safely and securely installed in Andrew's car, Andrew drove off with Happy Birthday wishes ringing in his ears from Lisa, Robert and Caroline for his mother, and still he hadn't opened his mouth and asked Lisa for a date.

Lisa opened the door of the boot room. 'Come on then Florence, let's go for a walk,' she said to the grinning wiggling Staffie. 'At least you are always keen to go somewhere with me!'

Chapter Thirteen

Wednesday 22nd April 2015, 10.00am

DS Patty Coxon was sitting at her desk in Swanwick Police Station, the north policing hub for the County of Brackenshire, looking at the latest information from PC McClure of the Woodford Police on the case of the vandalism at Williamson Antiques. Woodford and the surrounding villages were hardly Crime Central, usually all the police had to deal with were the typical rural crimes of thefts of heating oil, red diesel being used to power non-farm vehicles, minor drug offences, a few burglaries, and frequent traffic accidents.

The crime committed at the antiques centre was curious because no intelligence had been received about it either before or after, and nothing else had happened which could be related to it. There was just one incident the police had on file that could be linked, although Patty was well aware it was a very precarious connection. It was an unsolved assault and possible attempted mugging on the husband of one of the stallholders a few months before. As with the attack on the antiques centre there appeared to be no information or motive for the assault on James Wilde in February, and Patty knew she was clutching at straws in trying to link the two crimes, because although his wife's stock had been damaged during the attack on the antiques centre, so had every one else's.

Patty got up from her desk, stretched, took her glasses off and walked over to the corner of the large work room where the kettle was constantly in use. She made herself another cup of coffee, added a dash of milk, and ambled back to her desk, her face frowning in concentration as she endeavoured to find something substantial to investigate in either of the two cases.

Whoever had attacked the stock in the antiques centre had entered and exited the premises without leaving any trace, and you needed a good head for heights and be fairly fit and athletic to climb the ladder and then break a window before climbing in. The people were so thorough in their destruction of the items, and yet able to avoid detection by the surveillance cameras which were switched on and working, that it was unlikely to be a one-off incident. Plus they must have had inside knowledge to avoid the, admittedly minimal, security systems in place. If Williamson Antiques had been an easy target then the many thieving criminals in the UK would have targeted it long ago.

Patty had talked to her police colleagues in Woodford who were familiar with the victims, and they had all come to the conclusion it must have been a grudge against the owner, Cliff Williamson, although they didn't have anything to base that on. There wasn't even a wall of silence in the antiques trade, just a black hole, she thought grimly to herself. The most recent report from PC McClure didn't contain anything new, and she was beginning to think they needed another crime to be committed if they were ever going to solve this case.

Patty sighed, and turned her attention to the next case on her list, this time to a tip off about local and illegal sales of pornographic films. Apparently someone in the area had been producing and selling a series of 'Reader's Wives' type films for several years, and the person who had anonymously sent in the tip-off calculated the pornographers had pocketed in excess of three million pound tax-free.

She had seen some of the films. They were hilarious! Each film was set in a bedroom poorly disguised to look like something else, for example a barn or a prison cell or in one memorable case the cab of a fire engine. Each had a 'storyline' lasting about thirty minutes, which always started with the female doing something sexually explicit to herself on her own, before the male knocked on the door and she stopped what she was doing to let him into the room. They all appeared to 'star' the same heterosexual couple judging by their bodies, of which much could be seen although the actors' heads and faces were disguised by heavy make-up or covered in masks, and elaborate wigs were also a regular part of the costumes both parties wore. There were three fixed camera positions and the couple always engaged in the same sexual positions in the same order in each film she had seen. The scenes were explicit, but nothing which broke the pornography laws in the UK. They were just in very bad taste on so many other levels, not least the costumes and the acting. The man was strong and athletic with well-defined muscles and clearly took care of his health and fitness. And she was sure that if that was the same woman then she had had at least two surgical enhancements to her breasts over the years, they looked as though they had gone up several cup sizes whilst the rest of her body had stayed more or less the same! If it hadn't been for the illegal earnings aspect home movies like this would never have reached the attention of the police and the HMRC.

74

Chapter Fourteen

Wednesday 22nd April 2015, 10.00am

Andrew Dover took a deep breath and pushed open the door of The Woodford Tearooms, determined that after his failure on Saturday then today was the day he would finally pluck up the courage to ask Lisa out on a date. Over the last few weeks since he booked her to make his mum's birthday cake they had managed to have a few conversations with each other without too much blushing and falling over their words, but he still hadn't been able to take that next step. He was annoyed with himself for not making a move when he collected the cake from her house. Every time he thought the moment was right something happened to interrupt them, and the moment was gone.

Lisa looked up as the little cow bell tinkled to notify that a customer was entering the room, and smiled a welcome, admiring as she always did his gorgeous brown eyes which awoke something primeval deep inside her and sent her brain into a tizz. Andrew couldn't stop the big wide smile spreading across his face when he saw her, but 'Andrew, over here!' called Tony Cookson. As Andrew made his way over to Tony, weaving between the wooden chairs with their pretty coloured padded cushions neatly placed around tables of varying sizes with matching tablecloths, he was aware of Lisa's eyes following him.

'Hi Tony, sorry I kept you waiting,' he apologised. 'I just popped into Black's Auctions to view this weekend's sale, and before I knew it I was half an hour late. There is a lovely portrait miniature by John Boyle in there, and some Napoleonic medals. Did you see them? Any idea who put them in?'

This was partly true, in reality Andrew was late because he had been rehearsing how he was going to ask Lisa out whilst he was viewing the auction, but he was genuinely interested in the portrait miniature and the medals, as well as some of the Victorian jewellery. Auction houses are not allowed to tell anyone who has put the items in for sale, so antiques dealers are always trying to guess whether or not they come from one of their fellow dealers, in which case they can have an idea of where the item originated from and whether or not it is worth buying or if it will have already done the rounds and been seen by anyone they may wish to sell it on to. However if it had come from a private house and therefore termed fresh-to-the-market then the chances are it will be much easier to sell on quickly for a good price. There is also always the chance that if the seller is an ordinary member of the public then they may not know precisely what the item is, and so if it has also been mis-catalogued by the auction house then a dealer who knows its true value can pick up a bargain.

'That's OK mate,' said Tony. 'Gave me a chance to catch up on my auction sales results from the weekend. Yes I saw the portrait miniature and the jewellery, must have missed the medals. I think the jewellery has come from Simon Maxwell-Lewis, not his usual way of selling jewellery, I thought he always sold it straight to Joanna Wilde. But then I should think all of you who have lost stock when next door was attacked will have to change your modus operandi for a while?'

'True for dealers like him, I suppose, he does seem to have been hit very hard. I hadn't realised he made so much from selling that furniture of his in the antiques centre,' mused Andrew. 'I think I'll have a crack at buying the medals anyway, I have an online buyer who I think would like them. I'll have to ask Joanna about the jewellery and see why she hasn't bought it straight from Simon. I am sure her business must have taken a big knock from the attack on next door but she still appears to have plenty of stock and plenty of cash, so there must be another reason.'

Tony picked up the menu 'What are you having? I could do with some more coffee.' He turned around and called 'Lisa, could I have another black coffee please?'

'Yes, anything else?' she asked, looking at Andrew.

'Oh a coffee for me too please, but I'll have milk with mine. Thanks Lisa. And I'll have a cheese toastie please, I'm starving.'

'Oh yes a cheese toastie for me too, that's a good idea, thanks Lisa.' agreed Tony. 'So, tell me about these medals?'

The two men were soon engrossed in discussing the medals Andrew had seen in the auction, and then moved on to the amazing result one of their fellow dealers had at a different auction the previous week with a music box she had bought for three hundred pounds at an antiques fair the year before, and it had sold for seven thousand pounds.

Lisa was then kept busy as other customers came and went for the next hour, although she kept peeking over at Andrew and catching his eye as he was doing the same to her. By eleven o'clock Gemma had appeared, and the two sisters settled down to the routine of Wednesday lunchtimes which were always busy, so it was with a plummeting sense of disappointment that she noticed his chair was empty and she realised he had left without saying goodbye. She went over to clear the table of coffee cups and cake plates – both men had later succumbed to chocolate brownies – and wondered when she would see him again.

The day after his mother's birthday party Andrew had delivered an enormous bouquet of flowers to Lisa's house, which Caroline had received for her and left on the kitchen table so she saw them as soon as she walked through her front door. The card revealed they were a Thank You from his family for the birthday cake, which his mother had loved and had insisted lots of photographs were taken before anyone took a knife to it.

Lisa had created the cake in the form of a chocolate dance floor and decorated with a small band of edible musicians and several edible dancing couples. Rachael had told Lisa about her mum's former career as a professional ballroom dancer on the cruise ships, which was how she had met her future husband, Andrew and Rachael's father. He had been a trombone player, and twenty years older than her, and a widower. According to Rachael it had been love at first sight, and within weeks their romance had blossomed and the Captain of The Ship had conducted their marriage ceremony on board while sailing over the Pacific Ocean.

Her husband had died some years ago after a long illness, and their mother had found True Love again with a former school friend, although claimed she had no plans to marry him, but Rachael wasn't so sure and was hoping there would be An Announcement soon.

Lisa wasn't home when Andrew delivered the flowers, and after shyly thanking him the next time he came into the tearooms, had only spoken to him in reference to food and drink orders since then, but she had been desperately trying to work out how to engage him in conversation other than 'and would you like butter on your roll?' or 'yes, those scones were made fresh today!'

She sighed, beginning to think maybe she wasn't ready for a new romantic relationship just yet, and wiped down the tablecloth before turning to take the order of the three young mums who had come in for a quick early lunch before collecting their children from nursery.

If only she could pluck up courage to ask him out. But where? Where did people go for a 'date' these days? The Ship Inn or the Italian in Woodford were the only two places she could think of, but then what would they talk about all evening when they could barely string two words together for the few minutes they spent in each others company now. The cinema? Did people still go to the cinema for a date? No that would not do either, what about all the time spent waiting for the film to start, they would have to talk then, either that or sit in awkward silence. And what film would they see? All her kids seemed to watch were horror and teen movies, Lisa had no idea what other films were shown at the cinema, she hadn't been for over twenty years when Braveheart and the Die Hard films were showing. Mmmmh, Bruce Willis, Mel Gibson, those were the days, she smiled at the memories.

The cowbell tinkled as a tall, lean, grey haired man entered the tearooms. He looked around and seeing an empty table headed for it whilst taking off his jacket. Gemma watched open mouthed, he was the most gorgeous man she had ever seen! She signalled to her sister that she would take his order and eagerly rushed over, pad and pen in hand.

'Good morning! Have you been here before?' she asked.

'Good morning!' he replied with a smile, looking up at her so she could see he had gorgeous deep blue eyes designed for gazing into, and making her body tingle. 'No, this is my first time. I'm starving, thought I'd grab some lunch before my meeting this afternoon. What do you recommend?'

Lisa watched enviously as her sister and the stranger easily fell into conversation, her sister showing no sign of embarrassment, no reddening of her cheeks or faltering over her words. The two women were very similar in appearance but almost completely different in personality; Lisa was quieter and liked to think things through before committing to anything, exploring every angle for possible dangers and pitfalls, whereas Gemma was more impulsive and outgoing.

Lisa sighed, why couldn't she have that ease and confidence with Andrew? Even now that she was finally able to hold a conversation with him, the topics were limited to what he would like to eat and drink in the tearooms. How hard could it be to expand into a wider range of subjects?

'Oh my goodness isn't he lovely!' gushed Gemma as she rushed into the kitchen. 'Don't worry about serving him, I'll take care of it,' she winked.

The lunchtime rush picked up, but Gemma still managed to be extremely attentive to the stranger whose name was Peter Isaac, a vet who specialised in horses, and who had an interview with Jackie Martin at Woodford Equine Veterinary Clinic that afternoon.

By the time he was ready to leave the tearooms Peter and Gemma had arranged to meet up in The Ship Inn later that day once she had finished work, to celebrate or commiserate depending on the outcome of the job interview.

Lisa was pleased for her sister, and even more determined to devise a way to spend time with Andrew, away from the tearooms.

Chapter Fifteen

Wednesday 22nd April 2015, 6.45pm

'Pint, Cliff?' offered James Wilde, as Cliff walked in through the door of The Ship Inn.

'Great, thanks James, just what I need after today.'

'What have you been doing?'

Cliff took his baseball cap off and rubbed his hand over his head. 'Trying to get some paperwork finished and phone calls made while the electricians have been working putting in the new cameras. The deadline for re-opening the antiques centre is looming and there aren't enough stallholders yet. I have been ringing round all the old ones and not enough people want to come back in while this crime is still unsolved.'

James felt sorry for Cliff, he looked so tired and miserable. 'Here you are,' he said as he passed Cliff his pint. 'Are the police still no closer to solving the crime?'

'I haven't heard a thing, either from them or from anyone in the antiques trade. Nothing else seems to have happened anywhere which could be related. I was a bit worried it was a personal attack on me but if that was the case then surely they would have attacked me or my home or even my family by now? All very strange. Oh well, thanks for this,' and he raised his glass in a toast to James.

Over the next few minutes they were joined by a few more Regulars, and their conversation was interrupted so everyone could be greeted as they came through the door. There was much shuffling around finding chairs, tables, ordering drinks, some ordering food, trips to the toilets, others nipping outside for a cigarette.

Once there was a lull in new arrivals James and Cliff found themselves next to each other again.

'How was the antiques fair over in Kent yesterday?' asked James.

'Oh it was really good, thank you,' Cliff visibly brightened up. 'That one is always full of gear, I bought this stonking pair of portrait miniatures, and I really reckon them, they are of a Georgian couple. Here, have a look,' he said as he pulled a bundle of tissue paper out of the inside pocket of his denim jacket. James looked obligingly at them, he really wasn't interested in antiques but had perfected the 'Oh how interesting' look after being married to an antiques dealer for all this time. Cliff carried on regardless. 'They'll go in Paul's Art auction in October, should make a tidy profit with any luck. Although at this rate they'll be the only income I'll have by then,' and he sank back into his gloomy reverie.

'What have you got there?' Sarah Handley had spotted Cliff's portrait miniatures.

'Oh you'll like these Sarah,' said Cliff, grateful to find someone genuinely interested in the treasure he had found. 'Two examples of the Limner's Art at its finest.'

'Oh these are beautiful,' she exclaimed. 'Look at the quality! The frames are good too. I wonder who the artist is? Looks like they could have been painted by Penelope Carwardine, here in the corner are her initials P.C. I love her work. Difficult to get hold of though Cliff, you've done well here. What a find! A shame nothing is written on the back to show who they are, but with a bit of research I bet you could find out.'

Cliff picked up on Sarah's hopeful expression. 'Go on then,' he laughed. 'Have a look for me, let me know when you find something.'

'Yes!' she said, before turning away to serve a patiently waiting customer at the end of the bar.

As soon as she had gone Cliff resumed his gloomy expression and his shoulders slumped back down.

James sighed, and turned as Tony Cookson appeared at the bar. 'Evening Tony, I hope you can help me cheer Cliff up, he's on a right downer today.'

'What's up Cliff? I thought you had a good time yesterday at the fair?'

'Oh I did, yesterday was good. It's today that's the problem. I can't drum up much interest for the antiques centre. I wish the police would pull their fingers out and hurry up and solve this mystery. I think they've given up and the details are lost deep in a filing cabinet somewhere.'

'Do they still use filing cabinets?' mused Tony. 'I'd have thought everything was on computers these days.'

'Yup,' said James, 'Computers and the internet are the only way to disseminate information. My business couldn't operate without them.'

'Oh don't say that,' groaned Cliff. 'I hate the bloody things. Thanks to internet auction sites and television programmes everyone's a bloody expert. It is killing the antiques trade.'

'Yes you're right there,' agreed Tony. 'All these wannabes think they are at a car boot sale when they go to an antiques market. They go around asking for Trade or Best price as though they have earned it! What have they got to Trade with? Bloody cheek, I start to raise the price if they annoy me.'

'At least you lot expect to have a bit of a deal,' Mike Handley joined in their conversation from the other side of the bar. 'I had some red trousered wally in here trying to haggle with me about the price of a bottle of wine at the weekend! I had to chuck him out in the end. As he went he was making all sorts of threats about never coming in here again, silly arse, didn't seem to realise we don't want customers who won't pay the advertised price. It's not as though he comes in here regularly, I know he prefers to eat at The Bat and Ball in Swanwick because the Landlord was telling me about him and his bargaining tactics a few months ago. Well they are welcome to him.'

'Ha ha you've cheered me up, there is always someone worse off!' laughed Cliff. 'Another drink anyone?'

'No, thanks,' said Tony. 'It's my turn to cook tonight so I'd better get back.'

'What's on the menu tonight Tony, what are you cooking for Lesley?' asked Cliff.

'Thai Prawn with jasmine rice, Lesley's favourite. What are you cooking for Rebecca then Cliff?' said Tony, cheekily. It was a standing joke that Cliff couldn't even cook toast, everyone knew Rebecca did all the cooking in their house.

'No need for me to cook, Rebecca loves it, she's brilliant, I couldn't possibly compete with her in the kitchen. You run off home and put your Chef's apron on, I'm having another pint. James, one for you?'.

'Oh I'll keep you company for another Cliff, thank you. Joanna will be here later on, we're eating A La Ship tonight.'

Chapter Sixteen

Wednesday 22nd April 2015, 6.45pm

'Well, how did your interview go?' asked Gemma. He really was very good looking. 'Did you get the job?' she asked hopefully.

'Yes I did!' said Peter. 'You are looking at the new Equine Vet for Woodford Equine Veterinary Practice. I hope you are in the mood for a celebration Gemma, what would you like to drink?'

'Ooooh no I'll buy, you're the one celebrating. Would you like Champagne or a pint?'

'I'd rather have a pint please,' he laughed, 'and no, I'm paying this evening, this is my treat. Sarah has set up a tab for me. I am staying here tonight in one of their B&B rooms, so put your money away. Sarah!' he called over to the bar. 'Another pint please, and Gemma what will you have? Champagne or a pint?'

'I'd rather have a Pimms!' she said with a grin.

'Now that sounds like a very good idea,' said Sarah. 'It's a beautiful evening, why don't you two go out into the garden. The sunset over the hills will be stunning in another hour or so. I'll bring your drinks out as soon as I have made up the Pimms.'

As the pair of them made their way out to the garden they passed Cliff just as he was walking back to his seat from the bar.

'That is Cliff Williamson. Jackie Martin, your new boss, is his mother-in-law' whispered Gemma.

Peter frowned, there was something about the way Cliff walked that reminded Peter of someone he had seen, but he didn't recognise Cliff's face. He wondered if they had met previously somewhere else.

'What does Cliff do?' he asked Gemma.

'Oh, he is an antiques dealer. Well a bit more than that, he has an antiques centre, Williamson Antiques, or at least he used to. Someone broke in a couple of months ago and trashed the place, so it has been closed since then. He is trying to pull everything together so he can re-open it in July, but I am not sure if he is going to be able to. The antiques trade has been spooked by the attack, no one seems to know who was behind it, and an awful lot of people lost thousands, if not hundreds of thousands of pounds in the attack. Poor man is working night and day trying to build enough interest from other dealers. Lisa and I really hope he can do it, he is a nice man and has a lovely wife and children so it would be a shame if it all fell apart because of some random act of vandalism.'

'Ah yes, I read about that online when I was researching this area as part of my preparation for the interview today.' said Peter. 'Nothing was stolen then?'

'No, that is why it is so strange. Who would break into an antiques centre and not steal anything?'

It would be several months before Peter realised where he had seen Cliff before, and when he did he was glad he hadn't recognised him on that first occasion, although just maybe the questions of 'who' and 'why' surrounding the crime at the antiques centre would have been answered a lot sooner than they were.

'Let's eat too shall we?' said Gemma. 'No, we'll go halves, I don't want you to pay for my food as well as my drinks. I'll take a couple of menus with me, we can order when Sarah comes out with the drinks.'

Once they were settled with their drinks in The Ship Inn's garden, Gemma and Peter carried on comfortably chatting as they had in the tearooms earlier, telling each other all about their families and ex-partners. Peter also had two children, both girls and a bit older than Gemma's sons, and had separated from his wife two years earlier. He had moved out of the family house in Shropshire and was now temporarily living with his mum who was only twenty minutes from his former home but an hour away from his surgery, which was proving to be too far away to be workable for much longer. On the nights he was On Duty he was sleeping in the surgery so he could be close at hand if there was an emergency. Peter had spent the last year or so trying to decide whether to buy somewhere close to the surgery, or move away out of the area to another veterinary practice. Now that both his daughters were settled in careers and relationships of their own, and his divorce from his wife was almost finalised, he was ready to move on, both emotionally and geographically.

Peter had really enjoyed working for the equine practice in Shropshire, but his wife was heavily involved in the competition world up there so they had no choice but to bump into each other regularly at various horse shows. Now that she was in a relationship and her new man was usually by her side, Peter had decided he needed to move away. Brackenshire was far enough away from Shropshire that he wouldn't be seeing his ex-wife and her partner every week, but close enough he could see his daughters every month.

The air had grown chilly as the sun sank down behind the hills, so Gemma and Peter decided to carry on their conversation inside the pub, where they both tucked in to a meal of garlic prawns followed by seafood linguine, washed down with chilled white wine, and then as they were celebrating Peter's new job, chocolate profiteroles, before sharing a cafetiere of coffee.

Finally the evening was drawing to a close. Peter walked with Gemma the ten minutes back to her house, where he gave her a chaste but warm kiss on the cheek, and they arranged to meet up again in a month's time for another evening meal, choosing the day before he started his new job for their next date.

As she closed her front door Gemma hugged herself. What a lovely gorgeous man! For the first time since her marriage had broken up she was seriously considering a relationship. Peter was so easy to talk to, fun, sexy obviously, quite a bit taller than her with those beautiful blue eyes and almost-but-not-quite-white hair, and when he had leaned in to kiss her cheek his hand had sent lightning shocks up her arm where it touched her skin, and his lips were soft and smooth on her face.

Yes, Gemma was very much looking forward to Peter Isaac moving into the village.

Peter was thinking along the same lines as Gemma, although his romantic past was a lot messier than hers, and a lot more recent. When he had discovered his wife was having an affair with the farrier he had not been surprised. He had always known she was an outrageous flirt, and he long suspected that she had been having liaisons throughout their twenty-seven-year marriage but had turned a blind eye to them, blaming himself for the long hours he worked, often late into the evenings and at night, usually bone tired when he came to bed so conversation let alone making love was the last thing on his mind for weeks at a time. But this last one was different. The others had been brief and largely anonymous, but her affair with the farrier was blatant, in his face, and in his bed. He had left that day and moved in with one of his colleagues and his wife, but had foolishly got entangled with the wife who wasn't particularly attractive but Peter had felt the need to be wanted and she certainly wanted him, so he quickly moved out of their house and into his mother's before his colleague became aware of what was going on under his own roof. As far as Peter knew his colleague was still in the dark, and he wanted it to stay that way if at all possible.

Over the next few months his female clients and his friends all seemed determined to set him up with someone new, but he just wanted to be left alone and nurse his broken heart. He had loved his wife, and been prepared to overlook her affairs. He did not have the energy or the enthusiasm to start all over again.

Two of his friends, a couple he had known since they were all at school together and whose marriage had lasted for over thirty years, had persevered and succeeded in setting Peter up with a couple of dating experiences. Because of their own track record Peter had been a little bit more inclined to listen to them, but Peter hadn't particularly liked either of the two women his friends had deemed 'perfect' for him, and the experiences had put him off trying again.

The first attempt at dating had been very strained, the conversation was stilted, and the sex was expected (by her) and perfunctory (by him), and neither bothered to call the other one again. He hadn't slept with anyone except his wife for more than thirty years, and despite all the pain and heartache she had put him through she was still the only woman he desired. He was very shaken up by the whole dating experience, and wondered if he would ever be able to make love to a woman again, or if he was destined to be celibate for the rest of his life. At only fifty two years old this wasn't a prospect he wanted to settle for.

The second attempt at dating was even more mortifying for Peter. The lady was a friend of a friend of the married couple, and initially all was going well. They met at a party and spent the evening chatting, and then went out a week later for a meal and again the conversation flowed. At the end of the evening the lady was very keen to go to bed with Peter, but after his last experience he was not eager to rush anything and wanted to wait a while longer. She clearly felt rejected and he assumed he wouldn't be seeing her again, which was a shame as he had enjoyed their time together and would have been happy to allow the relationship to progress slowly.

He was really pleased and a little relieved when she phoned him a week later and invited him to come to her house for a meal, and by this time had talked himself into speeding the dating process up more quickly than he had originally planned. He spruced himself up in preparation for what he was sure was going to be a fun evening of lively conversation, and then with any luck a night of passion. The meal was delicious, she was a super cook, the conversation was witty and sparkling, loaded with sexual tension, and Peter found the lady very attractive. He knew he had been right to wait, but now he was ready.

After dinner they sat down together on her huge sofa and she suggested they watch a film. His nerves had started to creep back by this time, as it was clear that sex was firmly on the evening's agenda, so he agreed a film would be a good idea, thinking it would give him time to tame the nervous butterflies in his stomach.

But then the film started.....it was a porn film, a badly made porn film (are there any others?) involving a woman scantily clad in something which was meant to be a horse rider's outfit, doing lots of bending down movements so the viewers could see either her impressive cleavage or firm rounded buttocks, and occasionally both. She appeared to be in a bedroom full of horse tack, there were saddles and bridles and pitch forks placed in view of the camera, plus some very new-looking brushes which had clearly never been within a few hundred metres of a real horse, and of course the obligatory whips of various lengths and colours. Peter was getting increasingly uncomfortable, but probably not in the way his new lady friend had hoped. The woman on screen stopped what she was doing to herself with one of the brushes and then there was a knock on the door of the 'tack room' (Peter couldn't help but be distracted by the poor timing in the sequence, although his lady friend seemed to be anticipating something very exciting, her eyes glued to the screen, he had a suspicion she had watched this one before) and the woman teetered over to the door (honestly, thought Peter, who wears heels like that in a stable yard? She would do herself an injury if she tried to put her feet in the stirrups in those boots.) When she opened the door in walked a man, also scantily dressed, although from the little he was wearing and carrying it was clear he was meant to be a farrier. Well that was it, Peter hurriedly made his excuses and left, resolving to remain a celibate singleton for the rest of his life.

Those experiences had terrified him, and made him wonder if his wife had been right in their final we-can-never-come-back-from-this argument about his lack of sexual capabilities. But tonight being with Gemma had been like a breath of fresh air, so easy to talk to, very beautiful, seemed to genuinely like him and be interested in his plans. She didn't appear to have any agenda, hadn't tried to jump him, or make him watch a video, or relive the disastrous events in his marriage, and the only tension in the air was sexual – about which he was relieved!

He too was very much looking forward to starting his new life in the village next month.

Chapter Seventeen

Thursday 23rd April 2015, 12 noon

It was half term so Rebecca was enjoying some quality mother-daughter time with Charlotte, and treating her to lunch at The Woodford Tearooms, with her mum, Jackie.

'Hi Nana!' called Charlotte, as Jackie walked in.

'Hi Mum,' said Rebecca as she got up to hug and kiss her mother. 'You are looking gorgeous as usual, new top? That colour suits you.'

'Yes it is! I love this colour, I bought it from the boutique in the High Street last week, so when you invited me here for lunch I was really pleased to have an opportunity to wear it. What are you two drinking?'

'Fiery ginger beer!' said Charlotte, holding her glass up. 'It's delicious.'

'And you Rebecca?'

'Oh a glass of dry white, it's such a lovely sunny day I feel as though summer is on its way so thought I'd toast it.'

'Good idea, I'll have one of those too. I am celebrating because I employed a new vet yesterday, so should be able to return to my part-time hours again. Such a shame Alastair decided to retire but I am hoping this chap will be a good replacement for him. No point being the boss if I have to do all the work too!'

'Ooooh tell us all about him Mum!' said Rebecca eagerly.

'His name is Peter Isaac, a very experienced equine vet who has a lovely way with horses, and seems to know a lot about barefoot rehabilitation for tendon and ligament injuries too which has been a bit of a gap in our knowledge at the practice. Neither Alastair nor I have had much experience of it, in fact I haven't had any, but as an increasing number of our clients are either keeping their horses barefoot, or are having the shoes taken off when they go lame, I am hoping Peter will be able to work with them and use his previous knowledge and experiences to help them and educate me.

'While I think of it, I am on the look out for somewhere he can rent for a while, so if you hear of anyone who has a cottage or an annexe could you let me know please?'

'Will do Mum. Have you thought of asking the Higston family? They have a few small cottages which they rent out, one of them may be available.'

'Hi ladies, are you ready to order?' Gemma appeared, 'Was that Peter Isaac you were talking about? Your new vet?'

'Yes we were. Do you know him?' asked Jackie.

'Well, we had a lovely evening in The Ship Inn last night. I met him in here yesterday, he popped in before his interview with you, and afterwards we went and celebrated his appointment. He is very keen to get started. I am hoping to see a lot more of him next month onwards,' she smiled happily, and winked at Rebecca. 'Right, food, what would you all like to eat today?'

Once everyone had ordered, Rebecca and Jackie started to discuss the upcoming Woodford Summer Fete. Rebecca was the Woodford Summer Fete Coordinator, and Jackie was involved with the charity which would be benefiting from the fete-goers' generosity, and was also going to be supervising the Horse Show as usual in her capacity as the local equine vet. The village green, where the annual fete was held, was not up to hosting a big event with cross-country jumps and numerous Showing rings, but did have enough room for an 80x80 foot area to be roped off to allow for a series of fun showing classes such as Horse with the Prettiest Tail, Best Dressed Pair (the theme for that year was Horror), and Oldest Horse & Rider Combination.

'How many entries have you had in total Mum?' asked Rebecca, pen and paper at the ready.

'Not as many as last year, we are down to forty-two horses this year, but that should make it much easier to cope with the timetable. Last year's record fifty-seven entries was a bit of a challenge to coordinate!' laughed Jackie. 'Although I think in the end we were only running one hour and forty minutes late. Better than the three hours overrun in 2012 when we had the Olympics Theme for the fancy dress, that was a nightmare. I still think those two women who managed to come as the X-country Jump with their horses should have won, it was brilliant, and how they managed to ride their horses perfectly in time so they didn't drop any bits of the jump was astonishing! At least the sun was shining on us that year, I really hope we are lucky with the weather this year, muddy ground conditions are not ideal.'

'And are all the Classes well supported again?'

'All except the Most Likely to be Featured in a Thelwell Picture I'm pleased to report. I don't think we should be promoting fat ponies and would like to drop that Class, plus we have only had two entries so hopefully the rest of the local equestrian community is feeling the same.'

'Ah, that's a shame!' exclaimed Charlotte. 'Those ponies are so cute and so funny. I love those books.'

'Hmmh,' said her Nana, frowning. 'But you do realise how serious obesity is don't you Charlotte? One of the worst parts of my job is when I have to put a horse or pony to sleep due to poor management.'

'Well, yes, of course I know that poor diet and obesity is not good for anyone, ponies or humans, everyone knows that, people are always banging on about it. But you have to admit they are cute Nana, and funny. Maybe you could re-name the class: 'Slimmer Than a Thelwell Pony But Just As Funny'? After all it is ponies outwitting their owners which make those cartoons so brilliant, not the size of them.'

'Clever girl!' exclaimed Jackie with a big smile on her face, beaming at her granddaughter. 'Yes, I'll try to get that accepted by the committee for next year.' She retrieved her handbag from under her chair and pulled out her diary to write a note at the back for the 2016 Fete.

'Good, that's all sorted then,' said Rebecca firmly before the discussion could move any further off topic, keen to tick a few more points off her list. 'I have checked with John Higston and he is happy to organise fencing off the Show Ring, and also the Horse Walk from the Maxwell-Lewis' field to the Ring as he did last year. Mrs Maxwell-Lewis has kindly offered the use of the paddock in front of her farmhouse again this year for the horse lorry park. That's OK isn't it Mum? It all worked very well last time, I thought.'

'Yes it did, much better than trying to have everyone in another penned off area next to the ring, much easier and safer to have all the trailers and lorries in a different field. Plus the access to the Maxwell-Lewis' property is better able to cope with all the lorries and 4x4s with trailers than the Farnham Road entrance to The Green if the weather is a bit on the damp side. Although we will need marshals and maybe a one way system for the High Street this time. It was traffic chaos last year, probably the only part of the fete which didn't run relatively smoothly?'

'OK Mum, I'll have a think about who I can ask. Maybe the local football club would like to help? They offered their services last year for taking down the marquees and we didn't really need all of them.' She made a note on her list to contact the Woodford Football Club's chairman.

Gemma appeared with a tray carrying their lunches. 'Are you talking about the Fete?' she asked.

'Yes we are, my main topic of conversation now for the next month,' laughed Rebecca. 'Are you and Lisa still on track to run the refreshment tent, is there anything you need from me?'

'All under control, thanks,' said Gemma. 'We will do the same as last year. We'll set up on the morning although we will bring all the tables and chairs straight over after closing on the Sunday and leave them stacked in the marquee. Sarah and Mike are letting us use their water and electricity as usual, so the urns and washing up stations are operational. We'll have all the cups and saucers and plates there by 9.00am on the morning of the fete. Everybody will bring their baked donations to the marquee between 10.00-11.00am, I will be there to help them with Nathan and Caroline, while Lisa, Daniel and Robert all drive around the area separately collecting from those people who aren't able to transport their own contributions. We have a rota of five ladies and gents doing one hour shifts throughout the afternoon to do the serving, taking money, and clearing tables, so we'll be the ones boiling the water and washing up, and Lisa has worked out a rota for us too.'

'Great, so our Fete meeting next week should be a quick run through of everything as planned, hopefully not too many surprises. I have managed to catch up with almost everyone this week and they all seem to be looking forward to it. Please thank your family,' she said, smiling at Gemma. 'That refreshments tent was a nightmare when I first took over as the fete coordinator, but it runs so smoothly now you all take care of it I don't need to do anything! Do you remember the year the helpers all fell out with each other and started taking their cakes away within half an hour of the Fete opening?'

'Ha ha yes, that was brilliant!' laughed Charlotte.

'Thankfully before my time,' grinned Gemma, 'but we are glad to help. I hope the weather's kind!'

'Me too,' said Rebecca, 'me too!'

Chapter Eighteen

Saturday 23rd May 2015, 12.30pm

'Hellooooo!' called Gemma, as she pushed open the unlocked front door. 'Are you ready for lunch? I've brought sandwiches and cake as requested.'

'Gemma!' Peter stopped unpacking the box of bathroom towels and soaps and came rushing over to give her a big hug. She had wondered what to wear and ummmed and aaaahhhed over various 'casual' outfits and hairstyles, but in the end decided not to change a thing and opted to keep her Woodford Tearooms uniform on, and her long blond curly hair firmly under control in a French plait. Peter thought she looked wonderful.

'Oh how lovely to see you,' he said. 'Thank you for taking time off work to come and keep me company Gemma. Who have you left in charge of the tearooms?' He was dressed in traditional Moving In clothes of scruffy jeans and a paint-stained T-shirt, so Gemma felt quite well-dressed next to him and was glad she hadn't dressed up for the lunchtime date.

'Oh it's OK, I've put my children to work instead, they are both helping Lisa while I'm gone. That's the beauty of having students in the family, they always need money! Here you are, I have made cheese rolls and chicken sandwiches, with flapjack to follow. I've also brought teabags and milk, and four Woodford

Tearooms mugs as a house-warming present,' she grinned cheekily. 'I hope you found your kettle.'

'Oh yes, I packed the kettle very carefully so it was the first thing I could unpack. I thought we could eat outside AND I have a tablecloth for the table!'

The pair of them worked together quickly to carry all they needed outside to the garden, and were soon sitting down to eat in the sunshine.

Peter was not due to start work until the following Tuesday, but had come down a few days earlier so he could settle into the little cottage Jackie had found for him on one of the local country estates. He was pleased he could spend some time with Gemma before the County's horses' medical needs took over most of his attention. The cottage was a former Gatehouse made from the local green stone, fairly dark inside but Peter knew it would be warm and cosy in the winter, with a rayburn in the kitchen for cooking and hot water, and it also heated a radiator upstairs in his bedroom and in the bathroom, and had a small open fireplace in the sitting room. He would be happy to live here for a while until he knew in which direction his life was heading.

'So,' said Gemma, as she wiped the crumbs from a chicken sandwich from her mouth, 'what are your plans for the next few days? It is Bank Holiday on Monday, the village are having their annual fete and Lisa and I are running the refreshments tent, so I won't be able to show you around then I'm afraid. I have to go back to work this afternoon, but am free all day tomorrow if you would like a local guide? Lisa and her kids are opening the tearooms tomorrow. You can meet Suzy if you like, we can take her for a walk somewhere.'

'Suzy?'

'My Staffie. Lisa has her sister, Florence, we adopted them from the Swanwick Animal Shelter last year, gorgeous dogs both of them.'

'Oh I love Staffies!' exclaimed Peter delightedly. 'Although I think my favourite dogs are German Shepherds. Hopefully once my life is a bit more settled I can find one to come and live with me.'

'Ah yes, they are lovely dogs too, but tend to be a bit big and a bit hairy for the type of walks we do. At least with our Staffies they are short haired, small, and extremely easy to wash and dry and leave in front of the Aga before we go to work,' grinned Gemma. 'I should think a GS would either take ten times as long to wash off, or would still be wet when I got home!'

'Yes you could be right,' laughed Peter. 'Are you doing anything tonight? If not would you like to meet at The Ship Inn again?' he asked hopefully, suddenly aware of just how much time he wanted to spend with this woman.

'Yes, we could meet there, or you could come to my house for dinner. We usually have takeaway fish and chips on a Saturday night, just me and Lisa and whichever of our children are around, you are very welcome to join us.'

Peter took a moment to think about it. On the one hand he had been looking forward to spending time alone with Gemma, but the idea of seeing her surrounded by her family was an appealing one. 'Well if that's OK and I'm not intruding I would love to come and have fish and chips.'

'Great, just turn up around seven o'clock. Robert, Lisa's son, will go and get them when we have all decided what we're having.'

They finished off the rolls, sandwiches and flapjack, before Gemma had to go back to the tearooms and Peter carried on with his unpacking.

When Gemma walked in she was surprised to see her sister and Andrew Dover deep in conversation sitting together on the window seat. She scooted into the kitchen where her sons Nathan and Daniel were peering round the corner of the serving hatch watching the couple in the window. 'What's going on?' she asked eagerly.

'Aunty Lisa has finally managed to have a proper conversation with him,' said Nathan, rolling his eyes. At six foot two inches tall, with dark hair, blue eyes, and a light dusting of freckles on his tanned face Nathan had no difficulty with attracting or talking to girls, and his Aunt's ineptness at engaging a man who clearly liked her in conversation had been a source of great amusement to him over the last few months.

'Well, he started it,' said Daniel, who looked similar to his brother except that he took after his mother and Aunt and had blond curly hair. 'He asked her what was in the parsnip soup,' he said disgustedly, 'and they've been talking for about fifteen minutes now!'

'Hurray,' whispered Gemma, watching her sister. A small smile crept over her lips as she saw how animated Lisa was being, a far cry from the stuttering blushing woman of the last few months. 'Long may they continue to talk,' she said, turning away. 'Come on you two, there must be something else you can be doing other than spying on your Aunt!'

'Nope, all the lunches are finished, everyone in here has been served, all the washing-up has been put in the dishwasher or washed up in the sinks, and all the empty tables have been cleared. We have been Perfect

Workers this lunchtime while you've been A Lady Who Lunches,' said Nathan.

'How was lunch?' asked Daniel, curiously.

'Oh, you know,' said Gemma airily, and quickly left the kitchen before her sons could start to interrogate her. 'Oh yes,' she called over her shoulder, 'he's coming for fish and chips tonight if you want to meet him. His name is Peter,' she called as she quickly moved to the other end of the tearooms and started straightening chairs around the tables.

'I think we'd better,' said Daniel, looking at his brother.

'Yup' agreed Nathan.

Chapter Nineteen

Saturday 23rd May 2015, 7.00pm

The whole family were waiting for Peter's arrival, including the dogs Florence and Suzy, so when he walked up to the front door Gemma opened it before he could ring the doorbell.

'Hi Peter, come on in, we're all in the kitchen.' They greeted each other with a quick peck on the cheek, and walked into the kitchen together where Lisa, Caroline, Nathan, Daniel and Robert were all seated around the table.

'Blimey,' Peter laughed. 'I thought the job interview was last month!'

It was exactly the right thing to say, and everyone burst out laughing with him. As this was the first man either Gemma or Lisa had brought into the family circle, everyone was unsure how to behave, and Gemma's sons were both trying to be adult about the evening, aiming to find the right balance between looking out for their mother and supporting her in whatever she decided to do. As far as they knew their father hadn't found anyone new to share his life with, and they had agreed not to tell him about Peter unless or until their mum wanted them too. Lisa's children were watching their cousins' reactions with interest, both were aware of their own mother's interest in Andrew Dover, and they both liked what they had seen of him, but they wondered how long it would be before he, too, was welcomed to join one of their family Saturday evenings. It was unusual for all four of the children to be there, and Gemma was pleased everyone had made the effort so that Peter could see the whole family at once, plus it would enable her to see how he fitted in with them. He wasn't far wrong with his Job Interview analogy.

The attention quickly moved away from the newcomer at their dining table to more important matters, namely the decision whether to order five or six portions of chips for the seven of them, and who was having mushy peas, who was having battered sausage, who was having haddock, who was having cod. Once everyone had decided, and Robert had the list written down, plus a few extra items to buy from the supermarket next door to the fish and chip shop, he and Nathan left to fetch the food.

Drinks were next, and once everyone around the table had a glass or a mug in front of them, the inquisition started. Gemma allowed Daniel and Caroline to question Peter about his work and his own children, both of which he seemed more than happy to chat about, and after a few minutes she steered the conversation around to the Woodford Summer Fete.

'Do you think your daughters would like to come?' she asked.

'I know they are both keen to come and see where I have moved to, I'll ask them, hang on a moment,' he said, and pulled out his phone to quickly type a couple of text messages 'So, tell me all about this fete, although if you are serving teas and coffees I don't suppose you see much of it do you?'

'No, not really,' said Lisa. 'But we have a little wander around the stalls before the fete officially opens, which means we have a chance to reserve any plants we may want, and buy raffle tickets, and so on. The Woodford Summer Fete is probably similar to all other village fetes you have been to, with stalls and games designed to part visitors from their money. It is very well supported both by people willing to give items for sale, and people willing to buy them, and usually makes substantial amounts of money for whichever charity we are supporting.

'None of the local businesses, except The Ship Inn, are open on the day of the fete, mainly because all the business owners and workers are enjoying themselves there! It is a real community family event. Probably the main things we miss seeing are the Dog Show and the Horse Show, judging by some of the stories I hear in the tearooms they can be hilarious. But we still manage to enjoy ourselves, don't we?' She looked around the table at the rest of her family for their agreement.

'Oh yes,' chimed in Caroline. 'The Dog Show is brilliant. Remember last year they tried to make a tunnel out of cardboard boxes and first Florence, then the Cookson's labrador Alfie, jumped on top of it and squashed it! So funny, best part of the fete that year was watching all those adults being beaten in every class by the children, regardless of how well-behaved or well-turned out the adults' dogs were. They are all good sports though, and of course everyone ends up with a rosette.'

'And what about the Horse Show?' asked Peter.

'Well, yes I suppose you would be interested in that one!' laughed Gemma. 'Sorry, I have never watched any of it, have you?' she looked around the table. Everyone shook their heads.

'No, it is on the other side of The Green,' explained Lisa. 'It is not easy to run over and watch for a few minutes, and I am not very keen on horses, they are big and scary. It is a popular event, though, and well supported with competitors. Some of the fancy dress costumes are very inventive. You'll have to tell us all about it this year Peter.'

'I do hope it doesn't rain again,' said Gemma. 'Rebecca Williamson is a genius at organising the fete, but even she can't organise the weather too.'

'Ah Rebecca Williamson, married to Cliff Williamson who you pointed out to me in the pub, and therefore daughter of my new boss Jackie Martin?' asked Peter.

'That's right, Rebecca has been running the fete since before we started helping out. I think she is doing a really good job, I certainly wouldn't want to do it!' said Gemma.

'Oh, nor me,' agreed Lisa, 'horrible job, all those different people with their own ideas about how things should be, whether or not they are right. We are fortunate that we work alongside Mike and Sarah at The Ship Inn, and between the four of us (ahem, a little correction from Daniel) between the *eight* of us (Gemma laughed) and we have a few local volunteers who support us, we provide all the refreshments. That is why they are the only ones who remain open. Also they allow everyone to use their toilets which saves money on hiring any. Mike and Sarah are a great couple, very hard-working and community-minded.'

'When I stayed there last month Sarah was telling me they have been running that pub for over ten years, they really like it here,' said Peter.

'That's good, we like them too. Hope they stay for a few more years, it is not easy running a pub these days, but they seem to make it work for them as well as the town,' said Gemma. 'Aha, that sounds and smells like our food arriving!' as the two boys appeared through the back door, both carrying several bags between them, and within minutes all the food was distributed, drinks were topped up, and everyone sat down to the serious task of eating their Saturday Night Fish 'n Chips.

Chapter Twenty

Sunday 24th May 2015, 9.45.am

The following morning Lisa arrived at The Woodford Tearooms to open up for the day.

The Bartletts never knew from one week to the next how busy a Sunday would be. Some days they would have four customers in total all day and one of the sisters could easily manage on their own, using the quiet time as an opportunity to catch up on preparing food for the next few days, or trying out new recipes to add to their menu. Other Sundays they would be inundated with hungry locals and tourists and would need to call in extra help as the day rushed by.

As this was the first weekend of a half-term holiday for the local schools Lisa was expecting a busy day, so had brought her daughter Caroline in to work with her, and Gemma's son Nathan was due to come in for the lunchtime rush at twelve noon. Mother and daughter worked quietly and efficiently waking up the kitchen in preparation for supplying the hungry and thirsty locals who enjoyed a leisurely read of the newspapers whilst drinking coffee and eating toast, before the mixture of locals and tourists who would be arriving for brunch after either a heavy night celebrating something in the town or an early morning run, cycle ride, or horse ride around the beautiful local countryside.

Once the urns and the ovens were switched on, and the fridges and cupboards were re-stocked with delicious cakes, pastries, salads and meats, Lisa set to work preparing the day's lunchtime specials of chilli bean and veggie wraps, pea and ham soup, salmon salad, and beef lasagne.

Meanwhile Caroline was quickly restoring the eating area from its night-time slumbering state to the day-time welcoming and inviting atmosphere which encouraged the customers to linger over 'one more' drink or cake. Once the tables and chairs were arranged with table cloths and cushions, and fresh flowers she had picked from their garden that morning, some still with morning dew sitting prettily on them, were decorating every table, Caroline pulled up the functional black out blinds which covered the windows when the tearooms were not open for business, before unlocking the front door.

'Good morning Nicola!' she said as she held the door open for Nicola, her arms full of one newspaper, three magazines, a jacket and a bag.

'Morning Caroline, morning Lisa!' she called through to the kitchen area. 'Such a lovely sunny day I am going to park myself over in the window to make the most of it.'

'Good morning Nicola, pot of tea and a chocolate croissant?' asked Lisa,

'Yes please, the usual' grinned Nicola, as she placed her reading material carefully on the table, narrowly avoiding the china cup which held the delicately coloured pink and yellow snapdragons adorning her chosen table.

The next time the cowbell tinkled it was Sarah Handley who, as usual, was joining Nicola for a quiet hour before the busy pub Sunday lunch trade took over the rest of her day.

112

'Good morning Sarah, cappuccino and a flapjack?' asked Lisa, as she walked over to Nicola's table carrying her tea and pastry on a tray.

'Hi Lisa, yes please, you know us so well,' grinned Sarah, as she sat down.

'Are you and Mike ready for the Fete tomorrow?' asked Nicola. 'Do you need a hand?'

'Thanks Nicola, I think we have everything under control, but I am sure we can find something for you to do if you are at a loose end during the day,' said Sarah, as she burrowed into her bag. 'Look at my latest acquisition, isn't it beautiful?'

'Oh that is lovely, and so elegant!' exclaimed Nicola, as Sarah passed her the three strand pearl bracelet with a portrait miniature of a girl built into the clasp. 'Where did you buy it?'

'I saw it in Paul's auction catalogue last week, went and had a look on Thursday evening when he had the Viewing. I fell in love with it, and left a commission bid with him because I couldn't spare the time to go to the auction yesterday.'

'Oh isn't that gorgeous!' exclaimed Caroline, as she arrived at their table with Sarah's breakfast. 'Can I try it on please?'

'Yes you can, it will probably fit around your wrist, mine is too big,' said Sarah, a note of envy creeping into her voice.

'Who is the girl?' asked Caroline, once Nicola had secured the gold clasp.

'Her name is Clara Allsopp and she was about eight years old in this painting. If I undo the clasp for you, turn the portrait miniature over and look at the back.'

'Urgh, is that hair?' asked Caroline, almost flinging the jewellery back at Sarah.

'Yes it is!' laughed Sarah, 'Nothing to be frightened of.'

'Why is it there?' asked Nicola, as she took the piece from Sarah and started to examine it.

'You must have seen these before Nicola, working where you do!' exclaimed Sarah. 'Have you never seen a portrait miniature with decoration to the reverse made from the hair of the painting's subject? Isn't it intricate, all those weaves and plaits. Although the hair isn't always that of the sitter, I should think it was in this case, just look at that glorious red colour. The artist has captured it in the painting perfectly.'

'Nope, I have never seen that on the back of portrait miniatures in the antiques centre, although I probably will now. Is this a family you are researching Sarah?'

'Yes, I went off on a bit of a tangent from my own family and ended up following the line of someone else who was a neighbour on the 1841 census. It was an amazing stroke of luck to spot this in Paul's catalogue last week. I would love to know how this piece of jewellery came to be commissioned, whether it was a love token from her father to her mother, or whether it was made after she died so her mother could keep a reminder of her daughter.'

'Gross,' commented Caroline, as she walked away.

After the success of the family dinner the night before Gemma was even keener to explore her relationship with Peter. Before he left at the end of the evening they arranged to spend the following day together, so while her sister and niece were working hard in the kitchen of their tearooms, Gemma and Peter were taking Florence and Suzy, the Staffies, for a ten mile circular walk along some of the footpaths and by-ways of Brackenshire. They stopped near the end of their walk at the Higston's Farm Shop in Brackendon, the village next to Woodford, for their Sunday lunch. When Lisa was quizzing Gemma for the finer details of their date later that day, as they worked together preparing for the fete, all Gemma could tell her was that they talked and talked and talked about everything and nothing, and that the weather was beautiful, that the countryside was wonderful, all the time beaming from ear to ear.

Chapter Twenty One

Sunday 24th May 2015, 4.00pm

Meanwhile Rebecca Williamson was checking and re-checking her lists, working non-stop to make sure everything went as close to plan as possible, spending most of the day on The Green as the marquees and smaller tents were put up, and the various show rings and walkways were marked out. She was surrounded by volunteers giving up their Sunday (and Monday), and all three of her children were helping too, along with several of their friends. Cliff rarely came to these events, and today was no exception as he was busy working away, buying at a couple of antiques fairs in the Midlands.

By four o'clock the infrastructure for the 2015 Woodford Summer Fete was in place, and Rebecca knew she would have an early start in the morning to help set up the stalls and games which would bring in the public and hopefully encourage them to donate as much cash as they could spare.

Woodford Summer Fete was held every year on The Green, a large open piece of common land which was over-looked by the cottages and houses on the other side of Farnham Road, and ran along to the beer garden of The Ship Inn on the corner where the High Street began and was separated from The Green by several businesses, including The Woodford Tearooms and Williamson Antiques. Access to the Maxwell-

Lewis Farm came off the High Street and followed the edge of The Green parallel to Farnham Road, until it went through a gap in the hedge which ran on up to Farnham Road and separated The Green from the fields behind. The Green was a popular space for the locals, with a duck pond, a cricket pitch, and a few trees providing shelter or shade depending on the weather along the hedge line. Rebecca took one last look around The Green, in awe as she was every year at how the popular town open space could be transformed into a mini-village in a matter of hours, before getting into her car and heading back home, hoping the weather gods would be kind and keep the rain away for another twenty-four hours.

Just as she was putting the kettle on to boil in her kitchen and starting to think about preparing the family's evening meal, she received a panicky phone call from the electrician who volunteered every year to ensure power was distributed safely around the fete. He was on The Green with the technician in charge of the sound system, but there was a last-minute hitch because the town's PA equipment had gone missing from its secure location in the Church hall. It took an hour for Rebecca to track it down to its last known whereabouts at the Football Club, by telephoning everyone she could think of and sitting by the phone waiting for it to ring with news, and another twenty minutes before she had located the only key holder who hadn't gone away for the half-term break.

Crisis averted, Rebecca turned her attention back to her family and prepared the chicken for the oven, before she started peeling potatoes ready for the traditional Sunday Roast. First Michael appeared, and started to help her to prepare the vegetables, then Nicholas came down from his room and laid the table without being nagged to, and finally Charlotte came home from the local riding stables just in time to stir the gravy. By half past seven the whole family – minus Cliff – were sitting down together around the kitchen table, excitedly chattering about their day or quietly ploughing their way through their meal.

Chapter Twenty Two

Monday 25th May 2015, 12 noon

The morning of the Woodford Summer Fete had brought with it the inevitable rain. Over the years the town of Woodford had become adept at coping with the British summertime weather, and although on occasion it would be extremely hot and the volunteer medical team would be kept busy with various visitors and stallholders succumbing to the unaccustomed heat of the sunshine, more often than not the day was a wet one.

Rebecca had been coordinating the Woodford Summer Fete for five years now, originally volunteering to man the Bash The Rat stand with the help of Nicholas and Michael when they were young (used to cost her a fortune as they LOVED it!), then she was promoted (?) to the dreaded Bric-a-Brac tent where all the locals would take advantage of the opportunity to dump their unwanted and often unusable and therefore unsaleable items, before finding herself with the title of Woodford Summer Fete Coordinator for 2011 as nominated by the other volunteers at the 2010 Wash-Up Party.

It was a role she tackled with her usual common sense and good humour, both of which can be in short supply when trying to mediate between warring factions on the Flower Stall or behind the urn in the refreshment tent, and after the first two very challenging fetes in 2011 and 2012 she had found her rhythm and was usually able to anticipate problems before they became battles. She used her people-charming abilities to delegate the various roles sensibly so the little disputes were resolved quickly, and the major problems could be tackled by those best placed to find the solutions.

Rebecca relied on her trusty paper file full of lists, photographs of stalls, plans for events which were successful in the past, and addresses of Could Not Run the Fete Without volunteers whose particular skills were essential to the smooth running of the annual event. Challenges she had successfully resolved with the help of her trusty supporters included: finding a replacement generator at the last minute; hunting down a large enough vehicle to transport the various posts and ropes which were used to mark out the layout of the Fete; and, her greatest achievement to date, persuading the two rival gardening groups, the Woodford Gardeners and the Brackendon Horticulture & Allotments Society to work together and run the popular and lucrative plant stall. Rebecca also relied on the email folders which in some cases duplicated her paper file but definitely made communicating quicker than telephone or committee meetings did.

She was ably assisted by the Woodford Summer Fete Treasurer, Sarah Handley, who was also an excellent Go To person for anything Rebecca may need, such as sourcing the most reasonable providers of rosettes for the Dog Show or persuading local businesses to donate fabulous prizes for the raffle. Sarah was one of those people for whom the well-worn advice 'if you want something done, ask a busy person' was well-suited.

Every year the Woodford Summer Fete raised money for a different local charity, and those charities who were lucky enough to be chosen for a year when the weather was dry and sunny always received a far larger donation than the others, but nevertheless several thousand pounds were gifted every year by the generous private and business inhabitants of Woodford and the surrounding villages. Traditionally the fete was opened by someone related to that year's chosen charity, and the 2015 Fete was due to be opened at half past twelve by the Chairman of the local Riding for the Disabled Association, Rebecca's mum and local Equine Veterinary Surgeon, Jackie Martin.

As the time approached everyone was relieved that the rain clouds disappeared to be replaced by blue sky and warm sunshine, which instantly brought a smile to everybody's face.

The Higston Family were always stalwarts of the fete, and their generosity in offering their time, expertise and farm vehicles was invaluable. Their tractors and trailers were used for fetching and carrying equipment too big for the town's cars and vans, and for doubling up as podiums. It was onto the back of one of their trailers, which had been decorated with bunting and equipped with the formerly misplaced PA system, that Jackie climbed up and positioned herself with an excellent view of the fete. After a brief speech detailing a little about the RDA's work and their local branch's recent news, plus a few house-keeping announcements mainly concerning toilets and refreshments, she announced the 2015 Woodford Summer Fete open!

The crowds of people hurried through the four entrance lines, throwing their one pound coins into the buckets held by the volunteers, and rushed to grab the few bargains in the Bric-a-Brac tent and the many bargains in the Plant tent. The popular local Swanwick Band were keeping everybody entertained with their music, and the Master of Ceremonies, Paul Black, was using his skills as an auctioneer to make regular announcements ensuring everyone knew about the huge variety of Stalls, and about the raffle tickets which were available from three strategic points. It was also the MC's task to use his vantage point high up on the trailer to do a running commentary on the Dog Show and the Horse Show, making sure all the fete goers knew which Classes were starting when, and the names of the first three placed contestants in each Class. Paul was working hard as usual to attempt to look as though his role was easy, which it wasn't as he was constantly having pieces of paper with names and times thrust at him by the runners for the two Shows, as well as remembering to advertise the less popular stalls and games without sounding desperate.

Both Peter Isaac's daughters, Alison and Jennifer, had come down for the day and had brought Jennifer's greyhound Lucy with them, first arriving at his cottage for Brunch before the three of them drove over to the fete. Gemma had given him permission to park in the driveway of her cottage which was conveniently opposite The Green, and they were there ready for the Opening of the Fete, loudly applauding Jackie's opening speech before Peter, Jennifer and Lucy the greyhound headed for the Horse Show, while Alison headed for the Arts & Crafts tent. Jennifer had followed in her father's footsteps and qualified as an equine vet, while Alison had followed in her mother's footsteps and qualified as a riding instructor with the British Horse Society and enjoyed competing her two horses Ernie & Flo in various riding club events whenever she had the chance. She had brought some photos of her horses and was hoping there would be an artist who could draw a lifelike picture of them. She didn't find an artist, but by the time she found her father and sister again she had succeeded in buying a jar of locally produced honey, a silver cushion with a black stylised horse's head, and had entered Lucy into a couple of the classes in the Dog Show.

'Dad! Jennifer! This is wonderful!' she beamed at them. 'What a beautiful place. How is the Horse Show?'

'Oh, very tense,' said her father. 'We are just waiting to see if the Judge keeps that little black pony dressed as a dragon with the tiny boy in a Knight's Suit of Armour minus the head in first place, or if she chooses our favourite, the bay ex-racehorse who has been dressed up as a spider and is terrifying all the other competitors, both horses and humans!'

'Brilliant! I should have brought Ernie down with me, we could have painted him to look like a skeleton and I could wear your headless ghost costume Jennifer.'

'Good idea. Maybe next year? Anyone want a cuppa, I'm so thirsty,' said Jennifer.

'I'll go and get them,' volunteered their father. 'Tea? Coffee?'

'Oh no, we'll all go shall we? We want to meet Gemma!' Jennifer linked arms with her dad and led the way before he could find a reasonable excuse not to go with them. It wasn't that he was ashamed of either of his daughters or of Gemma, he was just very nervous that they wouldn't like each other, and make life awkward for him just as he thought he had something to look forward to.

He needn't have worried. For one thing Gemma was extremely busy tucked away at the back of the marquee sorting trays of dirty and clean cups and saucers so didn't have time for more than a quick 'Hi'; for another his daughters were impressed with all the teamwork on display with Gemma and Lisa and their children. Plus the cakes they all succumbed to were delicious.

Before long it was time for the first of Lucy's classes in the Dog Show. Alison had put her name down for Dog with the Cutest Eyelashes and Dog with the Longest Tail, and the family were delighted when she won the second of her two classes. Proudly sporting a pale blue rosette on her collar, Lucy led the way back to the Horse Show in time for the family to watch the start of the Handy Pony class, which seemed to be filled with middle-aged women and their Hunters, the humans all giggling and falling over when trying to walk the flower pot line or dropping the raw eggs off their spoons so they broke, the horses looking bemused, and the crowd loudly shouting encouragement whilst taking photos and videos which they planned to post online as soon as they could get an internet signal.

The rain stayed away much to everyone's relief until the Fete officially closed at four o'clock, and just as importantly it stayed away for the rest of the afternoon and on into the evening as the mammoth task of clearing the site was completed. By seven o'clock the only evidence of the 2015 Woodford Summer Fete was the muddy tyre tracks and churned up grass from numerous vehicles entering and leaving the site, and evidence of human feet and horses' hooves. Rebecca was always amazed at how quickly the site was cleared after an event as big as this one.

She joined all the other fete volunteers for the after-fete party in The Ship Inn, where many pints of locally brewed cider and beer, and glasses of wine, were consumed, along with plates of Mike Handley's famous (in Brackenshire) shepherd's pie, made with

Higston's lamb mince and topped with mashed potato cooked perfectly so it had a crispy crust, and mushroom pie with four types of mushroom deliciously baked in a mouth-watering gravy under a home-made pastry lid, all amply supported with great bowls of vegetables. Just before the food was served Sarah and Nicola, who had been helping to count the money, were able to announce that before all the pledges were paid (probably amounting to £2700) this year's total to donate to the RDA was approximately £11 000. The cheer that went up was deafening, before the pub fell silent other than the noises of several dozen people tucking into the Pie of their choice, or in quite a few cases Pies.

Once everyone had filled their bellies, and the plates and dishes had been cleared away, it was time for all the thank you's. Rebecca had made a point of going around to every stall during the afternoon and thanking each person individually, but this was her chance to publicly thank the behind-the-scenes people like John Higston and his family, Mrs Maxwell-Lewis and her son Simon, Gemma and Lisa Bartlett and their families, and of course Mike and Sarah Handley. She was a gentle and amusing Speaker, and the fete volunteers had quickly learned that these after-fete speeches would not be a long and boring list of thank you's, but more a humorous round-up of the time and effort they had all put into creating the successful event over the last twelve months since the last one, in which Rebecca managed to skilfully include every single person who had contributed to the event.

The fifteen minutes went very quickly, and at the end Rebecca sat down to roaring applause and cheers, before having to stand up again much to her embarrassment as Paul presented her with an enormous bunch of flowers and bottle of champagne as her own thank you from the other volunteers.

All over for this year, the planning for the 2016 Woodford Summer Fete would start next week.

Chapter Twenty Three

Friday 26th June 2015, 6.00pm

The last few months had been hard work for Cliff, and he now felt drained, both emotionally and financially.

Once everything had been cleared away and he and his team of Nicola, Barry and Des had set to work re-designing and re-building the antiques business, Cliff finally started to feel a tinge of excitement about his future again. There were a few little details he took the opportunity to change in the previous layout of the stands, and he hoped that the new cabinets with more effective lighting would also enhance the appearance and therefore the saleability of the antiques they would display.

There was one big stumbling block to the re-development however, Cliff was still having great difficulty in persuading anyone to place their trust, and therefore their quality stock, in his hands. Although the majority of the dealers felt great sympathy for him, there were one or two who had turned from sympathy to animosity, blaming Cliff for the loss of their stock and the subsequent large hole in their income, and once mistrust is started it spreads like a highly contagious disease, particularly in an industry dealing in fine and rare and often very expensive items. The antiques world thrives on trust – you have to be able to trust that the person you are dealing with is honestly answering your questions about how they came to be in a position to sell the item, what price they paid for it, how long they have owned it, and who else they have shown it to before bringing it to you. You also have to trust your own instinct and knowledge. Successful antiques dealers have incredible memories for who bought what and for how much last week, last year, sometimes thirty plus years ago. They are also often willing to operate a sort of Buy Now Pay Later deal, whereby the seller will allow the buyer to take their three thousand pound Chinese silver and jade box away for five days and pay for it once they have sold it to someone else, or when they have completed a different deal with other stock.

Obviously there is a criminal element in the antiques trade, as in all walks of life, but anyone who thinks they can run a successful antiques business dealing with reliable and trustworthy antiques dealers by cheating and lying to them, never succeed. The people who are known to be dodgy both in their financial dealings and in their business relationships are rarely successful in the legitimate antiques world, because the trustworthy people won't deal with them. It only takes one ill-founded accusation, one incident where someone sells an item as an amber brooch and it turns out to be bakelite, one occasion where someone knowingly sells a stolen bronze figure and claims they bought it privately from the home owner, and that person will struggle to make a living from legitimate business and will have to work extra hard for a long time before anyone forgives. Although no one forgets. No one wants to be tarred with that brush.

Cliff couldn't blame the people who no longer wanted to be associated with him. Until he knew who was behind the destruction and why this had happened he was as concerned as they were. There didn't seem to be anyone else to blame, and as is always the case many human beings need someone to blame for their misfortunes. There was still no news, no leads, no rumours, nothing. There had also been no other attacks, either aimed at Cliff or any other dealers, for which he was grateful. The whole thing was a devastating and very expensive experience for which he had no idea why or if it would happen again.

Once it became clear that the dealers would not be flocking to sell through his antiques centre he had given up trying to entice them, and instead had resigned himself to the fact he would now need to buy in a lot more of his own stock than before in order to fill up the newly painted shelves and new glass cabinets. For several years he had been able to deal in antiques of his choosing at a leisurely pace, taking months and years to move something on, but in the short term he would need to buy items he knew he could quickly sell. Quick sales usually mean low profit, and at the moment Cliff needed as much money as he could earn so this business model was not one he planned on putting into practice for any longer than was absolutely necessary.

Cliff was fairly versatile in the antiques he dealt in, and had a good basic knowledge, but his personal favourites were Oriental. He had originally become interested in dealing in Oriental works of art when he found a book in Emily's shop about The Silk Road, and had fallen in love with the amazing history of the transcontinental trading routes, how they had developed and adapted over the decades as supply and demand changed, and how by the late seventeenth century the trade in Oriental works of art had opened up a whole new market to the wealthy British buyers. They were introduced to colours and patterns they had never seen before, the exotic materials of ivory, jade and porcelain were exciting and different to those they were used to, and the quality was exceptional. Cliff's appreciation of oriental antiques grew the more he dealt in them. He loved them with a passion, and appreciated the skills of the craftsmen who had created them.

He sighed and shook his head. He knew that for the foreseeable future he was going to need a quick turnaround on his investments, no time for appreciating quality, he would have to sacrifice long term profit for short term cash flow. The only way he would be able to put Williamson Antiques back on the map as a place the antiques trade would want to regularly visit was by putting on a decent show of volume of stock, with a few quality items dotted around the place to entice the buyers in and create the desire to put their hands in their pockets and hand over their money.

Fortunately Cliff did have a solid reputation in the local antiques trade, and was well-liked, and as nothing had come to light about The Attack the trade had moved on from talking about it as their sole topic of conversation, and other scandals had moved into the rumour spotlight. There were some of the original dealers who had chosen to stay and support him, and two new dealers had also put their trust in him, but even these rents and proposed sales were not going to be enough to cover the costs. Cliff had to spend far more on replacing and repairing fixtures and fittings, plus additional expense on installing extra cameras so any future crime could never go undetected again, than the original cost of total surveillance by cameras would have cost him when he installed the system fifteen years before. The crippling part was that he had to pay his bills before receiving any form of payout from the insurance company, who were not eager to give him financial support in the near or even long term future because they had also been under the impression Cliff had installed a complete alarm and surveillance system. He was over his credit limits on his cards, his overdraft was astronomical with the bank, he had sold Rebecca's super-duper top-of-the-range Range Rover with only twelve thousand miles on the clock for about half of its value, and his own pride and joy Mercedes sports car for twenty thousand pounds less than its list price, in order to have the cash to pay for the necessary work.

He took one last look around his antiques centre as it stood ready to open for business at last the next day, too exhausted and drained to feel much in the way of pride or even hope.

He switched the lights off, locked the lobby door, set the alarm, locked the outer door, and went to the pub where he was greeted like a long-lost friend by the Regulars. He soon had a pint in his hand and a smile on his face while his friends chattered about the finishing touches they had planned for the festivities the next day. And he finally dared to allow a little bit of that missing hope to creep back into his soul.

Chapter Twenty Four

Friday 26ᵗʰ June 2015, 8.00pm

Not everyone was feeling waves of goodwill towards Cliff Williamson. Sat at the end of the bar was someone who most definitely was not wishing him well for the next day or for the future. This person *could not believe* the bloody man had been able to pick himself and his business up from the literally smashed and broken pieces on the floor ready to start it all again the next day. Was the man indestructible?

The person at the end of the bar had been so pleased with themselves when they had committed the crime at Williamson Antiques in the early hours of Monday March 9th. They had been dancing around the room as they destroyed everything they possibly could, gleefully imagining Cliff's face when he discovered what had happened, positive that he would never guess it had been them.

But they had also been sure there was no way he would have been able to rise from the debris, like some bloody phoenix from the ashes. They had been surprised that so many people had been willing to help the man this person knew to be a conceited bastard completely devoid of any morals. Maybe instead of attacking his business, which the person had done believing it was the only thing Cliff really cared about, perhaps they should destroy something else of Cliff's?

Look at him, downing yet another pint bought by some bloody do-gooder. Could no one else see what an evil and selfish double-crossing bastard the man was?

Even snitching to the police about Cliff's money-making sideline didn't seem to have resulted in any action by the authorities, and no one else appeared to be aware of it. The attacker had expected Cliff to be on the receiving end of mass condemnation and ridicule at the very least by now, the most they had hoped for was a lengthy prison sentence for him.

The perpetrator had truly believed they were far more intelligent than Cliff, and that he was too stupid and immoral to have received any help and support from the people around him. The person was furious that Cliff had been able to achieve as much as he had in the last four months.

For the first time since the attack on Williamson Antiques the person felt a little twinge of doubt about their own cleverness.

Had they got away with it scot-free after all?

Chapter Twenty Five

Saturday 27th June 2015, 12 noon

For the second time in his life, Cliff Williamson was orchestrating the Grand Opening of Williamson Antiques, only today he felt a lot less excited and a lot more exhausted than the first time eighteen years before, plus to be honest he had a small hangover from allowing himself to be led astray by the Regulars the night before, and had drunk one too many of the whiskies he had started drinking once the pints appeared to be running straight through his system.

The place looked a sad shadow of its former self. Out of the twenty-seven stallholders filling thirty six stands and cabinets in March only ten had agreed to come back, although he had managed to persuade a couple of new people to take a cabinet each. Rather than spreading the paltry sixteen stands to cover the whole saleroom, Cliff had kept the majority of the antiques and all of the cabinets towards the front, and had designed a T-shape so the architectural and garden stock was laid out as if leading the buyers down a path to the far end of the space where the door to the yard could still be easily used for moving the often heavy and awkward-to-handle items out of the building. He had erected a line of Victorian screens to close off the big empty holes and shape the T, in fact the place looked very similar to how it did when he had first opened his antiques centre, but for Cliff it was devoid of the excitement for the future he had enjoyed bac.. then. He had been there, done that, and it had been taken away from him without any warning, and apparently without any reason.

Just for the day he had shifted the screens back so there was room in front of them for the pub and the tearooms to provide refreshments. Both the Handleys and the Bartletts had kindly agreed to set up a bar and a tea-and-cake stand, and also to donate a percentage of their takings to the local swimming pool committee's fund-raising efforts to keep the pool open throughout the summer, but Cliff still felt bad that he couldn't afford to provide any free drinks or nibbles to those who had made the effort to support him. All his money was sunk into re-opening Williamson Antiques, he literally didn't have enough for one bottle of fizz. But he was determined to put on a brave face, even though he was scrutinising every person who walked through the door to see if they could have been behind the devastation four months previously. Whoever it was, and why ever they did it, if they were here they would see he wasn't beaten.

Rebecca had managed to conjure up a pair of giant scissors from somewhere, and a huge red ribbon which she and Des had strung up in front of the counter. She had been as devastated as Cliff by The Attack, and also scared in case whoever had done it might go for their children, or even herself or Cliff. She had tried to discuss her fears with Cliff but he wouldn't talk about it with her. She felt he didn't care about them and was focussing all his fears and concerns on another attack on the business.

Whereas Cliff had spent the last few months with nothing on his mind but how to restore his business, his behaviour throughout the day The Attack had been discovered had finally made Rebecca face something she had been ignoring for several years. In fact now the thought was in her head she realised the truth had been there all of their married life: that she did not count for anything meaningful in his world, she was there as window-dressing only.

She was used to him disappearing for a few hours, not answering his phone or returning her calls or texts, they had rarely attended any social functions together, and it was a miracle they had more than one child as their sex life had been virtually non-existent after those admittedly frequent and mind-blowing love-making sessions during the weeks they were engaged.

Rebecca believed that you should make the best of what you have, and when she looked around at other people's husbands and at the fathers of her children's friends she was often very glad that Cliff had chosen her. She could honestly say she wouldn't have swapped him for any of them!

But since March 9th when she realised that she hadn't even entered his thoughts she was wondering if life would be better if he wasn't such a large part of it. She loved being a mother and a home-maker, and would have loved being a good wife to a good husband, and up until four months ago that is exactly what she thought they were; a team who supported each other, brought the best out of each other, loved one another.

She didn't see anything demeaning about her chosen home-maker life, although her mother did and would sometimes make comments to that effect in the way mothers do, those frustrating and annoying little barbs which you end up reverting to child-like defensive behaviour to rebut.

Look at her mother! A very successful career woman, who apparently had it all: the career, her own business, successful marriage, two children, her health, good looks….until her husband, Rebecca's father, just walked out one day, saying he couldn't cope with the constraints of married family life and wanted to 'find himself'. They had occasionally received news from him over the years via post and email, but since Rebecca was fourteen years old she had never seen or spoken with her father again.

She could vividly remember her mother's face as her father walked out of the back door of their home, the look of disbelief, mild derision, fear, shock, grief, fury all flashed across her face as the three of them followed his progress down the garden and out through the gate, where he disappeared from view. Rebecca and her sister had been old enough to understand he had left home, but they were confused about why, and they both missed him very much for the first few weeks. She still did. She would have loved for him to walk through the door now. She imagined she would run up to him and hug him so tightly. But then other times she felt cross, angry, hurt. How could he abandon them? Her sister, she knew, wanted nothing to do with their father, but Rebecca was sure he must have had very good reasons for leaving them, and would like one day to hear his explanation.

Her mother's words infiltrated her thoughts:

'All men will treat you like a doormat if you let them!' was one of her mother's favourite, and frequent, sayings. Rebecca had always rolled her eyes and said 'Mother!' but her eyes had been opened on the night of March 9th, and even though she was perfectly happy with herself and her life, she had spent the last few months noticing the way Cliff behaved towards her, and found it both lacking in respect and void of love.

It wasn't just the fact he hadn't bothered to call her to tell her what was going on, let alone wanted or needed her by his side at a traumatic event in his life, or even the fact that he was at home when Nicola had phoned him with the news and yet all he had said as he rushed out of the door was 'See ya later, love, gotta go.' Since the 9th March she had finally realised that as far as Cliff was concerned, the only parts she played in his life were: to clean the house he treated as a hotel; to obtain, prepare and put food on the table, or more often in the oven or in the fridge so HE could heat it up and put it on the table and eat on his own; and to bring up their children. Although even that last one she wasn't sure he actually would notice if she stopped, as sadly she realised their children also had no place in Cliff's world other than to illustrate his image as a Family Man. When was the last time he had said more than 'Morning' or 'Good night' to any of them? For a while she had tried to find out if they were bothered by his treatment of them, but it had come as a shock to her to realise that for them, their father's behaviour was normal and they were fine with it.

How had this happened? Why hadn't she noticed before that she was, in effect, a single parent with a lodger who paid all the bills and who slept most nights in bed next to her?

She knew he worked hard and kept long hours, and when he wasn't at the antiques centre during opening hours he was driving all over the country looking for bargains and keeping up-to-date with the antiques world, which is vital or you get left behind and make expensive mistakes, or worse you just stop operating as an antiques dealer and your business disappears. They had seen too many dealers fall into financial ruin because they refused to move with the ever-changing times, dealers who kept turning up at a certain market week after week because it had once been the heart of the UK antiques world, even though they had been losing money for the last five years; dealers who had made fortunes from specific types of antiques like pewter or ivory, and were now systematically losing their fortunes because those antiques were no longer the collectable, saleable, and valuable commodity they had once been. Fashions change, demands change, prices change.

Rebecca had known from the beginning of their romance that the antiques centre was Cliff's priority, and she had been happy with the status quo. His attitude suited her, she didn't want a man who was possessive and clingy, who wanted to be by her side every second, who wanted to know who she was with and where she was going. Rebecca wanted a man who, like Cliff, had his own interests, his own projects, and who was successful in his own world. Cliff certainly fitted her criteria.

But that day had forced her to recognise that there was little or no connection, emotion, passion, *feelings* in this marriage. As Rebecca thought about it all she realised that she didn't feel anything either, other than a sense of loss. No hatred or blame, love or desire, nothing.

Right, she took a deep breath and squared her shoulders.

She either had to be happy with this situation, which up until March 9th she was sure she had been, or she needed to do something about it because clearly Cliff was content with their marriage in this state.

Or was he?

Now she had started to question her own feelings she found she was unsure about his. Well, she decided, regardless of Cliff she had tested her own feelings, and concluded she was not happy with this situation! If she was going to share her life with someone then she did want it to mean something more to them than this, otherwise why bother? She had a hollow feeling inside, which she hadn't been aware of before.

So, how to proceed?

Rebecca had quietly been canvassing opinions from her friends about her situation and how to resolve it, without actually spelling anything out in detail because that would then make it real, and she wasn't ready for that. Her mother wasn't the only one who had thought Cliff's behaviour in not telling her about the attack on the antiques centre was outrageous, and Christine had commented more than once on his decision not to include her in that time of crisis.

After four months Rebecca felt she was almost ready, she just needed to be able to find that last bit of courage. She had a mantra, something she had learned about from Christine a few years ago but up until now hadn't understood the purpose or the power of it. Rebecca had not paid much attention to Christine's self-discoveries as they all sounded a bit woo-woo and self-centred to her, but over the last few months she had started to realise what it was all about and had even attended and enjoyed a workshop about self-awareness. Up until The Attack Rebecca had been happy with her life, her appearance, she had a beautiful family, an active and fulfilling commitment to various voluntary groups in the area, a lovely group of friends with whom she shared the ups and downs of bringing up children, wine, and Zumba sessions. But now The Attack had raised some issues she hadn't been aware of, and she strongly felt there was something missing in her world. She just needed the courage to do something about the deficiency.

One of Christine's favourite mantras in times of stress was 'I need to close this door, to enable another door to open.' Rebecca tested it and far from being woo-woo or cringingly embarrassing as she had previously thought, she found it fitted her current way of thinking, and chose to try it out for herself. What was going to be on the other side of the new door she wasn't sure, but she was ready for it!

Although, she faltered, maybe not quite yet, the advantage of closing a door was you could open it again, surely? She wasn't ready, she could carry on as before for a little while longer, after all here she was dutifully smiling and standing by Cliff's side as he prepared to launch his business. Rebecca had ensured she had been by his side whenever possible over the last few months, asking him about his plans and achievements, commiserating when things didn't go smoothly, making sure the children didn't add to his worries, his clothes were always laundered ready for him to wear, their meals were nutritious and filling, the house was a comfortable refuge for him to come home to after the exhausting challenges he was facing. She had been a regular visitor to the antiques centre as the repairs and installation of new fixtures and fittings were taking place, running out for any necessary hardware, tools, decorations as required, saving Cliff and his team hours in time by collecting and delivering items from shops and customers. Rebecca had been determined to support her husband in any way she could in those months leading up to the re-opening of his business.

And that was another thing, she mused, it was always his business, never theirs. She was happy to leave her job when she was pregnant, even though there was a wonderful children's nursery in Woodford, and her mum and Cliff's mother were very keen to help out with Grandmother Duties when they could. But Rebecca knew she wanted to be with her baby all the time, and Cliff could financially support them so her wages weren't needed. Her boss didn't want her to go and had made it clear she was welcome back any time; he would find a way to make room for her on his staff.

Once Nicholas was born her feelings were so strong she knew that as she was lucky enough to have the option she really didn't want to leave him with other people, however trustworthy and loving they were. The smell of him, sound of him, feel of him, she absolutely loved being a mum, and as Cliff was happy for her to choose whether to return to work or stay at home, she stayed with her baby.

Williamson Antiques was Cliff's baby, and although Rebecca had tried to be involved in the beginning, had wanted to be a part of what was so obviously a major element of his life, Cliff didn't encourage her, and once Child No.1 came along it wasn't practical for a few weeks, and then the weeks became months, and there never seemed to be a reason for her to do more than show an interest when Cliff came home at night to give them something to chat about together. Child No.2 had quickly followed, and for the last seventeen years her life had been happily focussed on her children, and she was content.

This re-launch had taken a considerable amount of effort by Cliff, and he was ably assisted by Nicola, Des and Barry, plus the stallholders who remained loyal to him had also given up a lot of time to get the antiques centre to a point where they all could start to earn some money from it again. Rebecca had proved herself to him that she could be more involved, but all her offers of permanent help had been gently turned down by Cliff, and for the first time in their married life she felt that as rejection, there had been no 'choice', he didn't want or need her to be at his side, running his business with him.

It was his rejection of her clear wishes and abilities to be more involved in his world that had brought things to a head, and she knew her own needs and aspirations had changed. Up until then she had happily moved through her life making choices and decisions which suited her without any conflict with what Cliff thought or wanted. But now things weren't as simple or easy as they had been for the last eighteen years.

She thought about her friends and family and all the ups and downs they had lived through, all the trauma and heartbreaks, the arguments and discordance which had plagued some people's lives, and smiled quietly and a little sadly to herself. Yes, she had a good life, she and Cliff and their children had not had any great upheavals or disagreements beyond 'You're not going out in that!' and 'No, you can't spend all morning watching telly you have HOMEWORK!'. But now she knew nothing would be the same again.

Well, if she was really honest then she was the only one who had altered. Cliff had always behaved in that way and she had always been content for him to do so. But no, not any more.

Rebecca realised she had no particular desire to transform her marriage, which saddened her that she cared so little after eighteen years and three children. She knew she had put a lot of effort into trying to be involved with Cliff's life over the last few months, but now it felt like hitting a square peg into a round hole, and it was time to stop. He didn't need the things she wanted to give him. She could see it wouldn't be fair to expect Cliff to change too, after all with hindsight he had been this way for eighteen years, it was highly unlikely he would suddenly become a passionate lover and caring husband and attentive father to their children. He had been a good provider of material things, she mused.

All Cliff wanted was to deal in antiques and run his antiques centre, to enjoy the banter with the dealers and the public who walked through the doors or those he met on his road trips to the antiques fairs around the country, to go next door to the tearooms for tea and cake and more discussions about antiques, or up the road to the pub for a few pints or a dram of whisky (or quite a lot of whisky judging by the smell of him when he did eventually clamber into their/her bed some nights!). In fact, she smiled gently to herself, it was just as well he went running most mornings or he would have grown to the size of a house.

She would break it to him gently, once she had worked out what 'it' was going to be, and she wondered what his reaction would be. Would he be surprised? Relieved? Devastated? She quickly moved on from that, it would be awful if he was devastated, but no, that wasn't likely, after all he didn't put much effort into their home life so nothing much would change for him.

She assumed that for a while they would continue to share the house and probably carry on with the whole dinner in the oven/in the fridge/ on the table charade, but they would no longer be sharing a bed, and would no longer maintain this pretence of a marriage. There

144

was no hurry, she would take her time to decide just what it was she wanted to do with the rest of her life.

A job was probably the first thing she needed to sort out, and once she was employed and earning her own money......oh that was going to be hard after all these years! What on earth was she going to do? Who would employ her? She didn't have any skills needed for the modern day workplace. Rebecca felt her resolve weakening, maybe she didn't need to rock the boat, after all what was so wrong with the way things were? But no, Rebecca knew that everything was wrong now, for her, and only she could make the necessary changes. And if that meant re-training so she was employable then while she had a roof over her head and her bills were being paid for then she needed to pluck up all of her courage and put it to positive use.

But wasn't that being very disloyal to Cliff? Using his generosity to enable her to leave him? Betraying his trust in her? No!!!! Her resolve strengthened as she reminded herself that her loyalty and trust towards him was not needed or wanted, and she wouldn't be taking anything he wasn't willingly giving her. Right, yes, re-training for something....

Cliff had no idea that anything was different about his marriage, no inkling about his wife's thoughts. To him she was a cheerful companion, the mother of his children, and most importantly a signal to the world that he was happily married family man. Oblivious to the turmoil which was going on inside the person standing next to him, once there were a decent number of people in the room, and a few minutes after the appointed time, Cliff called for everyone's attention and gave a short prepared speech:

'Thank you so much for turning out today to support me. As you can imagine the last few months have been very challenging, and a lot of hard work and effort, but as you can see despite a few last minute hiccups (yes, thought Nicola, the wrong size light bulbs were supplied with the cabinets, thank goodness for Rebecca shooting out in her car and sourcing correct ones that morning!) it has all come together so that we can open today. Thank you to all the stallholders who have come back, and welcome to our newest additions, I hope you will be profitable members of our team! Of course thank you to Nicola, Des and Barry who have stayed with me despite an uncertain future, I really couldn't have done it without them.

'Please do have a good look around at all the fine and rare antiques we have on display, ask us any questions about the stock and we will do our best to answer them, and of course don't hesitate to buy something!

'The Woodford Tearooms and The Ship Inn are all set up at the back there to help fill your bellies too, they are kindly donating some of their takings today to the Woodford Swimming Pool fund, so come on, get your money out!'

And with a big smile and a flourish he cut through the ribbon and declared that Williamson Antiques were open! Everyone cheered and clapped, and then either headed straight to the food and drink or started to peruse the antique items on display.

Except for two people.

Rebecca was one of them. She stood rooted to the spot where he had left her, wondering if she was the only one to notice Cliff hadn't mentioned any contribution from her towards today's successful re-launch of Williamson Antiques in his speech. She had been standing right next to him! Did her support mean nothing? All those evenings spent listening about his troubles of the day, the problems with coordinating the decorating, reassuring him when the absence of people he had counted as friends grew too big for him to cope with, the running around all over Brackenshire looking for the right colour paint to finish one small section when the Special Offer paint had run out, all those bloody meals re-heated in the microwave when they had been lovingly prepared four hours earlier? Rebecca could feel the resolve to change her life, which had been ebbing away, strengthening again with a rush. How often had that dismissal of her existence happened and she had not noticed?

In that moment Rebecca truly understood the saying 'Ignorance is Bliss'.

The other person whose feet were incapable of moving was someone who had only come along today to check that it really was all up and running and not some unfunny trick being played on them by the rest of the town. They could not believe their eyes at the sight of the antiques centre looking all fresh and bright and clean and busy. Yes, there were clearly far fewer stalls than before, but enough dealers had put their faith back into Cliff Williamson to make it a workable business. And look at all these people here cheering and supporting *Cliff bloody Williamson*, even though the tight bastard hadn't put his hand in his pocket to provide even a few sausage rolls and a glass of cheap plonk! Was everybody else mad?

If he wanted to bring Cliff down he was clearly going to have to do something else. He had really thought that ruining Cliff's business would be payback for the all-consuming jealousy he had been feeling ever since he had found out Cliff's nasty little secret, and when

147

that hadn't worked dropping the information off to the police about Cliff's 'other' money-making activities in the expectation that his credibility as a trustworthy business man would be shot down in flames. But no, neither action had succeeded in shutting this man down, here he was surrounded by laughing and smiling people, all wishing him success in his legitimate business.

Then a smile broke out on the man's face as he looked at one person in the room. He knew for certain what he would do next. It was a shame it was going to destroy that person's life, and would affect quite a few other people too, one of whom he had believed would become his wife a few months before. But then trashing the antiques centre had affected both of those people, and many more besides, including himself.

In fact thinking about it, this was a much better plan, he could kill the two secret birds with one stone and finally exact his revenge.

Yes, the man thought smugly, as he made his way over to the bar, this was going to hit Cliff where it hurts.

Smiling he raised his glass to Cliff who looked surprised that this man of all people should be wishing him well. Watch out mate, you won't know what's hit you.

Chapter Twenty Six

Tuesday 14th July 2015, 11.00am

Emboldened by the fun family evening spent when Gemma invited Peter to join them for their Saturday Night Fish 'n Chips, and gaining a little more confidence from how smoothly Gemma and Peter's romance was blossoming, Lisa plucked up the courage to ask Andrew Dover out for a date, determined to ask him the next time he came into The Woodford Tearooms.

Andrew had tried several times to ask Lisa out, but each time had been distracted by someone, and then lost his nerve.

So it was perhaps fate that determined that as Lisa went to pull out onto the roundabout the person who had been indicating left to come off the roundabout the turning before hers changed their mind at the last second and kept on coming round, so Lisa braked, and Andrew ran into the back of her car.

He was out of his car like a shot 'Oh no no no no, Lisa, are you alright, are you hurt, are you OK, I am so so so sorry, I can't believe I did that, are you alright?'

Lisa was shaken, but unhurt, and she looked up at him and smiled weakly. 'I'm fine Andrew, but are you OK?'

He stopped to think, he hadn't even thought about himself, but the airbag had given his face a fair old punch, and he realised his lip was bleeding.

'Oh, I'm fine too. Look if you are OK to drive, keep on going up to The Ship Inn's car park and I'll follow, at a distance don't worry! We can have a look at the damage then and I'll phone my insurance company.'

The Ship Inn was a couple of minutes along Farnham road, and once there they could see that the only damage was to Andrew's car where he had effectively driven into the tow bar on Lisa's. As it was almost lunchtime Andrew persuaded Lisa to come and have a pub lunch with him, and so, finally, they had their first date.

And they didn't stop talking for the first hour, both thankful the other was relatively undamaged from their car accident, and both relieved to finally be sitting down together at the same table, chatting, away from the tearooms.

When they eventually stopped talking for a moment Sarah rushed over with a couple of menus.

'Hello you two!' she said, with a broad grin, pleased to see that one of them had finally plucked up the courage to ask the other out. 'Are you planning to eat here today, or have you just popped in for a drink?'

'Oh yes, food, I'm starving!' Andrew hadn't realised how hungry he was.

They ordered, and then carried on chatting, asking each other all the questions they had been longing to ask for months, sharing stories, revealing wishes for the future, and generally getting on Very Well Indeed, as Sarah and Mike observed from behind the bar.

When Sarah came back over with their food, she said 'Oh Andrew, is that your portrait miniature in the cabinet in Williamson Antiques?'

'The one by Gervase Spencer? Yes that's mine. Do you like it?'

'I love it, just a shame there is no name to say who the sitter is.'

'Sarah, how did you become interested in portrait miniatures?' asked Lisa.

'Oh, well, I was tracing a branch of my Family Tree, and had jumped a few generations following something else, when I got a bit side-tracked reading about King Henry VIII and how he came to marry Anne of Cleves. Apparently he was shown a portrait miniature of her before he met her, and although he approved of her looks in the painting when they finally met each other in real life he thought she bore little resemblance to the artist's impression, and the King was rather displeased. That story tickled my imagination, so I started to notice portrait miniatures in shops and at antiques fairs. I had never noticed them before, and then I realised some of them were named so I began to look up their family histories when I had a bit of spare time, and now I have about forty of them! If you are interested you should pop up to London, to the Victoria & Albert museum where they have the national collection on display. Absolutely fascinating, well to me it is. Anyway, enjoy your lunch, let me know if you need anything else.'

'Is that true? About King Henry VIII and the portrait miniature of Anne of Cleves?' Lisa turned to Andrew after Sarah had left them.

'Who knows, but it is certainly a story I have heard before,' confirmed Andrew.

'Ah aren't they a lovely couple, good to see Lisa enjoying herself away from her work.' Sarah and Mike stood, companionably leaning together as they watched Lisa and Andrew enjoy their First Proper Date together.

Chapter Twenty Seven

Saturday 18th July 2015, 6.30pm

Cliff sank heavily into his leather chair in the living room with a groan, drained his pre-dinner whisky, and sighed. It had been another long, hard day at the antiques centre, with far more customers through the door than antiques sold; he had only taken twelve pounds all day – and that was for a modern vase.

Williamson Antiques had been back in business for three weeks, and after the initial buzz of the Opening Day there had been very few customers and even fewer sales. Admittedly summer is usually a quiet time in the antiques trade, but Cliff had been poring over his meticulously recorded sales figures for the last few years and this was definitely far worse than any previous year. If something didn't change soon he was in grave danger of going bankrupt, which would mean he would lose everything: his business; his reputation; this house.

He had briefly contemplated putting the house up for sale and moving the whole family into the flat above the antiques centre, at least that way he wouldn't lose that building which he was so proud of. He was sure he could make them all fit, and had even paced out the floor to see where he could erect plasterboard as room dividers, working out that the boys could share a bedroom, Charlotte could have her own room, and he and Rebecca would probably have to sleep in what would become the sitting room, and there wouldn't be a separate dining room so all their meals would be prepared in the kitchenette and then eaten in the sitting room/their bedroom. He did still consider that to be an option, although having three teenagers stomping around upstairs, with their loud music and constant use of the tiny bathroom might not be the best atmosphere in which to increase sales downstairs. In addition it would mean losing valuable office and works space for the business.

Rebecca and their three children were out for the evening, all at different places celebrating the end of term. Rebecca was meeting some of the other mums at the fabulous local Italian restaurant Amore, and the children were round at various friends' houses and would all be back according to their specific curfews.

He sighed again, and heaved himself back out of the chair to go and put the individual shepherd's pie Rebecca had made for him earlier in the day into the oven as per her instructions, before re-filling his glass with whisky and collapsing back into his chair. Peace and quiet. If it wasn't for all his financial worries this was Cliff's idea of heaven.

As he sat there his thoughts turned to the next morning's plans. Tomorrow was going to be an early start, he had to get to the Drayton Flea Market in time to grab something worth selling, and was catching a lift with Tony Cookson. He had the week's cash takings in his pocket, a total of four hundred and seventy pounds, so he really was going to be on the lookout for bargains, and bargains he could turn around quickly. No use buying something to put into auction and wait several weeks for the payout, if it even sold, there were no guarantees. He had no desire to pay the auction fees either, even though most of the auction houses he used gave him a much reduced percentage seller's fee, but just at the moment even those charges were eating far too much into the Loss column in his accounts.

What a way to earn a living. Or not as it seemed at the moment.

Cliff's mind started running over the events of the last few months, as it had done every single night since March 9th. Who had done it? And why? Someone must know something, and yet there were absolutely no rumours, or at least none which had come to his ears, and anyone who knows anything about the antiques trade knows what a hot-bed of gossip and rumour-mongering it is. Obviously he had rivals in the business, fallings out with various people over the years only to make it up again with some of them so they could carry on trading together, although some remained sworn enemies due to real or imagined dastardly deals where one of them made a real or imagined fortune out of the other.

The antiques trade is a funny place, where the dealers will go out of their way to help each other when times are tough, share information, show-off what they have bought and how much for, sob about what they have bought and how much for, and yet one real or imagined slight in a sale room and all of the shared history counts for nothing, they will never trade with each other again. But he could not think of a single person he may have upset who could: a) fit through the toilet window, even with the glass smashed out or b) pay someone else to do it in order to destroy all those antiques – a dealer in antiques just couldn't do that!

No other business premises in Woodford or even the surrounding Counties had been similarly targeted before or since. The police seemed to have formed the opinion it was a personal attack on Cliff through his business, although who the attackers were they didn't have any clues.

Who?

Why?

Without knowing the answers to those two questions Cliff couldn't know whether or not they would come back a second time. And this worried him.

Chapter Twenty Eight

Sunday 19th July 2015, 6.15am

'Good morning!' Tony was always so cheerful, whatever time of the day.

'Morning,' grunted Cliff as he hauled himself up into the passenger seat of Tony's blue Mercedes Vito van. It was funny, he pondered, he was fine if he was going out for a run as he did most mornings, but if he had to get up early for any other reason it was a real effort and he disliked it.

Tony was a chubby man of medium height with a mop of grey curly hair, and the sort of warm grey eyes which just invite you to smile with him, although their charm was lost on Cliff that morning. The van wound its way through the country lanes as Tony and Cliff chatted about who had sold what to whom, and who had bought a disaster, who had had a 'lucky' buy and speculated on where the dealer would sell it.

The monthly Drayton Flea Market was held on a disused airstrip, which meant the sellers were happy their vans and tables would not get sucked into the mud, and the buyers were happy they could wander around looking at the stock instead of walking in a muddy puddle.

'Looks like a good number of sellers here today' observed Tony forty minutes later as they drove past the stationary queue of assorted vans and cars, some with trailers loaded up behind and covered with tarpaulin sheets.

'Mmmh,' said Cliff, grumpily. 'Too many buyers here already for my liking.'

Although the market wasn't due to open to the public for free until half past eight, you could buy a ten pound ticket and get in at the same time as the sellers at seven o'clock, so once Tony and Cliff had bought their tickets they split up and went rushing from one stall to the next as the sellers were trying to set up their tables as quickly as possible, bringing out items they knew certain buyers would be interested in when they appeared. It was pot luck where the outside sellers would be as pre-booked stalls were only available to those people who wanted to be warm and dry inside one of the former aircraft hangars which had now been converted into a useful hall, with a café and toilets. The café was always well-run with affordable teas and coffee and delicious bacon sandwiches and home-made cakes, whereas the toilets were…well, better not to dwell on the state of the lavatories.

Most of the sellers Cliff was interested in buying from were usually stalled outside, whereas Tony was a postcard dealer, so his usual suppliers were sensibly installed indoors, but the half past eight rule was strictly adhered to for the hall otherwise it would be chaos as the sellers tried to unload several boxes of their stock from their cars and carry them through to their stalls, while buyers got in everybody's way desperately trying to be the first to see what was for sale.

Tony also dealt in military memorabilia, although if he was honest he was more of a collector than a dealer. He had a Man Cave in the garden, which looked like an ordinary wooden shed on the outside, but inside was

158

a secure strong room in which he stored medals, clothing, weapons and photos mainly from World Wars 1 and 2. His wife Lesley was banned from entering his shed, for which she was very pleased as the thought of all the reminders of war and death were not inviting to her. There was one particular dealer of militaria who always stalled outside, and for Tony it was well worth paying the extortionate ten pound entry fee to meet up with Mark Kenyon, a very tall thin man who also had grey curly hair and grey eyes, but had the opposite effect to Tony in that you wanted to take a step back from this sad and washed-out looking man who seemed to radiate ill-health and despair. He travelled down from Shropshire every month for this fair, and always had a box of goodies he had selected with Tony in mind.

'Good morning Mark! What have you got for me?'

'Morning Tony, come on I'll show you, it's in the front of the van,' Mark said, with his usual morose lack of enthusiasm. Despite his outward appearance Mark was a successful antiques dealer, who was financially well off and could have retired several years ago. It was a mystery to all the other dealers why he kept turning up at fairs and markets, when he appeared to find the whole experience so depressing.

Tony spent the next half an hour happily sorting through three boxes and a bag of militaria, bidding Mark on the contents, and walking away with a spring in his step and a huge grin on his face to find Cliff so the pair of them could carry the newly acquired stock through the market ground to the buyers' carpark.

On their way they passed a stall belonging to one of the former stallholders at the antiques centre, Simon Maxwell-Lewis, whose stall of furniture, beautifully displayed, had been thoroughly smashed into unusable

159

pieces, and who still held Cliff entirely responsible for the loss of his stock. Simon was an average looking bloke with nothing remarkable to distinguish him from anyone else, except for the air of menace which he now seemed to carry with him everywhere. He was a fitness freak, and regularly competed in triathlons, and had even completed a couple of Iron Man competitions, but despite Cliff's penchant for fitness and running the two had never been mates, even before The Attack, and they certainly wouldn't be now. As usual, he loudly called out a greeting which, predictably for Simon, was mainly vulgar insults ill-disguised as bonhomie. Cliff muttered a polite 'Morning' back.

Any sorrow and empathy Cliff had felt for the man in those first few dreadful weeks after the attack on the antiques centre had long since been replaced with a determination never to deal with him again, or put any business his way in the future, and he certainly didn't want anyone with that aggressive attitude stalled out in his antiques centre, even though he was desperate for stallholders. Simon had always been a touchy tricky client, one of the dealers who would take offence easily, and moan that so-and-so's stock was detracting from his own, that his stock wasn't selling as well as he thought it should because of, in his view but no one else's, another stallholder's lack of quality items or unreasonably cheap prices or the way they displayed their stock on their own stand. Nevertheless Cliff had felt sorry for him in the early days, as he did for all the stallholders. They had lost tens of thousands of pounds in stock, and in some cases hundreds of thousands of pounds, and in at least three cases it meant the end of their business.

Those people who had lost their businesses had not been professional dealers, but were retired teachers and salesmen who received good pensions and had been enjoying turning what had been a hobby into a bit of cash. All the same the loss of their stock had certainly been a major emotional blow to them, and Cliff had been desperately sorry for them as they were all lovely people and would be on a tighter financial budget than before, but he was slightly comforted by the knowledge they were not in any danger of losing their homes or entering into bankruptcy, as he and a couple of the others were.

The professional dealers only used the antiques centre as one of their outlets, it doesn't pay to put all your eggs in one basket whatever business you are in, and their items on the stalls and in the cabinets which had been destroyed were only a percentage of their total stock – admittedly in some cases over half of their stock had been on display for sale at the antiques centre, but they were still able to keep trading, as was the case for Simon. Despite his penchant for constantly complaining about other stall holders, and ability to bring a discordant air into the antiques centre just by walking in through the door, Cliff had been happy to have him in there because his stock was one of the highest sellers and brought many people in who also bought from other stallholder's stands and cabinets, but not anymore. Not that he had asked to come back, but Cliff was ready to politely rebuff him if he did.

By the time the flea market had opened to the non-fee paying public Cliff had bought all he wanted too, but he had to wait around for Tony to scour the stalls in the Hall so he bought himself a cup of tea and a bacon roll, and sat down on one of the plastic chairs with three other dealers. The subject of the vandalism in his antiques centre had long since been exhausted in the previous four months, so he was glad to have some respite from the puzzle and engage in a lively debate about whether or not a bronze bowl one of the other dealers had bought was a three hundred year old Tibetan incense bowl or a Chinese forty year old reproduction, the difference being whether or not he had bought a bargain for thirty pounds which he would be able to re-sell for five thousand pounds, or an expensive fifteen pound pot pourri container.

Chapter Twenty Nine

Monday 20th July 2015, 8.20am

Nicola coaxed the heavy key into the awkward lock as the gorgeous morning sunshine smiled down on her, and unlocked the front door to Williamson Antiques at the first attempt. Alarm code entered carefully, the two locks on the inner door opened with precision, the six light switches flicked on 1,2,3……since that awful morning when she had been shocked by the sight of the destruction of all those beautiful items in front of her, Nicola took care when opening up the antiques centre, paying attention to any details she may have missed even though the police were sure this wasn't the way the vandals had entered the building.

The experience had changed something for her, she had lost the sense of excitement she had felt for the past eighteen years at what the new day would bring, and no longer smiled with pride as she opened the lobby door and saw how beautiful the saleroom looked. Now she would pause with a sense of trepidation just in case….but no, everything looked as though it was where it was meant to be, and in the condition it had been left in the previous afternoon when she and Barry had closed up at a quarter past four.

She sighed, and wondered if she would ever feel the same again, the crime had unnerved her and she had been reluctant to be the one to open up on the mornings she was first in, but a job was a job, and one of her responsibilities, and therefore part of her salary, was to open or close the antiques centre on the days she was working there.

It was fortunate that she, Des and Barry had been able to continue to work for Cliff during the months between The Attack and the Grand Opening, she couldn't imagine where he had produced their wages from but had noticed he and Rebecca were no longer driving flash motors. Nicola knew Cliff had found her help invaluable in the last few weeks when it came to dealing with the paperwork, emails and phone calls from suppliers, prospective clients, and impatient buyers who didn't seem to understand they were closed because they were not in a position to be open to the public.

She continued with the Opening Up sequence, which included going up to the kitchen and putting the kettle on to boil, make herself a cup of tea before switching on the till and the computer, turning the Closed sign around to Open, and was soon sitting down behind the counter with her drink.

Ten minutes later Joanna Wilde came bouncing in through the door, eager to show Nicola her latest haul of goodies from a private house call. Joanna was one of the ten dealers who had agreed to come back after the attack, in fact Joanna had been one of the original dealers who had rented a cabinet when Cliff first opened the antiques centre eighteen years before. Joanna's husband, James, one of Cliff's regular drinking companions in The Ship Inn, worked for the firm of solicitors who had originally handled the sale of the property to Cliff when Emily Grant had died, and it had been her husband who had first sounded

Cliff out about the possibility of his wife selling a few items of jewellery in there.

Joanna was one of those tall slender women exuding energy, she had gorgeous big dark eyes, curly dark hair cut into a layered bob and styled in a way it was long enough to bounce around when she did, with astonishingly large and pert breasts for such a slim frame, and a permanent tan. Nicola wondered, as she always did when she saw Joanna, if her breasts were real, and if she used a tanning bed or if she had a spray or cream tan.

'Good morning Nicola!' grinned Joanna as she opened up her bag and poured the contents out all over the counter. 'Look at all this treasure!'

Although Nicola appreciated beautiful things, like the Victorian ruby and opal ring which wouldn't even fit on her little finger, and the delicate pearl brooch Joanna was showing her, her practical nature couldn't see the point of buying such items which you couldn't or wouldn't wear regularly. Nevertheless she smiled, and oohed and aaaahed, going with Joanna's enthusiasm and clear love for her latest purchases. Once she had shown Nicola every piece, Joanna asked for the keys to her own cabinet and proceeded to spend the next half an hour inspecting and re-arranging the existing stock to make room for the new items.

'Ooooh has the modern diamond ring sold Nicola?' she asked.

'Yes! A young couple came in yesterday looking for something 'old' as their engagement ring, and they seemed to think it fitted that description.' Nicola grinned at Joanna, who rolled her eyes, both of them in silent agreement that something fifteen years old did not fit the description of 'old', particularly when there were four other diamond rings in that cabinet, all of which were over one hundred years old according to their eighteen carat gold hallmarks.

By ten o'clock two of the other stallholders had been in to inspect their cabinets and stands, and to question Nicola about what they had sold over the weekend; the phone had rung at least seven times with enquiries about opening times, one cold caller claiming whoever answered needed to resolve their PPI insurance claims; and Cliff had also rung in to check all was OK and to say he would be there later that morning. He didn't sound happy that so far there had not been any customers through the door, although at that time of year the Public were more likely to be heading to the beach forty minutes away on a beautiful summer day, and the Trade had all headed to their holiday homes in Spain or Turkey.

Just as Nicola was trying to decide whether to make a second cup of tea or to open the bottle of ice-cold cloudy lemonade in the fridge, the lobby door was flung open with extreme force, and in charged Rebecca Williamson with an uncharacteristically furious look on her face.

'You Bitch!' she yelled. 'You Fucking Bitch!'

Chapter Thirty

Monday 20th July 2015, 10.12am

Nicola froze in shock. Rebecca Williamson was one of the most pleasant people you could meet, and certainly Nicola had never heard her swear, let alone shout any form of abuse at anyone! She felt some relief when she realised Rebecca's fury was not aimed at her, and then a feeling of curiosity and intrigue when she saw who Rebecca was striding towards in the same fast aggressive pace she had come through the door. Joanna was clearly as shocked as everyone else by this unexpected turn of events and stood rooted to the spot as Rebecca advanced on her furiously, before swinging her arm back, fist clenched, and punching Joanna in the face.

By this time everyone in the antiques centre (including the elderly woman and her daughter, the first customers of the day, typical, thought Nicola) had stopped what they were doing and were watching the drama unfold in front of them until that punch at which point several people sprang to help Joanna and prevent Rebecca from doing any more harm. This meant that there were five witnesses who could describe in accurate detail to PC McClure and PCSO Boston that it was indeed Rebecca Williamson, stalwart of the Woodford Secondary School's PTA, Woodford Summer Fete Coordinator, and all-round good egg, who had broken Joanna Wilde's nose with a single punch.

Rebecca's aim had been to exact revenge on the woman who she had just been informed was having an affair with her husband, and who, with the recent discoveries about her own life in mind, Rebecca blamed for taking up her husband's time and energy while she, Rebecca, was single-handedly parenting their teenagers.

She succeeded in that aim, but also with that single punch Rebecca Williamson positioned herself firmly as the Number One Suspect for The Attack on Williamson Antiques in March.

Chapter Thirty One

Monday 20th July 2015, 2.00pm

'I can't believe it. I can't believe it. I just can't believe it. Can you believe it?' Cliff was sitting in the tearooms with his head in his hands, while Paul Black and Tony Cookson sat on the other side of the table watching him. Secretly, Paul was loving every minute of it. Although they had been friends for a long time, he had always been a little bit jealous of Cliff both professionally and personally, and held a torch for Rebecca, but today he had particular reason to feel resentment. He was annoyed that Cliff had managed to have a secret affair with Joanna Wilde whilst maintaining a wife and children, while he, Paul, hadn't even been able to keep either of his two wives, let alone a mistress on the side.

As soon as he heard the news of Rebecca's assault on Joanna, Paul had rushed to the antiques centre along with every antiques dealer within a thirty mile radius, apparently. The ambulance was quickly on the scene, and the paramedics had taken Joanna to hospital because as well as the broken nose, Rebecca had knocked her out for a short time, so she was under observation for concussion. The police had taken Rebecca away, who, by the time they arrived, had collapsed in a heap on the floor sobbing loudly, completely inconsolable until the police turned up and then she stood, accepted the tissues Nicola had been trying to give her for the last few minutes, and walked out with her head held high.

Nicola and Des had cleared up as best they could the mess of Joanna's blood on both the floor and the cabinets in the vicinity, all the time exclaiming about how out of character Rebecca's behaviour was, and asking each other over and over again if they had known about the affair. Neither of them did, so they continued to ask each other who could have known, and who had told Rebecca.

Next door Cliff was asking similar questions, but with a lot less animation than his two employees.

'How did she find out? Who told her?' he groaned.

'Ooh yes, tell us all the details!' said Paul a bit too eagerly, which earned him a glare from Tony.

'Do you think she did all that damage to your stock in March?' asked Paul, keen to exact as much misery from Cliff while he could. 'Although if she knew then, why did she wait until now to punch Joanna's lights out? Oooh has she punched you too?' he asked.

'That's enough Paul' said Tony, sharply. 'Now is not the time to start rumours. Cliff, rather than sitting here asking questions neither of us can answer, don't you think you really should be at the police station so you can bring Rebecca home as soon as the police have finished questioning her.'

'Home! Home! She's not bloody well setting foot in my house ever again!' yelled Cliff. 'What the hell did she think she was doing, assaulting poor Joanna like that! And Paul's right, what if she did try and damn near bloody well succeed in ruining my business, our business, the business which pays for a roof over her head and clothes on her back. Bloody woman. There is no way I am letting her back in my house. Absolutely no way. She can sleep on the streets for all I care. Poor

Joanna, there's a chance she's going to need plastic surgery after this. Oh no.' A horrible thought suddenly occurred to him. 'I hope she's not going to expect me to pay for it. James can well afford it, he can pay. I'm not bloody paying, those procedures are bloody expensive aren't they. Oh no, James, what if he knows?'

'Ooooh maybe he'll come in and punch you on the nose' exclaimed Paul. 'And yes those procedures are expensive, running into the tens of thousands of pounds. Plus the cost of paying for her psychological trauma. This is going to cost you mate,' said Paul.

'Paul!' Tony tried not to shout, loathe to draw any more attention to them from the other customers in the tearooms. 'Will you please shut up!'

'You're bloody loving this aren't you,' said Cliff, looking at Paul miserably.

'No, I'm not' said Paul contritely, and not entirely truthfully. 'But who'd have thought your Rebecca could have behaved like that! Apparently she was F-ing and blinding all the way up the High Street before she nearly took those doors off their hinges and drop-kicked Joanna!'

'PAUL' Tony shouted. 'This situation is bad enough without you exaggerating every detail, now SHUT UP!'

Finally Paul realised that the events were serious, and he was adding to his friend's misery. He leaned forward and put his hand on Cliff's arm.

'Sorry mate, I'll stop winding you up now. I was just taken by surprise that you have never said anything to me about bouncing around on the bed with the delectable Joanna Wilde. I am only behaving like a jealous idiot, just ignore me.'

His words barely registered with Cliff, who was so wrapped in the awful realisation his adulterous behaviour could have been responsible for his dire business situation.

'Oh what am I going to do!' wailed Cliff, 'Just as I'm starting to get back on my feet she comes along and tears it all down again! I'm never going to get any dealers in if my bloody wife is going to go around assaulting them and putting them in hospital am I!'

'That's enough!' said a loud and angry female voice.

The three men looked up, startled.

'How you can manage to make yourself the victim in all this is just typical of your selfish attitude.' Standing with her hands on her hips and looking furious was Nicola.

'Whaaaat???' stammered Cliff, not used to anyone speaking to him like this, let alone his mild-mannered quietly efficient Assistant, Nicola Stacey. What on earth was going on with the women in his life?

'You. You. You,' said Nicola, raising her voice and jabbing her finger at him, her cheeks going pink. 'You and Joanna must have been having a right laugh at James and Rebecca all these years, patting yourselves on the back at going undetected, congratulating each other on your deceptions, being *pleased* with how successfully you have betrayed Rebecca and James' trust in you both. And now the rug has been pulled out from under Rebecca's feet, everything she believed about her life with you has been proved a lie, she is clearly devastated, and all you can do is vilify her. Shame on you Cliff Williamson. Shame on you.'

And with that she turned on her heel and stalked out of the tearooms, leaving the three men staring after her open mouthed, even Paul was lost for words for once. Her outburst and subsequent exit from the room had a

172

galvanising effect on the other customers who all started to share wide eyed looks across their tables before a series of conspiratorial whispers filled the brief silence. What a very exciting place Woodford was turning out to be today, thought Gemma, with mixed feelings that yet again bad luck for Cliff Williamson was proving to be good business for her.

Chapter Thirty Two

Monday 20th July 2015, 2.30pm

'Blimey!' exclaimed Paul, as all three men sat watching Nicola's rapidly retreating back, and forgetting about his recent apology to Cliff. 'What's got into her? She's always so quiet. You haven't been bonking her too have you Cliff?'

'No I bloody haven't!' howled Cliff, clearly at the end of his tether with Paul. 'She's just being a typical woman, irrational and emotional, sounding off when it's none of her business.' By now the tearooms were agog with the tableau being played out in front them, and Cliff's statement was met with a collective intake of breath from the mainly female audience.

'Well she has got a point,' said Tony, quietly. 'This particular can of worms is now wide open, and it is all of your own making Cliff, yours and Joanna's, so just maybe you need to do some damage limitation and fast. All very well making a quick decision not to support Rebecca from now on, but where will she go? Who is going to look after the kids and your animal menagerie, or are you chucking them out too? We know you can't cook. Do you even know how to work the washing machine? I don't think that kicking your betrayed wife out on her ear is going to help your campaign to prove yourself as a trustworthy businessman. You are having a hard enough time of it convincing dealers into Williamson Antiques with their precious stock, let alone the local buying public, Cliff. And what about James? What if he decides to react in the same way? Surely even he can't still be ignorant of what has been going on all this time. How do you know Rebecca even wants to stay with you? I'm not sure Lesley would stand by me if she found out I'd been having an affair.'

'Oh shut up Tony, I don't have the answers to any of those questions. I can't believe this is happening. What a bloody awful year I'm having.'

Cliff was silent for a few moments, re-assessing the situation. 'Right, yes, I think the best thing would be to go and collect Rebecca from the police station and see if we can sort something out. I'll leave Joanna for James to look after. Although if Rebecca did trash my antiques centre I am well within my rights to make her sling her hook, and she can take the kids and the cats and dogs and bloody rabbits too!'

By the time Cliff had made it to Woodford Police Station, Rebecca had already been released, and collected by her mum and driven back home. Cliff's indignant fury which he had been vainly hanging onto suddenly dissipated as he started to realise the enormity of what was happening, and his own role in the drama, so it was with slow heavy steps that he walked up the path to his front door.

Oh bloody hell, now what! Just as it dawned on him his front door key no longer fitted the front door lock, an upstairs window opened and Rebecca leaned out. It quickly became evident that her own fury was still very much alive.

'That's right, you cheating bastard, the locksmith came round and changed all of the locks. He finished twenty minutes ago. You took your time deciding whose side you were going to take didn't you? Well, thanks for that, you gave me the time to think so I have decided for you!' And with that she disappeared from view, only to re-appear and throw two suitcases out of the window. 'Let me know where you are staying so I can tell my solicitor where she can contact you!' She yelled, before slamming the window shut.

Cliff stood on the path, shoulders sagging, all the emotion and energy of the last few hours catching up with him, leaving him drained and confused.

How had this happened?

Why?

Those same questions he had been asking for the last four months were now taking on another meaning, but still the answers were evading him.

'Rebecca! Rebecca!' He shouted, in what he hoped was a conciliatory tone. 'Come on love, we need to talk. I'm so sorry you found out about me and Joanna. I never meant to hurt you. Who told you? Let me in love, please. We need to talk about this. Obviously it's over now, me 'n her I mean, not you and me, you're the one I married Rebecca, come on open the door please?'

The window was flung open again, and Rebecca's face appeared. 'Well that just sums it up doesn't it. You're sorry I found out? Really? That is what you are sorry for? Sorry that you were found out, not sorry for all the lies, the years of deception, all those missed school plays, unable to take the kids swimming or to their friends' birthday parties, or even their own birthday parties. Always 'Too Busy' working. Yeah right, I think we all now know what you were too busy doing, or who I should say. I'm not going to tell you who told me, but I am very grateful to him. And' she said triumphantly, waving a photograph out of the window 'he gave me the evidence to prove it! You are disgusting, you revolt me, GO AWAY.'

'Oh Rebecca please let's not do this standing in the street, let me in love, please.' Cliff was starting to panic now, this was all a bit too real for his liking, he had never imagined Rebecca would find out about him and Joanna, and he certainly hadn't envisaged that he would be the one thrown out on the street if she did.

'Stop calling me that! Love? Love? You don't know the meaning of the word you bastard. I Loved you, I gave up my career to be your wife, run your home, raise your kids, pick up your dirty washing, do all the shopping. And I found out you have been cheating on me the ENTIRE time?! Love! Fuck OFF!' She roared, and slammed the window shut again.

As she turned away she gave a wry smile, so that's why the Door Closing mantra hadn't quite worked for her, it was a Window Slamming mantra she had needed. Exhausted, she sank to the floor and bawled, crying big noisy snotty tears, until her mum appeared and sat on the floor with her, hugging her tightly and wishing she could do something to stop her daughter's pain. But there was nothing else she could do, other than to be there for her. This was her daughter's life and Rebecca would need to find her own way through this upheaval, just as Jackie had done when her own marriage had crashed and burned with no apparent warning.

Cliff decided to beat a hasty retreat before Rebecca opened the window again. It wasn't pleasant being shouted at when you live on an estate like theirs, and he could see several of their neighbours standing outside their houses or leaning out of their windows. He hurriedly grabbed the suitcases, shoved them in the boot of his car, and left.

It was only as he was driving away that the implications of Rebecca's actions and words hit home. She had been waving a photograph at him.

Cliff had to slam on the brakes to avoid driving into a neighbour's garden wall.

Chapter Thirty Three

Monday 20th July 2015, 6.00pm

There was one topic of discussion in The Ship Inn that evening.

No one seemed to have known Cliff and Joanna were having an affair, or at least if they did no one was admitting to it. There were quite a few women who were feeling envious of Joanna, Cliff Williamson was a rare man in Woodford being both gorgeous and successful, but everyone had thought he was a happily married family man and neither he nor Rebecca had ever given anyone cause to think he would be up for an extra-marital liaison. Rebecca was well-liked by the women in Woodford, plenty of people had been on committees or local groups with her, and they all knew her as a caring and responsible mother.

Even more men in the pub were openly full of admiration for Cliff, not only for having an affair with Joanna Wilde, the sort of woman both men and women would take the time to look up and down when she walked into a room, but to have managed to do it without anyone else knowing.

Although clearly at least one other person had known. Who that was no one knew as Rebecca had refused to name her source, and nobody had come forward to accept responsibility.

Opinion was divided about who was the more attractive: Rebecca or Joanna. Initially no one

179

considered James' feelings or future, and no one expressed surprise that Joanna would have cheated on him.

Facts were still sketchy, and the Regulars in The Ship Inn were unaware of the extent of Cliff and Joanna's relationship.

Their affair had been going on for about twenty years. It started a couple of years before Cliff and Rebecca had met, even before James had 'introduced' them with the suggestion that Joanna should have a cabinet in the proposed antiques centre, and had continued throughout the Williamson's courtship, engagement, wedding, and the births of their three children. They had been incredibly discrete, everyone was shocked both by the news of the affair and when the whole truth came out by the length of time it had been going on for.

As the evening wore on the general consensus of opinion in The Ship Inn was that Cliff was a fool for cheating on Rebecca, but that Joanna was probably a good choice if you wanted to have a bit on the side, and that it just goes to show that you don't know what goes on behind closed doors because everyone had thought that Cliff and Rebecca, and James and Joanna, were happily married. In fact James and Joanna had celebrated their Silver Wedding Anniversary earlier in the year, they were often in The Ship Inn together seemingly happy in each other's company. They were part of the regular crowd, and although Cliff was also one of the Regulars no one had ever seen any indication that there was something going on between him and Joanna, no sparks, no secret conversations, nothing.

By the time Mike Handley called Time speculation had already started as to whether Cliff was the one who had 'mugged' James in February, and that maybe it was James who had carried out The Attack on the antiques centre.

News had also reached the pub about Rebecca's decision to leave Cliff, and generally the Regulars were in agreement that she was right to do so.

No one had heard what had happened to James and Joanna, neither of whom had been seen since Joanna left the antiques centre in the ambulance although they all knew she had been discharged and was no longer at the hospital. Presumably James was now fully aware of what had been going on as normally by this time on a Monday evening he would have been propping up the bar engaging in the local gossip too.

Joining in with the speculation and rumour-mongering, expressing surprise at the news of the affair between Cliff and Joanna, and generally maintaining his place as a Regular at the pub was the man who had tried and failed to destroy Cliff's business first by trashing the antiques in the centre, then by tipping off the police about Cliff's 'other' business venture, and had succeeded in putting into motion the events of the day by giving Rebecca a photo of Cliff and Joanna in bed together.

Or to be precise, on a bed together, leaving nothing to the imagination.

He had waylaid Rebecca in the carpark of the farm shop as she was about to do her normal weekly shopping. Rebecca was a creature of habit and liked to get there early, and be in and out before the hungry elderly arrived for their Monday morning Pensioner's Special Breakfast, so the carpark was deserted as usual for that time in the morning when he had quickly slipped into the passenger seat of her car so they could talk quietly in relative privacy. At first she had been startled and scared when a man had opened the door and got in, but once she saw who it was she had been pleased to see him.

Until he had started to talk.

Rebecca had refused to believe him, even when he started to list dates and places and she knew Cliff wasn't at home with her on those days. He hadn't planned to show her the photograph, but he could see she wasn't going to take his word at face value and he was getting desperate. All the same he was taken aback by her reaction. He had expected sorrowful tears, maybe a little bit of wailing, and had even brought one of those handy packs of tissues with him imagining she would cry on his shoulder. But instead she had flown into a furious rage at the sight of the couple on the bed. Rather than offering a comforting arm he had hastily left before her shouting brought any attention to him.

He was sorry that Rebecca had been so upset, but he was overjoyed by the fact she had thrown Cliff out, and the fact that ungrateful slut Joanna had been injured too was a bonus as far as he was concerned. She deserved everything she got, just like her double-crossing husband.

At last he felt he could relax, sit back, and watch their lives unravel, finally getting his revenge for the way, the appalling way, the three of them had treated him. They would not get away with their deliberate attempts to cheat him out of his right to love, and to money.

Chapter Thirty Four

Wednesday 22nd July 2015, 11.45am

Gemma and Lisa were having a quick breather before the expected lunch time rush. A lull in customers had given them the opportunity to try a couple of new fruit smoothie recipes before committing them to the menu. Gemma was drinking a mango-based one, and Lisa was drinking a raspberry and pomegranate smoothie, both had added ice and were trying not to gulp the tasty, cooling drinks.

It was one of those gorgeous hot summer days, which for a market town like Woodford was terrible for the local economy because it meant the tourists would have headed to the beach, but the Bartletts had taken care to ensure theirs was a business which attracted locals as well as tourists, so they were sure of year-round business including on rare sunny days in the English summertime.

'So come on then little sister,' said Gemma with a gleam in her eye, 'how is the Romance of the Century going with Andrew?' she grinned slyly.

Lisa stopped sipping her drink for a moment and looked thoughtful. 'Er, not great,' she admitted.

'No?' enquired Gemma in a surprised tone. 'I thought you two were hitting it off really well! Has something happened?'

'Oh yes, we are' exclaimed Lisa. 'And no, nothing has happened. Well, that is the problem really. You know, we haven't…' she dropped her voice to a whisper and looked around furtively 'we haven't had sex.'

Gemma screamed with laughter 'Lisa Bartlett! You have only been seeing each other for a week, I should hope you haven't jumped into bed with him already. What are you like?!' she grinned and hugged her sister affectionately. 'Why on earth do you think you should have jumped each other's bones at this early stage in your relationship?'

'Well, yes, I know we have only been officially going out together for a week,' admitted Lisa, looking increasingly red-faced as her sister continued to snort and laugh. 'But we have been, you know, *interested* in each other for several months, and we have seen each other every day since the accident, so I would have thought things would have progressed further than a kiss on the cheek when we meet each other or say goodbye to each other.'

'Ah, I see, he is being very courteous and gentlemanly is he?' said Gemma, attempting and failing to add a conciliatory note to her voice.

'How long did it take before you and Peter slept together?' asked Lisa.

Now it was Gemma's turn to look embarrassed. 'Well, we haven't yet, we are taking our time to get to know each other properly. There is no hurry little sister, we're not desperate teenagers looking for a quick fumble and shag you know,' she said, a little defensively.

Both sisters were quiet for a few moments, each deep in thought about their own love lives, or lack of. The truth was that Gemma was nervous of sleeping with Peter. She had been comfortably married for a long time and was secretly terrified of going to bed with a new man. In the early days she and her husband had been full of lust and passion, making love every night, often several times a night, but babies had changed their relationship; pregnancy, giving birth, and sleep deprivation meant that the lust and passion, although still there, had dampened down considerably, and they had fallen into a two or three times a month and never twice in one night arrangement for a number of years. Sex with her now ex-husband had become fun and companiable and routine, just as their working relationship had been, until it gradually faded away to being non-existent at the same time as their individual hopes and dreams separated from the happily married and like-minded business partners they had been.

The thought of being intimate with a man who would feel different, expect her to behave and respond in another way to the one she had grown used to, who liked things she didn't know about, who would touch her in places that age and child-birth had altered permanently, was terrifying. She fancied Peter, he made her whole body tingle every time they touched, she just had to catch a glimpse of him walking along the road or driving past and her heart shot up into her mouth. Also, she knew he was ready to take her to bed. But although she was keen, she wasn't prepared for that next step.

Gemma really enjoyed spending time with him. Peter was very intelligent, kept himself fit and healthy without being a nutrition or fitness-fanatic, didn't indulge in drugs other than a few pints of beer or glasses of wine every week that she was aware of, and got on well with her kids. She had met his daughters a couple of times now, and they had seemed very nice and friendly towards her, so no barriers to progressing with their relationship there.

Peter made her laugh with his funny anecdotes about his clients, and he was a kind man who cared about the health and well-being of the horses he treated, and also about their owners, often taking a lot longer at appointments than the receptionist had planned so was fast earning the reputation for turning up late which intensely annoyed some clients, but was appreciated by others who had been at the receiving end of his thoughtful and compassionate approach.

Jackie Martin wasn't quite so enamoured with her junior partner's time-keeping, but then she preferred to maintain a professional approach with clients, sticking to the point of the visit rather than discussing everything from feed to exercise routine to behaviour issues, as Peter regularly did during his veterinary visits. In the short time he had been working for her Jackie could see that their client list was already starting to split between those who asked for her, and those who asked for Peter, so she was prepared to wait a while longer to see if the natural split benefited the Practice's finances. It was clear that Peter was less inclined to prescribe treatments from which the Practice earned its money, but already word had spread and their client list had increased and the number of visits to private yards were higher than in previous years. Also, the local riding school manager who had always used the equine vets from Swanwick, had recently made enquiries about employing the Woodford Equine Vets with the proviso that Peter was their go-to-vet when possible.

He certainly had a different approach to equine welfare to the one she and her former partner Alastair had taken, and while theirs had worked very well for the last thirty years Jackie was wise enough to see that horse ownership had also changed significantly during that time. Increasingly horses would be equipped with knotted rope halters and long ropes rather than the beautiful leather head collars and short lead ropes she preferred, and more and more owners were taking on the responsibility of caring for their horses' hooves and managing them barefoot rather than relying on a farrier to shoe them every six weeks or so. Jackie was not comfortable with this particular latest fashion of shoeless horses, and it bothered her to see them running around with no protection on their hooves when she was Vet on Call at the local Endurance trials or TREC competitions. When she was the veterinary professional at the various equine events in the County she was always stringent about checking the soundness of barefoot horses at the checkpoints, and although she hadn't noticed any higher statistics for unsoundness in that group, she was noticing that their heart rates tended to be lower than the shod horses. Plus the barefoot trend was increasing in popularity, and as Peter was enthusiastic about horses performing barefoot and had positive experiences to relate to her, she was prepared to keep an eye on his methods, and their financial books, before making any judgements.

Meanwhile Lisa was feeling a tad frustrated. Unlike Gemma's, her marriage and sex-life with her husband had never been fun and companiable. It had been more like a competition to see how many times he could bring her to orgasm whilst skilfully holding his own back before eventually releasing both of them from the activity. There had been no romance or passion. Although at the time of their marriage break-up she had been devastated, crushed, and could never imagine ever trusting anyone to buy her a coffee let alone share her bed, the teasing build-up to finally dating Andrew had awakened all sorts of feeling she had never been aware of before, and now that they were finally a couple she was anxious to explore these new-found sensations. She desperately hoped it wasn't going to take as long to get Andrew into bed as it had to go on a date with him.

The cow bell rang and snapped the sisters out of their personal introspections, both looking up guiltily as a family of four trooped in through the door of the tearooms, clearly having spent too much time on the beach the day before judging by their red faces and stiff movements. Gemma and Lisa exchanged glances, both smiled encouragingly at the other, and they set to work.

Chapter Thirty Five

Saturday 1st August 2015, 8.30pm

Rebecca looked at herself nervously in the mirror. It was a long time since she had worn 'proper' work clothes having spent the last eighteen years mainly in jeans and T-shirts and flat shoes. The person staring back at her was wearing a sleeveless blouse, a long skirt, and open-toed sandals with two inch heels. Christine had treated her to a 'Back To Work' day at the Spa in Swanwick a few days before, and despite initial misgivings Rebecca thoroughly enjoyed the feeling of freedom and luxury and pampering. They had followed this up the next day with a shopping spree, Rebecca grateful for Christine's expert eye as they chose a capsule wardrobe of clothes suitable for her new job.

She relaxed a little bit and smiled, pleased with the image of herself in the cheval mirror Cliff had found for her when they first moved into this house. Through the turmoil of the last few weeks Rebecca had been determined not to look back on her marriage to Cliff as all bad, and reminding herself of the occasional thoughtful things he had done helped that process. She had loved this mirror when he brought it home, but remembered that a little part of her had wished he had included her in the decision since she would be the one using it most of the time and would have preferred the frame to be a different colour to suit the décor of her walk-in wardrobe, but she hadn't said anything then for fear of sounding ungrateful. Now she knew that in any future relationship she would not allow things like that to slide past her. It was possible to express an opinion without upsetting someone who loved and valued you.

Once she had time to sit down and assimilate all the facts, or at least those she was being made aware of, Rebecca had quickly come to terms with the knowledge her husband had been having an affair, and although she was initially crushed by the news of his infidelity, she knew she had stopped wanting to be married to Cliff Williamson several months before she found out about it. It didn't make all those years of unfaithfulness any less distressing, but she wasn't overwhelmed by the news as she felt she probably would have been if she had found out a few months before. Maybe she had always known there was someone else. It also neatly explained his emotional absence and their lack of a sex life, it was a relief to discover this was not due to anything she was responsible for although she felt like such a fool for thinking their marriage had been normal. She wondered at the last eighteen years of her life, had she really been as content as she had thought? Yes, she decided, she had been, but now she felt a sense of excitement and adventure, as well as trepidation, about what the future would bring.

Well, she thought to herself, if I had known a trip to a spa and another to a shopping centre was all it would take to get me back in the workplace I'd have done it years ago! She smiled at her mirror image, and then carefully took everything off before hanging her blouse and skirt on the outside of the wardrobe, ready for the morning.

Once she was more comfortably and normally dressed in pyjamas and slippers she went down stairs to join her children, who were all sitting watching television, but one glance outside convinced her that sitting out in the garden with a cup of mint tea and her book enjoying the stunning evening sunset would be far more relaxing than whatever was transfixing her children to the screen. She settled down in the cushions of her planter's chair, another of Cliff's purchases although this one she had wholly approved of, and rather than picking up her book she sat quietly, allowing the sounds of the families in the neighbouring gardens to wash over her, as she prepared herself for the next big change in her life.

Although the discovery of Cliff and Joanna's affair had been an enormous shock, in a funny way it had brought peace to Rebecca, it meant that she didn't have to be the one to end their marriage, or find a reason to explain the break-up to anyone. And as her new job had materialised so quickly she also didn't have time to hide away and mope, although even if she had wanted to having three teenage children to care for, whose own lives had also been severely jolted, was reason enough to make sure she got out of bed every morning, washed and dressed, and attempted to carry on as 'normal', whatever that was. Both her mother and Christine had been amazing sources of support, and she felt happier about leaving her comfort zone of home and voluntary committees to become an employee and part of a workplace, knowing that both women were ready to listen and advise if she needed them too.

As she had suspected the break-up of their marriage made little difference to the daily routine she and her children lived with, although the school holidays meant everything was a little different. In fact the only unexpected incident in the last two weeks was the apology note and flowers from Joanna Wilde. Even Christine couldn't find a woo-woo reason for that one!

Rebecca smiled as she thought of Christine, whose romance with Dave Truckell was moving at a fast pace. They certainly made a lovely couple. Rebecca had seen a lot of them over the last few months, although she was aware that Dave had stayed out of the way for the past fortnight so Christine could give extra time for Rebecca in case of breakdowns and hysterics or physical assaults. But since that day when she had behaved in such an uncharacteristic fashion – although she had never been confronted with a photograph of her husband in flagrante with another woman before, she reasoned – Rebecca's emotions had been lighter and less fettered than before. She supposed she had done most of her grieving in the months since she had realised her marriage was non-existent.

'Mum!' Michael's call broke into her thoughts.

'Yes darling?' she called back.

'Ah, we didn't know where you were. What are you doing out here in your PJs?!' All three of her children appeared, looking a little too smiley and jolly. Rebecca recognised those looks.

'What have you three been up to?' she asked, sternly.

'Nothing! Honest!' exclaimed Charlotte. 'Well, we have been up to something, but you'll like it. Come on Nick, give it to her!'

Nick stepped forward with a small gold-coloured gift bag, and presented it to Rebecca with great ceremony, bowing low and flourishing his arms and hands around wildly.

'Thank you darlings, this is a surprise!' she said, peering inside. And that did it. All the gentle tearful feelings and emotions which seemed to have been missing from the last fortnight came flooding out as she carefully picked out the coffee mug with her name and 'Best Mum in the World' written on it, a tiny little teddy bear mascot, a pen and pencil set with her name inscribed on them, and a framed photograph of her three babies all grown up and standing in line with their arms around each other, smiling directly into her eyes.

'Oh don't cry Mum, it's meant to make you happy, for your desk at work.' Charlotte was concerned now, as were her brothers.

'Oh I am happy,' sobbed Rebecca, 'so happy, I am crying because I am happy. What wonderful children you are, oh I do love you, all of you.' She stood up and the four of them had a big family hug, before she had to break free to go and find some tissues.

Yes, she thought, despite everything that has happened in the last few months we are all happy.

Chapter Thirty Six

Saturday 1st August 2015, 10.00pm

Someone else who was feeling 'happy' was Gemma. The conversation with Lisa in the tearooms earlier that week had caused her to spend a couple of days mulling over her feelings about Peter, about their possible future, and about her own needs. Peter had become a regular attendee of their Saturday night fish and chip suppers, her sons no longer felt the need to turn up every Saturday night to supervise and they had made other plans that night, as had Lisa and both of her children.

Peter had been the Vet on Duty the night before and was called out twice, once to a colicking horse who tragically died before he got there, and once to a very late foaling which had been successful.

The owners, a family named Stanwick, had no idea their mare Molly was pregnant. They had bought her in the spring, and mother, Kim, and daughter, Heather, had been having fun with her exploring the local countryside with their other mare, Maggie. It wasn't until the week before when Molly had started to be a bit 'girthy' and sluggish that they had suspected anything was amiss. At the time they thought she was grumpy because maybe they had overworked her a little, such was their enthusiasm for exploring the countryside around them, so they gave both horses a week off. The Stanwicks had been keeping the mares on a strict hard core track system which involved very little access to grass during the day but adlib access to hay, and now they decided that as the season was moving on and, in their previous experience, the worst danger time for laminitis of February to June was over, to open up the track and include a larger area of grass at night.

It was only when Heather had been giving both horses a thorough check and groom on the Friday afternoon that anyone had noticed Molly's udders were bagging up, but as there was no possible way she could have been pregnant – they thought – plus it was far too late in the year for any foals to be born, they spent the rest of the afternoon on the internet looking for other reasons for the mare's udders to be swollen.

In the end the whole family decided to camp up at the horses' fields just in case. It was a beautifully warm and dry night and they were used to camping and cooking outside, having already spent a few nights at their fields that summer.

Theirs was a basic but effective way of equine management. They had five acres of hillside covered in a variety of grasses and herbs, and plants 'smart' horse people would term as weeds but which the family knew through their research and experience were valuable in providing variety and opportunities for self-selection for their mares. The fields were surrounded by hedges and trees, the undulations in the hillside provided additional shelter, but the horses also had a large wooden shelter which they used to escape the flies during the day, plus there was a smaller barn for storing hay and other feed. The Stanwicks had owned horses all their lives, the land had originally belonged to Kim's family and she had grown up with ponies and horses to ride any time she wanted, and her husband Robin was born into a family who ran a riding school.

Over the years the Stanwicks had successfully developed their own method of managing their horses, who lived out all year round, with a permanent track section of hardcore leading from the wooden shelter with its concrete apron, to the rest of the land. They had created a variety of patterns for their moveable grass track sections, and with the use of a ride-on mower they were able to keep it short enough to provide a useful facility whose primary purpose was to encourage movement rather than feed. Robin's last horse, a locally bred Irish Draught horse named Swanwick Spinner, or Wicky as he was usually called by the family, had lived well into his twenties, regularly hacking and competing in riding club activities until the end. Wicky was the first of their horses to teach them a different way of equine management to the one they had previously known, and Molly was now the fourth horse they were looking after in this more relaxed style.

Nobody really believed she was going to give birth, but they were worried about her nonetheless, and no one felt like going to sleep so the eight year old son, twelve year old daughter, and both parents were sitting, well-wrapped, around a camp fire they were keeping alight with regular topping up of branches from some tree maintenance they had carried out in Spring, when Molly started to show signs of restlessness and Maggie also began to behave out of character.

Better to be safe than sorry, they called the Woodford Vets and spoke to Peter, who was on his way to his first call of the night but took a few minutes to give them a few things to look out for, and urged them to phone him immediately if anything started to change.

The equine department of the Woodford Equine Veterinary Practice is small, with only Jackie and Peter as the dedicated horse vets, and Alastair Wilkinson on stand-by in cases of emergency although officially he was retired, so Peter texted Jackie even at that late hour just as a heads-up in case he needed any back-up.

By the time he arrived at his first appointment the horse was already dead and had been for over half an hour. He walked into a full scale argument between the owner of the horse and the owner of the livery yard, in which the words 'sue' 'neglect' and '£250 000 horse' were being shouted. Peter left details about the removal of the horse for the inevitable post mortem, which would take place at the main equine hospital over the County border in Newbury, and left as quickly as he could, desperate to get away from the scene where a horse had lost its life and no one was grieving, other than for lost potential and money. He texted Jackie again with brief details, and letting her know she could go to bed after all, much to her relief.

When he arrived at the Stanwick's field the mare was very clearly about to give birth, so he and the family sat quietly drinking cups of tea and hot chocolate while nature safely took its course, and a beautiful, perfect colt was born in front of their eyes to a loving nurturing mother and a gently protective aunt.

Once the colt was up and feeding from his mother, and Peter had checked both mother and son by torchlight to ensure all was as it should be, he left the family with information about how to care for their newly expanded herd – they had spent most of the evening researching on the internet - and took his leave, confident that all three of those horses, the sum total of their worth probably coming to less than two percent of the dead horse, would be much better cared for and loved, and live longer and happier lives, than the one now lying unloved with its life extinct in a spotless expensive stable.

He was too wired from the beautiful scene he had witnessed to go home and sleep. Despite seeing hundreds of foalings he was always filled with awe and had shed a little tear at the brilliance of nature. He wanted to share his experience with someone so he texted Gemma on the off-chance she was also awake.

By now it was four o'clock in the morning and the dawn was just starting to show. Gemma had been fast asleep, and her first instinct when the bleeping of his text-message arrived was that one of her sons was in trouble, but when she saw Peter's message she lay back on her pillows with relief and texted him back. Thirty minutes later he arrived at her front door, she let him in quickly deciding not to give him a welcome hug because despite the protective overalls he had been wearing during the birth, he was in need of a wash so she showed him where the towels were and how to work the shower, put all of his clothing into the washing machine, and went to the kitchen to wait for him. Once he emerged smelling much sweeter and wearing one of Daniel's t-shirts and a pair of his boxer shorts, they sat out in the garden drinking tea and eating bacon sandwiches, sharing the crusts with Suzy who was being Very Well Behaved and Not Begging.

In no time at all it was seven o'clock and they both had to get ready for work. Peter's clothes hadn't had time to dry, so again Gemma raided Daniel's wardrobe which was surprisingly full considering he had moved out of her house two years' earlier, and found an old pair of tracksuit bottoms and some socks.

They arranged for Peter to come back to Gemma's that night for the traditional fish and chips and to collect his own clothes, and she shyly suggested he bring an overnight bag. His initial reaction was 'Yes please' and a big snoggy kiss and hug, but then he remembered he had had no sleep and knew he would be dead to the world by nine o'clock that night, so he explained and reluctantly declined her offer.

'Oh that's alright!' she exclaimed, 'I've been awake since four o'clock this morning you know, I'll be ready for a good night's sleep by then too, you can always sleep in the spare room if my snoring keeps you awake,' she winked.

The brief awkwardness was over, they were back to being Gemma and Peter again, both enjoying their full working day with smiles on their faces despite their lack of sleep the night before. Peter popped back to the Stanwick's fields to check everyone was OK, and was pleased to see that the colt was lying down fast asleep as only babies can, while mum and aunt stood over him, protecting and guarding him from predators. The male members of the human family had popped home for more provisions, but the mother and daughter were still there, neither wanting to leave the unexpected addition to their herd, both telling Peter they were going to be camping up there all summer, although he suspected that hot showers and soft beds may call after a few days.

They thanked Peter over and over again for coming out to what turned out to be a non-emergency in the middle of the night, and for coming back out free of charge that morning, and as he walked back to his car he smiled to himself, content in the knowledge that as traumatic a decision as it had been to leave his previous Practice where he was well-liked and respected and happy, his new life was even better than the one he had left behind in Shropshire.

Gemma's day was far busier and less awe-inspiring than Peter's, but nonetheless she was feeling the love for every customer who walked through the door of The Woodford Tearooms, welcoming everyone with a broad smile and cheery voice. Gemma was always a sunny person, but even Lisa noticed a definite up-lift to her mood.

'What's got into you then Gem?' she asked.

'What do you mean?'

'Well, you are practically hugging everybody who comes in here! It is lovely that you are so happy, but come on, spill the beans, what's going on. Anything to do with our handsome local horse doctor?'

'Yes,' sighed Gemma happily, and drifted off to welcome yet more customers as they came through the tinkling door.

Sure enough, by half past eight that evening both Gemma and Peter were desperate for bed, but not for the reasons of sleep deprivation they had both been anticipating, and with no children to inhibit them they proceeded to explore each other's bodies greedily and noisily before they had even left the sofa. Gemma's worries about her body, about not being good enough or experienced enough, had a brief surge to the forefront of her mind but then a particularly bold move by Peter thrust them from her thoughts.

Forever.

Chapter Thirty Seven

Saturday 22nd August 2015, 4.00pm

As the summer wore on Lisa became more and more disheartened about her romance with Andrew Dover. She couldn't help but compare her relationship with that of Gemma and Peter's, which seemed so easy and light and *fun.* By contrast she and Andrew were friendly and polite and, frankly, boring.

They met up a couple of times a week for dinner at The Ship Inn or a visit to the cinema, and that was it. She had invited him to join in with the family's Saturday night fish and chip suppers but he had always declined, pleading early starts for this antiques fair or that flea market, but Lisa was beginning to suspect he didn't want to join in with her boisterous family's gatherings. She had suggested enjoying the beautiful sunsets by taking Florence for a walk along one of the many footpaths through the fields near her cottage, or going down to the beach to enjoy the stunning views other people travelled for over five hours to see on holiday, but he always found a reason why a pub meal at The Ship Inn or a film at the cinema in Swanwick was a better option.

Gemma had revealed edited highlights of that first, and then subsequent, night she and Peter spent together. Peter had practically moved in with her and they were clearly very much in love. Obviously Lisa was overjoyed that her sister was sharing so much fun with someone as lovely as Peter, but a nasty little piece inside her soul was green with envy as she compared her romantic relationship with that of her sister's.

As Lisa started the process of closing up the tearooms for the night, washing everything down and making sure it was all pristine for Gemma when she opened up in the morning, Lisa thought about Andrew and wondered whether they had a future together, or if she should call things to a halt now. His was a solitary life, revolving around checking and adding to his stock in six different antiques centres, including Williamson Antiques, and buying more antiques at several different auctions, fairs and markets. He didn't appear to have any social life, or friends who were not involved with the antiques business, and although she couldn't fault his almost religious solo weekly Sunday lunches with his mother, she wanted to.

Suddenly overwhelmed with sadness Lisa knew what she had to do. After all those months of idolising him, anticipating how wonderful it would be to be kissed by him, held by him, going to bed (or anywhere!) with him, the reality of dating Andrew Dover was like wading through a bucket of cold plain over-cooked porridge; boring, stodgy, slow and pointless.

The cowbell rang as the door opened, and Paul Black walked in.

'Lisa! Are you OK?' he asked, concern creasing his usually smiling face. 'I was walking past and saw you, is everything alright?'

Lisa realised she was sitting at one of the tables facing the window looking out onto the High Street, with tears running down her face. She had no idea how long she had been there, and hurriedly stood up brushing away the tears and sniffing hard, embarrassed about what was happening to her.

'Oh, yes, thank you Paul, I'm fine,' she lied, not very convincingly.

'No, you are not,' he said, moving in closer. 'What has happened? Come on, you can tell me. Can I get you anything? A glass of water? A cup of tea? I think there might be a teabag around here somewhere,' he grinned, and with that Lisa's tears dried up for real and she laughed.

'Yes, you might be right,' she agreed, 'this is The Woodford Tearooms you know,' she smiled up at him, noticing for the first time how very brown his eyes were, lovely kind brown eyes, with gold flecks.

Oh no, no no no no, you *can't* fall in love with serial womanizer Paul Black, she told herself sternly.

Paul took a step back, shocked by the suddenly fierce expression on the face of the woman who only seconds earlier had looked sad and vulnerable and in need of a warm hug, like his daughter when she had learned she hadn't passed her Grade Three piano examination. Now Lisa looked like she was about to shout at him and start throwing things! Seeing his reaction Lisa quickly rearranged her face into a more reasonable and friendly one.

'Thank you Paul, but honestly I am fine, just have something on my mind that's all.'

Relieved that she was smiling again, Paul nodded, and went back out the door, calling over his shoulder as he went. 'If there is anything you need just ring, here's my card with my mobile number on it. We'll be in The Ship Inn for a drink if you'd like to join us, I am meeting Cliff and some of the other Regulars, and you are very welcome!'

Now that is one offer she would not be taking up, she thought to herself. There had been enough tearful, upset women through the tearooms' doors over the few years she had been working here, and her nephew Daniel's stories of his boss's love life were equally enlightening. Lisa had been in Woodford long enough to know that Paul Black was not someone to turn to when things were a bit rough. However yummy his eyes were.

Chapter Thirty Eight

Tuesday 25th August 2015, 7.00pm

Lisa took a deep breath, stood up straighter, shook back her hair, and walked through the open door of The Ship Inn. Andrew was already there, seated at 'their' table over in the corner of the Lounge, he had bought her a glass of red along with his usual pint of bitter and was looking at the food menu. Lisa felt a shiver of doubt pulse through her body as she saw how pleased he was to see her, and then remembered her resolve as she walked towards the table.

'Hi darling,' he said as he stood up and kissed her cheek.

Nope, nothing. She felt nothing. No tingle of excitement. No sexual frisson whizzed through her body. It was like being given a welcome kiss by a brother or uncle.

'Hi Andrew,' she said brightly. 'Thank you for the wine. Have you chosen what you want to eat tonight?'

Lasagne. He is going to have lasagne. He always ate lasagne at The Ship Inn, she didn't know why he was bothering to look at the menu but he always did.

'Oh I think I'll have lasagne tonight!' he said, passing her the menu.

Surprise surprise, she thought, and now he'll say 'And I think I'll have the ice cream for dessert.'

'And I think I will have the ice-cream for dessert. What are you going to have?' just as she expected,

Andrew spoke the same words he had been saying every Tuesday night for six weeks.

'Oh I think I am going to go wild and have a starter and a main course.' Lisa said, with a challenging tone to her voice, willing him to throw caution to the winds and join her.

'Oh really?' he said, looking disappointed. 'Oh well, you go ahead, I don't mind waiting a bit longer for my dinner.' A strong sense of martyrdom filled the air.

And with that she knew. The wine suddenly felt like an unpleasant medicine on her tongue, filling her mouth, her swallowing reflex seemed to have deserted her, and for a few seconds she was afraid she was going to spit it out, but she managed to take a deep breath through her nose and while breathing out was able to swallow the liquid down her throat where she felt it burning. Lisa gathered her scattered thoughts, and leant forward to put her hand on his arm.

Before she could bottle out, in a quiet voice she said 'Andrew, I am really sorry, but I don't think I can carry on. I do like you, but I don't think we are suited as a couple, and I think we should end it now.'

There, she had said it, exactly as she had been rehearsing for the last few days. It was all she and Gemma had been talking about, going over and over what he would say, what she would say, would there be tears, recriminations, would he suddenly declare undying love and sweep her of her feet at last. She sat back feeling panicked, her skin prickled, and all she could hear was white noise in her ears as the pub seemed to disappear from her consciousness, all her focus was on the man opposite she had just hurt so badly.

He sat there staring at her, his mouth slightly open. Oh no, she thought, what if he bursts into tears? What if he begs her not to do this? She and Gemma had rehearsed both of these scenarios, although they felt the first was unlikely, and as the second would have required some emotion Lisa was worried she may respond positively to it.

'Oh I am so glad,' he said. 'I have been thinking the same thing for a while now but didn't want to upset you.'

Well.

Of all the ways Lisa and Gemma had imagined the break-up to play out this was not one of them. Lisa felt a sudden urge to pick up her glass and throw the wine in his stupid face. She hadn't even wanted red that evening, she would have preferred a sparkling white. What an idiot she was! No wonder he didn't want to do anything as a 'couple'. All those weeks of missed sunsets, the two hour round trips to Swanwick only to spend a couple of hours or more sitting inside a cold air conditioned room watching films she didn't particularly want to see when the warm summer was passing them by outside, with its birds, butterflies, blue skies, warm breezes. Aaaargh!!! She was so cross she burst into tears.

Within seconds she could hear the scraping of chair legs on the stone floor of the pub and a pair of strong male arms encircled her, hugging her so her cheek was pressed into the curve between shoulder and collar bone of a well-defined male chest, a pleasant and stimulating mixture of laundry detergent, shower gel, and maleness filling her nostrils. Wow, she thought, Andrew? Then she heard his voice from the other side of the table say 'Hey, what do you think you are doing?' Ah, so not Andrew then. And then a second voice, also from the other side of the table 'I think it's time you leave now, mate, you've done enough damage for one evening.' She recognised that voice, it was Cliff Williamson!

'Oh dear, this is exactly what I didn't want to happen,' bleated Andrew.

So who?

'Well it has, so off you go,' said Cliff, firmly.

'Bye Lisa,' said Andrew. 'I am sorry you are upset.'

'You're OK now, he's gone,' said Paul Black, the owner of the disturbingly comforting arms and body.

Although she didn't want to leave the soothing smell and feel of Paul's reassurance, she knew she had to. She pulled away, wiping her eyes and nose with a table napkin and desperately hoped it wouldn't leave traces of red dye all over her face.

'I'm OK,' she tried to smile, and looked up at the two men. 'Honestly, I am, it was me who ended it so I don't know why I'm crying.'

'How did you find out?' asked Cliff curiously.

Lisa frowned as she looked from one concerned male face to the other and back again, puzzled by Cliff's question.

'Find out what?' she asked.

'That he was two-timing you.'

'Whaaaat?'

'Ah, you didn't know. Good one Cliff!' said Paul, glaring at his friend.

Lisa turned to Paul, who was still disturbingly close. 'Well come on then, tell me everything.' She was almost shouting, the anger re-surfacing, and conscious she was flipping through every emotion at an alarming speed. 'I only finished with him because he was so boring and never around for anything more than a pub meal or a trip to the cinema. What do you mean two-timing me?'

The men looked at each other, willing the other one to speak up. This was so far out of their comfort zones they had no idea how to proceed.

In the end Lisa's glare had settled on Paul as he was the closest, so realising he had pulled the short straw he explained that while he and Cliff were out on their early morning runs, they had regularly seen Andrew leaving the home of the wife of a man who worked away on 'security' in the Middle East for long periods of time. When Paul had walked past The Woodford Tearooms a few days before and seen Lisa sobbing into her apron he assumed she had just discovered the affair, and had warned Cliff when he arrived at the pub, so when they saw Andrew and Lisa meeting up in The Ship Inn that evening the pair of them had been watching and waiting for the fallout to occur. As soon as she had burst into tears they had jumped into action from their prime viewing seats on the stools at the bar.

Paul was watching her closely, he was intrigued by her reaction. Although he had been responsible for many a broken female heart due to two-timing, or even three-timing, he had never witnessed the moment of the big reveal, only the inevitable screaming and recriminations that followed a few hours later when the unfortunate victim eventually caught up with him. Lisa's reaction to Andrew had cut him to the core, the look of sheer fury when Andrew had told her he had only been going through the motions of being in a relationship with her for the last few weeks was something Paul had expected, but the way her face had crumpled and dissolved into tears had affected him in a way he never knew it was possible. He was a father, so was familiar with the tug on his heart strings when his babies had been young and dependent on him, and how that tug had grown and developed as they became

209

toddlers, children, and now teenagers, but this was different. It was more of a primeval instinctive sexual urge to gather Lisa up in his arms and carry her to his cave and keep her there, safe from harm and outside influences.

His attention was starting to unnerve Lisa, for whom recent events were still too fresh for her to absorb the astonishing turn-around of events. Neither she nor Gemma had thought of this scenario when they were running through Breaking Up With Andrew possibilities. Now all she wanted to do was get away from the pub and run to her sister. She gathered as much dignity as she could and stood up.

'OK, thanks for letting me know,' she said as calmly as she could, all the time keeping her eyes averted from theirs, and retrieving her bag from the back of the chair. She didn't want to forget that and have to come back in again. 'I think I'll go home now. Thank you, both, for coming to my rescue, and for explaining everything.'

She walked steadily away from them, trying to look composed and normal, although conscious that for the last few minutes she had been the Pub Entertainment, still worried about what damage the table napkin may have done to her complexion, and focused her whole being on getting out of the pub and back to the safety of her own home. She pulled her mobile out of her bag and phoned her sister.

'Gem? Oh Gem!' she said when Gemma answered, and promptly started crying again. Gemma had been waiting for her call, had asked Lisa if she could come to the pub, had promised to wait discreetly out of sight until The Break-up was over, but Lisa had refused her offer and was now rather regretting her decision.

'Where are you, still at The Ship Inn?'

'No, no,' Lisa sobbed down the phone, 'I'm on my way home.'

'Right, I'll meet you there. I'll let myself in and put the kettle on so we can have a cup of tea while you tell me all about it.'

At the sound of her sister's voice Lisa knew everything was being to be alright. Her first attempt at dating since her divorce had been a disaster. Public humiliation is never a life choice, but she had friends and family who loved her, and at least she hadn't gone to bed with him after all. She smiled with relief, so something good had come out of her shyness. She felt a strong sense of desolation mixed with freedom about the ending of her romance with Andrew, and thoughts of Paul Black and his sexy strong firm comforting body kept invading her mind. One day she would be happy with a man. It just wasn't going to be this day.

Chapter Thirty Nine

Friday 28th August 2015, 5.30pm

Happy wasn't the first word which came to mind when Cliff thought about his own state. Lonely would be more appropriate.

He was sitting behind the counter of the antiques centre, clock-watching, wishing the last two customers of the day would hurry up and either purchase something or take notice of the not-very-subtle hint he had made by switching off half of the lights to indicate it was now closing time.

Since July he had been staying in the flat at the antiques centre, quickly realising what a stupid idea it had been to even contemplate moving his family in there from the six bedroom/ four bathroom house they had been living in. It would have been impossible to move his wife and children into such a tiny space with just one small bathroom, and only a kitchenette instead of the massive kitchen/diner they were used to. Whatever had he been thinking?

Within a couple of days of moving in he was surprised to find he was desperately missing them all, despite the almost insignificant time he used to spend with them. He missed all the comings and goings, the noise, the pleas/ demands/ requests for a lift, the pleas/ demands/ requests for pocket money or worse, for his credit card so they could purchase something from the internet. He missed the evening conversations he and Rebecca used to have, even though he remembered being mildly irritated that she wanted to take up his time when all he wanted to do was sit in peace and quiet after spending all day with other people.

As he sat in his own little empire he reflected on how his family's lives had changed so far that year. Whereas his own life had been turned on its head, losing his business and then trying to regain it again, moving out of his home, losing both his wife and his mistress, he realised that for Rebecca and their children things appeared to have changed only slightly. The upheaval for them had been more emotional than physical. Probably the only major change was Rebecca's return to full-time paid employment, although the amount of unpaid time she had previously spent on various committees meant that even that wasn't a big adjustment for them to make. Cliff's life appeared to be the only one that had changed dramatically.

For the last two months he had a lot more time on his hands than ever before, now that the antiques centre was back up and running, his affair with Joanna was over, and he was no longer surrounded by his family when he was at home – although 'at home' was not the same place either.

It was a rather different Cliff who sank into his leather chair in the evenings, no longer was the first thing he reached for a glass of whisky, instead it was his laptop so he could communicate with one or more of his children. He realised that he knew more about them now, and had been more involved in their lives and they in his, than he had in all the years since the day each of them was born. In a funny sort of way the timing of the Whole Truth coming out had been a good one: the start of the summer holidays meant his children were out of their normal routine and without a school timetable and homework to occupy their time; this time of year brought the usual summer lull in the antiques trade for him; plus the fact he no longer felt the urge to travel all over the country every week to attend various antiques fairs now that his affair with Joanna was over. Probably for the first time in their lives Cliff had spent several hours with each of his children both individually and together, his attention focused on whichever child he was with as opposed to his previous behaviour of tolerating them until he could turn his mind back to things he was really interested in.

The Williamsons hadn't gone on a family summer holiday for a number of years, probably since Paul and Christine had separated, and even then Cliff had often missed the start or end of the holiday, or had nipped away for a couple of days in the middle of the holiday week to visit an antiques fair or flea market. Since then Rebecca would take the children out for day trips, either all three of them, or individually, and she arranged for the children to attend various camps depending on what each child wanted to do varying from a few days to a fortnight, but Cliff had never been involved in these arrangements.

For the first time since they were born Cliff had spent a whole day individually with each of his children, and he had loved it. It was humbling to realise they had no need of him and that he had to make an effort for them to want to be in his company. He had offered them summer holiday work in the antiques centre, but the boys already had jobs lined up (again, why did he not know they had both been working every school holiday for the last couple of years?), and Charlotte was planning to spend every spare minute, when she wasn't swimming, at the riding stables where her Nana had arranged for her to 'Own a Pony' for the holidays, which meant she was responsible for mucking out, grooming, and exercising a cheeky 14hh New Forest pony named Smokey.

Cliff's world had always been about appearances and acceptances outside of his immediate family, he had never felt the need to engage in family life, and so had put very little effort into his own. He now recognised that Rebecca was an amazing human being to have brought their children up to be such beautiful souls almost single-handedly, and belatedly he realised what a big role her mother and his own parents had in their upbringing.

He had also recently discovered that Nicholas had passed his driving test, how had he not even known he was learning to drive, let alone that he and Rebecca along with their close family had bought him a car for his seventeenth birthday? Rebecca had been saving money every month since Nicholas was born, putting it into a savings account, precisely for presents such as the driving lessons in the future. It turned out she had done this for each of their children, and despite Cliff's belief that he was the one who controlled the family's finances he had no idea about his children's savings accounts.

As he sat behind the counter of the antiques centre he contemplated his track record as a father and he cringed at the awful revelation of just how insignificant a contribution he had made to his children's lives.

Cliff had only just discovered that Michael was a fantastic singer with his own band which he had put together three years ago - again, how had Cliff missed this? He had known he sang a bit with a few friends,

215

but not the extent of either his ability or the quality of his musical business.

Charlotte was a regular competitor in national swimming competitions with a shelf full of trophies and medals - that he had known, although he hadn't bothered to find out at what an amazingly high level she was winning. He loved his children, something he hadn't really considered before, he missed them, and he wanted to be a significant part of their lives. He hoped he hadn't left it too late, he at least had the humility to realise he was going to have to work very hard to win their trust and affection.

All three children wanted to take their mother's side, they were all old enough to understand the extent of Cliff's betrayal, none of them could understand his behaviour, and what respect they had for him had disappeared in one afternoon. But he was still their Dad, and Rebecca had made sure they didn't feel they would be disloyal to her by having contact with their father, and that in her eyes contact with him was a Good Thing, and he knew he had to be grateful to her for that. They had all been a bit wary of his attempts to ingratiate himself into their lives, after all this was their Dad who was either not at home, or when he was at home would be sitting in that awful old leather chair with a glass of whisky in his hand. He had certainly never shown any interest in them, although neither was he mean nor nasty as some of their friends' fathers could be. It was their mother who they talked to, asked for help from, shouted at, kissed good night. This man who wanted to be their friend was something all three were unsure about at first, especially Nicholas and Michael, but Rebecca helped to smooth his way with the children so that he was finally starting to appreciate what his family really meant to him. It wasn't the

Family Portrait taken by the professional photographers in Swanwick which was carefully hung on the wall of Williamson Antiques, the 'family' business in which no member of his family had been allowed to be involved in.

Cliff was now truly ashamed of himself when he realised just how removed he had chosen to be from a life which he had up until recently viewed as necessary but inconvenient. He was also aware he had been given a second chance with his children, and was determined to make the most of it. He wasn't sure what future he had with Rebecca, but he knew he wanted to have a future with her. He desperately missed her.

Once Rebecca had calmed down, she and Cliff had been able to talk face-to-face without personal belongings being thrown from windows, and they had made their practical and financial arrangements fairly easily. Cliff had been disabused of the idea that Rebecca had been involved in the attack on his business, and to his shame he realised she was an innocent person caught up in his dramas whom he had tried to blame and hold responsible for his own actions. He was genuinely contrite about his treatment of her, and she in turn was too busy looking to her present day-to-day challenges to spend much time dwelling on the past.

During the last two months he had seen Rebecca on average once a week, and in that time he had started to see her as he had never really bothered to see her before. Cliff noticed her when she walked into a room, listened and appreciated what she was saying, admired how she wore her hair and noticed when she tried something a little different to her usual attire of jeans and T-shirt. He was a bit bothered about her work clothes, in which he thought she looked stunning, and was worried about all the attention she was receiving from the various clients of Black's Auctions, and particularly concerned that his good friend Paul would make a move on her.

After a few days living alone in the flat he had begged to come home – surprising even himself that he wanted to return to the family home with Rebecca and the children since peace and quiet away from them was all he had ever wanted when he was surrounded by them. He missed hearing about Rebecca's committees, who had said what about whom, who voted unexpectedly for this action or who had ganged together against that change. He missed the way she used to move around the house clearing up after everyone, always checking they had the right clothes for the morning, knowing who needed to be where and at what time. He missed her smiling face as she told him about Charlotte's swimming successes or about Michael's latest gig, even though he had never paid any attention to what she was actually saying, and he missed her interest in him, his day, his life.

But Rebecca had made it clear there was to be no reconciliation, unlike Cliff she was thriving in her relative freedom, enjoying the absence of the tired and often irritated presence in her house. Her home felt lighter. She hadn't realised Cliff always brought a faint oppressive atmosphere home with him until his regular over-night stays away from them became permanent. Even the dog seemed happier.

Her solicitors had also informed Cliff he was not going to be able to move back to the family home, so he had resigned himself to making the best of what he did have, although he wasn't happy about it.

He had failed to notice that the customers had left, and once he realised he quickly set the alarms and the security cameras, closed and locked the front doors, and made his way upstairs to his flat. He made himself a cup of tea before settling down in his old leather chair, and reflected on how much had changed in the last two months. Whoever had told Rebecca about his affair with Joanna – and she still wasn't saying who had done it - surely couldn't have foreseen the consequences?

He was surprised to find he was relieved his affair was over, and now he had some time to think about it he realised what a tremendous effort it had all been. Neither had spoken to the other one since the big reveal had been made. A friend of Joanna's had turned up the day after the assault and removed every single one of her items of stock from the antiques centre, and given Nicola instructions from Joanna to forward all monies owed to an address in Berkshire. The solicitors James Wilde worked for had offices in Newbury, so it was assumed by the locals that he and his wife had decided to make a go of things together, and in order to do that had needed to move away for a fresh start.

No charges had been brought against Rebecca. In fact the day after the assault Joanna had apologised to Rebecca with a card and huge bunch of flowers, which Cliff had seen a few days later when he finally went round to see his children. He was rather surprised by that, particularly in light of her husband's profession.

Joanna had taken a cabinet in one of the antiques shops in Hungerford, and by all accounts – as a number of dealers fell over themselves to inform him every week since she had left - was doing very well.

He missed Joanna's bright sunny flirty presence in the antiques centre and in The Ship Inn, but when he thought about it he found he didn't want to continue with the affair with her anyway, and realised it had become part of his weekly routine.

All the excitement they had felt together in the early days, the sheer fun of the deceit, the sex games, he was now conscious, had been empty and meaningless for a long time. He didn't even miss the sex the pair of them had engaged in several times a month for all those years, and whereas he had always thought of Joanna as an exciting and fulfilling lover, now the thought of her left him cold. She had a penchant for role playing which, after his initial awkwardness, Cliff had found to be a huge turn on, but now it all just seemed a bit desperate and sad and empty.

Their affair had been conducted in a series of hotel rooms around the country, depending on where there was an antiques fair taking place in a location which was too far to drive to and from in a day. Joanna would leave a bag for him at the antiques centre containing his costume with a brief plot line, as people were always leaving bags and boxes containing stock for him to look at this was perfectly normal behaviour and had never aroused any suspicion from anyone. She would turn up at whichever hotel they were staying in and set the scene in her room before he arrived, so he knew when he knocked on the door that as soon as it was opened there would be no time for pleasantries, they would be straight into whichever scene she had dreamt up for that day. He always played his part with enthusiasm, quickly adapting to whichever role she had chosen for him. He cringed inwardly and could feel the heat rise in his face as he ran through the list: a fireman, a policeman, an army officer, a farrier, a pilot, a captain of a cruise ship, a cowboy, and a farmer, oh there were plenty more and he felt red hot burning of embarrassment as he recalled various scenarios. Sitting there now, in his chair, in the flat over the antiques centre, he could not feel a flicker of arousal.

What had he been thinking?!

They tended to repeat the same plotline and costume within a three month timescale, and there had been quite a few varieties!

Once finished there was no lingering lovey-dovey cuddling, they would clean up and then separately go and join the rest of the antiques dealers who were also staying at the hotel in preparation for the antiques fair the next day, have a few drinks and some dinner, before retiring to their individual rooms for the night.

Paul had listened with obvious envy when Cliff had finally relented and told him about the mechanics of the affair, and not for the first time wondered how Cliff had managed to hook up with such a fascinating woman, and how he had kept it a secret from everyone, even his wife and his best friend.

Cliff missed the tension created by the necessary excitement, the anticipation, the act of sex, but he realised that he felt a lot happier without it, and had so much more time he could spend with his family. He was also a little perplexed to find he didn't miss Joanna. Even though they had regularly met for dinner in all those hotels they were always part of a group of antiques dealers, and also several times a week they would both be in The Ship Inn, but they were part of a group of Regulars. Other than those half hour sessions in the hotel bedrooms playing make-believe they had never spent any time alone with each other.

Cliff had no idea about her favourite music, what she liked to read, anything about her family. They weren't the sorts of topics covered either when they were alone in private together or with their groups of antiques dealers and/or pub locals. Even though they socialised in the pubs, and Joanna had been one of his clients at the antiques centre for the last eighteen years, and they had been as physically intimate as two human beings can be for the last twenty years, Cliff was suddenly hit by the revelation that he knew very little about Joanna Wilde. He didn't even know if she had a middle name!

One thing he was sure about, her husband James hadn't had a clue what was going on. He and Cliff had regularly bought each other drinks in the pub most evenings after work, in fact The Ship Inn's takings had dropped a bit since the affair had become public knowledge because not only was James no longer part of their clientele, but Cliff tended to only drop in for a quick pint now and then, once a week at most.

As he started to prepare his evening meal - no more re-heating food Rebecca had prepared for him, he had to learn to cook from scratch and was surprised to find how much he enjoyed it - Cliff felt a great sense of peace flow over him. Yes he had fucked up big time, but somehow good was coming out of the mess for him, and his children, and, he hoped, for Rebecca too.

After eating his meal he sank back down into his leather chair, and he counted his blessings, something he had always thought of as a trite phrase only spoken by the righteous. But that evening he realised how many blessings he did have in his life.

Grinning he leapt up out of his chair and left the flat and the antiques centre, jauntily walking up the High Street to the pub with his hands in his pockets, whistling.

Chapter Forty

Friday 25th September 2015, 7.30pm

Rebecca appeared to have turned her life around and was resuming the career she had left when she had their first baby, Nicholas. She was back working at Paul's auction house, although it had belonged to his father when she had worked there previously. Paul had been straight round to see Rebecca and offer her a job within two days of the bust-up between her and Joanna at the antiques centre, only waiting until he was sure she had thrown Cliff out of the house.

Employment at Black's Auctions suited Rebecca because the building was in Woodford and close to her home, and she could be flexible with her working hours enabling her to be on hand if the children needed her. Although, she mused, at thirteen, sixteen, and seventeen years old they were capable of getting themselves to and from school and their friends' houses now that Nicholas had passed his driving test and was eager to drive his car whenever possible. AND she regularly came home to find that Michael had cooked dinner for them all!

The only thing she wasn't able to do as much as she used to was accompany Charlotte to her swimming practice several times a week, but her father, Cliff, was becoming actively involved in his daughter's life by regularly transporting her to the pool, and he always stayed to watch her practice.

Rebecca reflected how sad it was that it had taken the break-up of their marriage for him to understand the joy of having children. Although judging by their children's easy acceptance of his involvement in their lives they hadn't been badly affected by his previous attitude and behaviour towards them.

She thought about him now as she stacked the dishwasher (not everything in her life had changed dramatically!) and tested her feelings for him. Where she had always believed she loved him she now realised she had felt fondness and benevolence, viewing him as a man who relied on her unstinting support so he could pursue his dreams, and she had been pleased to provide that support. She didn't blame him or feel any grievance against him for the way he had behaved towards her during their marriage because she had willingly accepted and condoned it, but the revelation of his affair with Joanna, and particularly when more of the details of it were revealed to her (by Paul, who had been only too keen to share the information once he knew it) had shone a different light on her marriage, and had tarnished it irreparably. Rebecca didn't feel love or anger or any great emotion towards Cliff, but she knew she could never trust him again, or view him as the reliable and honest man she had always believed him to be. She felt sorry for him.

She did feel stupid for not having a clue about what was going on, and she vowed she would NEVER feel like that about herself again.

Rebecca was thoroughly enjoying being back in the work place, she needn't have worried about how she was going to learn the necessary skills for paid employment because all those years of raising three children and the hours of unpaid volunteering for this committee and that fund-raising event had expanded her abilities far more than eighteen years working in Black's Auctions or even Williamson Antiques could ever have done.

Yes, she thought to herself, the last few months with the break-in at the antiques centre and the harsh gut-wrenching revelations about her husband with a woman she had counted as a friend, albeit not a close friend, had been terrible, the worst events in her life to date, as had those few hours she had spent at the police station. But today, this evening, life for her was good, and the slamming of one door (or in her case window) had allowed her to tentatively open another, behind which she found a life she rather preferred to the one she had so recently left behind.

Chapter Forty One

Friday 25th September 2015, 7.30pm

Not everybody was feeling the joy of life.

Simon Maxwell-Lewis sat at the end of the bar unable to remove the bad tempered expression from his face as he stared into the bottom of his pint glass. That fucker Cliff Williamson had just walked in, no *skipped* into the pub and bought a round of drinks for all the Regulars. Including him.

Simon had thought the bastard had finally got his come-uppance when the news of his affair with that slut Joanna Wilde became common knowledge, he was sure the man would be destroyed once Simon had shown Cliff's wife that photograph. But no, like one of those candles you can't blow out, here he was looking fitter and healthier than ever, flashing his cash around, and spreading his goodwill to all men.

Bastard.

His actions hadn't even ruined Joanna Wilde either, unbelievable, the bloody woman was still married and living with her husband, another double-crossing bastard, and she was still successfully trading in antiques.

Simon ground his teeth as he thought about the injustice of life. HE was struggling to make a living, he had no one who loved him except his mother, his whole life had been screwed up by these bloody people, and yet he was the only one suffering. It was wrong.

Time for Phase Three.

He had already dropped hints to the Authorities, but they hadn't acted on them. Time to spell it out.

Chapter Forty Two

Friday 25th September 2015, 7.30pm

James and Joanna Wilde grinned at each other and toasted their latest success with champagne. Yet another old country house turned over without anyone noticing a thing, they both had a good feeling about their new recruit Darren Marshall who could climb the outside of any of these old buildings with their numerous substantial cast iron down pipes and wide window ledges, and squeeze in through the ancient latched window frames. These places were rarely fitted with a decent security system, so no problems with alarms or cameras. Once he was in Darren could go straight to the valuables and pass them out to James and Joanna, and it would often be several days, or even weeks, and in some cases months and years, before anyone noticed their family heirlooms were missing. Many of these country houses had belonged to the same family for over sixty years, housing several generations at once, plus servants. But now there were often only two or three people left, their role as the caretakers of what had once been a lively bustling animated household but was now a dilapidated money pit. These remaining family members were often in their eighties, and usually reduced for economic and accessibility reasons to living in a few rooms in one wing, which made illegal access extremely easy even if they were at home.

With James' inside knowledge of the old buildings through his work as a family solicitor who made house calls, plus the technology now available in the form of camera phones and tablets, combined with Joanna's expertise in antiques, the couple had produced a highly successful and illegal business. The Wildes had been busy for a number of years during which they managed to relieve a few old families of several hundreds of thousands of pounds' worth of jewellery and other small antique items without any alarm being raised which could lead the suspicion back to them.

They had decided to look for a replacement for Simon Maxwell-Lewis, Darren's predecessor as the company's cat burglar, last year when his infatuation with Joanna had become a little too much to bear, but neither had realised that he had started to stalk her until the life-changing events a couple of months ago.

James had always known about Joanna's affair with Cliff Williamson, in fact it had originally been his idea. James was more of a watcher than a participator in sex, so together they had watched many hours of video footage of Cliff and Joanna over the years.

Cliff would have been horrified had he known.

James, being a natural entrepreneur, had set up an editing suite in their attic room and the Wildes had been profiting from Joanna's imaginative story lines and costume designing for the last twenty years. They had started by selling sex tapes and DVDs through a contact of James', and more recently had been making use of the internet to cut out the middle man.

The Wildes had earned a fortune over the years, all tax-free.

Both of them had been relieved when Rebecca appeared on the scene, indeed Joanna had been instrumental in putting the idea of respectable family image into Cliff's head, because it meant Cliff wouldn't want to get too serious about Joanna which could have complicated matters, and the fact he was happy to carry on bonking Joanna at every opportunity played into their hands.

However neither of them had meant any harm to anyone else involved in their sex-for-money scheme; that had never been their intention. Essentially both were shallow and selfish people, who were well-suited and deserved each other, but as always seems to happen in these cases innocent victims get swept up into their lives.

Joanna did feel very sorry for Rebecca, although when Simon had vindictively broken the news about her husband's affair with Joanna on that Monday morning, both the Wildes were unprepared for the strength of her reaction. Thank goodness they had never divulged information to Simon about the sex tape business!

Simon had been a good worker for a while, the three of them had worked well as a team for several years and they had profited from it, as well as having enormous fun, but although the warning signs about Simon had been there for quite a while it wasn't until earlier in the year that everything came to a head.

In February Simon had sent Joanna a Valentine's card, a massive heart-shaped box of chocolates, and a huge bunch of red roses, closely followed by a rather embarrassing declaration of his love and an attempt to push an expensive diamond ring onto her finger, as they sat in the Wildes' kitchen waiting for James to join them with the final details of their next Operation. Joanna had rejected his advances, gently she thought, but Simon had clearly not believed that she didn't feel for him in the same way he felt about her and decided to remove any obstacles in the way of their True Love.

It had been Simon who had attacked James in the bungled mugging, he knew where the Wildes were staying because the three of them were planning another raid. On that occasion they were due to burgle a Georgian house belonging to an elderly couple who had engaged James' firm to value the estate so they could pass it onto their children without paying excessive death duties. James and Joanna knew it was Simon who had attacked him, but they chose not to press charges in case their other lucrative business was exposed, but his actions made it clear they couldn't carry on working with him.

Simon hadn't calculated the loss of his job or his income into his plans for a life of love and romance with Joanna. He had no savings, and spent all of his legal and ill-gotten gains on financially propping up the family dairy farm. His feelings of rejection were multiplied as he not only lost any close contact with the woman he was sure was going to be his wife, but also was promptly kicked out of their business partnership and therefore a useful source of both antiques stock and money.

He had been careful over the years not to draw attention to the illegal sideline to his legitimate antiques business, leaking his undeclared income into the farm by paying cash-in-hand for daily maintenance repairs rather than anything which would require capital expenditure. His mother ran the farm day-to-day, and was grateful for her son's financial contributions, never questioning too closely where his pocket full of £50 notes came from, just pleased that her non-farming son was willing to spend his own money on the failing family business.

Simon had not made any extravagant purchases for himself or the farm, indeed he still lived with his mum in the old farm house he had grown up in, and preferred to drive vans with several thousands of miles on the clock so he could spend hours touching up paintwork or making oil changes on the farm's sweeping gravel driveway.

Although the Wildes immediately cut off all contact with him, Simon couldn't let go, but it wasn't until a couple of weeks after he had declared his love to Joanna that he discovered the Wilde's 'other' money-making sideline. Smarting from her refusal to leave James and move in with him, obsessing about her every move, unable to stop thinking about how he could prove to her that life with him would be infinitely better than life with James, Simon had started to follow her everywhere. He followed her up to a hotel in Lincolnshire, where she was going to be buying at an antiques fair the next day, and then realised to his horror what was going on between her and Cliff. He was so furious that not only would she not leave her husband for him she was also enjoying debasing herself with another man. To add insult to his wounded pride he was incensed to discover that the long series of porn films he had been enjoying while holed up in his bedroom at home in the old farmhouse for years, were of Joanna and Cliff! He had no idea until that day, and when he eventually made it safely back home he made a huge bonfire and burned the lot of them.

Simon sneered as he thought about that other man, Cliff Williamson, what on earth did she see in him? Simon had seen an awful lot more of Cliff than he would have liked when he was spying on them through her hotel bedroom window, not least because Joanna's choice for Cliff that day had been a Cowboy costume, and long leather chaps do not leave *anything* to the imagination when worn on their own without under- or outer-wear.

Simon had been so upset that he had rushed back to Woodford and made use of the night time darkness, and his previously garnered knowledge due to the burglar's intrinsic thought-process of always working out how to by-pass security systems, to his advantage on the spur of the moment. He had been ecstatic as he trashed the cabinets, stamped on the silver, ripped up the linen, hurled the china, and his particular favourite, twisting and squashing the jewellery. The violence had been therapeutic for him as he systematically destroyed every antique he could, all the time seeing that grotesque image of Joanna and Cliff clamped together in orgasm, willing it to fade from his memory.

Looking around he suddenly realised he had left all the furniture untouched, even those of his rival dealers, so he had quickly and quietly damaged everything he could, aware of how much noise he had been making, but unaware of how long he had been there, worrying about just how unbalanced his behaviour had been. It was with a lot more care and a lot less enthusiasm that he left Williamson Antiques the way he had entered.

While Joanna and James were celebrating their latest thievery with champagne, and Cliff was (still blissfully unaware of his Star Status in nine hundred and thirty six sex films) celebrating his first week in profit in the antiques centre since the Grand Re-Opening with a cup of tea and slice of chocolate cake from The Woodford Tearooms, Simon Maxwell-Lewis was huddled up in his bedroom at his mother's house plotting his next and, he hoped, final Act of Revenge on the unsuspecting three people he held responsible for ruining his life.

Chapter Forty Three

Tuesday 29th September 2015, 10.00am

Sarah Handley was having a lovely day off. She had purchased a portrait miniature of a Victorian naval officer named George Deacon at a flea market in August, and had been struggling to stick to her Family History time parameters because his was such an interesting, and local, family. She was woken up by the sunrise and had been lost in the Deacon family history ever since, relishing her time alone after the hectic weekend in the pub. Sarah had followed the lineage of his eldest son, also George, up to the present day, and as the town hall clock struck ten o'clock the address of his great great great grandson appeared on her screen.

Sarah sat back with a smile on her face. She always had mixed feelings when her research was successful like this because it meant the end of that particular line. Although in this case the great great great grandson Frederick, and his parents David and Margaret Barker, lived in Swanwick Manor which was a mere hour away from Woodford. Sarah wondered if they knew of their family tree, and if they would be interested in spending an afternoon chatting to her about it. It may lead to more information about another branch, she thought excitedly!

George Deacon and his wife had produced three sons and two daughters, so she might find more relatives living locally. David and Margaret Barker of

234

Swanwick Manor had their telephone number listed on BT's online phone book, Sarah checked the time before picking up her phone – she had once made the mistake of ringing one family for a similar request, only to realise that it was a quarter past six in the morning, and the answer to her polite request, not surprisingly was 'no'.

On dialling the number she reached the Barker's answerphone, so she left a message containing her telephone number and briefly explaining who she was, again a lesson learned that Mrs Sarah Handley, publican of The Ship Inn in Woodford, was more likely to be positively received than 'Sarah who has some information about your family history'.

Pleased with her morning's work she went off to make herself a cup of tea, but before the kettle had boiled Mrs Margaret Barker had returned her call, and kindly invited her to come and have afternoon tea with her at Swanwick Manor.

Chapter Forty Four

Tuesday 29th September 2015, 3.30pm

Wow, what a beautiful house, thought Sarah as she drove up the long winding private road which led to Swanwick Manor. It appeared and then disappeared from view, alternately obscured and then revealed by the trees so carefully planted years before. She loved Georgian architecture, and from what she could see of the grounds and the house, Swanwick Manor was a good example and had been maintained in its original design.

Mrs Barker had told her to park to the left of the house and enter through the small wrought iron gate which opened into a beautiful walled garden. Although originally this would have been the kitchen garden for the house, now it was planted mainly with shrubs, bushes and raised flowerbeds where once there would have been all the garden produce the occupants of the manor house would have required throughout the year. Sarah could see that there were some fruit and vegetables growing there too, also in raised beds, as well as a small selection of herbs in tubs near the conservatory, or garden room as it would probably be described on estate agents' particulars, and she was thrilled to see what looked like the original lean-to greenhouse along one wall. So absorbed in the taking in of every detail, she forgot why she was there.

'Hello, are you Sarah Handley?' enquired a voice behind her.

Sarah jumped and spun round all in one movement.

'Oh sorry dear, I didn't mean to startle you!' smiled the tiny old lady seated in a wheelchair at a table which had been set for tea for two people. 'I am Margaret Barker,' she continued, holding out her hand in greeting.

'Oh, yes, yes I am,' stammered Sarah, still trying to pull herself together. 'Sorry, you did make me jump, I didn't realise anyone else was in here, what a beautiful garden,' she said, slightly breathlessly.

'Have you lived here long Mrs Barker?' she asked, her researcher's instincts kicking in as her composure returned, although she roughly knew the answer to her question thanks to the census records.

Sarah had found over the years that it helped to ask a question you knew the answer to in the beginning of her family history interviews, so she could assess how willing the person was to share their personal information.

'Oh please call me Margaret, Mrs Barker was my mother-in-law!' the old lady laughed, with a pretend shudder. 'A very loud bossy woman, may she rest in peace. Yes, we moved here when we married fifty-seven years ago, and raised our three children here too. Swanwick Manor was bought by my husband's grandparents in 1923, and this is where they brought their children up. They lived here in the Manor with David's uncle until they both died within a few months of each other in 1962. David and his parents lived in one of the gate houses on the other side of the estate, but when we were married his grandfather offered us a suite of rooms here in this house on the second floor, and we have lived here ever since. Of course I wasn't in this thing in those days,' she continued, gesturing to her wheelchair. (Marvellous, thought Sarah to herself, a talker!) 'Broke my pelvis in a hunting accident five years ago, haven't been able to walk since. Still, it doesn't stop me from getting around this garden, I do nearly all the work in here, just need a little bit of help when things are too high or too low for me to reach. Now, would you like milk or lemon in your tea, dear?'

Sarah and Margaret spent a happy hour as Margaret talked about her life and her beloved house and garden, and also about her horses and her daredevil riding adventures over the years. She had bred Irish Draught horses, breeding up to three foals a year using her own home-bred horses so she could be as sure of their good temperament and conformation as possible. Margaret always started the youngsters herself when they were about four years old, before selling them on at seven years old as fully trained hunters. She rode all the stallions and the mares too, participating in local Riding Club dressage and jumping competitions, ensuring all the horses had a purpose other than breeding, and then selling them on when the time was right and replacing them with home-grown colts and fillies. Sarah resolved to look up the stud name 'Swanwick' when she got home, as she looked at the lady in front of her and marvelled at how such a tiny woman could have managed to handle and school the horses safely.

Sarah had been a keen horse rider up until her late teens. She and Nicola used to spend all their spare time up at the local riding stables mucking out, grooming, poo-picking the fields, in return for free riding lessons, and the opportunities to escort rides out in the Brackenshire countryside. She wasn't sure when boys had replaced horses in their lives, but in a matter of

238

weeks glamming up for the cinema, pubs and nightclubs had become more important. Sitting here with this seventy-six year old lady she felt a desire to get back on a horse, it was never too late, after all Margaret Barker had still been riding up until the accident.

And that was a tragic story. She had been out on her last horse, a home-bred of course, twenty three year old grey mare called Swanwick Silver Star, who had collapsed from a suspected heart attack as they were walking along the road towards the Hunt Meet, something they did three times a week during the Hunting season. Margaret confided that she always told people her paralysis was the result of a hunting accident, because it was more dramatic than the plain truth, although Sarah thought that having a 700kg horse collapse and die on top of you, breaking your pelvis, in any situation was dramatic enough, without embellishing it further.

The sound of tyres on gravel pulling up outside the walled garden brought an end to their conversation, and after a few minutes a tall handsome man in his early fifties opened the gate, followed by an equally tall man in his seventies.

'Ah hello darling!' exclaimed Margaret. 'Sarah, this is my son Frederick and my husband David. This is Sarah Handley, the lady who has come to share some of our family history with us.'

The two men said hello to Sarah and shook her hand, David sat down at the table, and Frederick – Fred as he introduced himself – took the empty tea things away, saying he was going to make a fresh pot and would anyone like some more cake?

Once Fred had returned with the fresh pot of tea and clean cups, plus slices of delicious Victoria sponge cake, Sarah opened her bag and brought out her paperwork and the portrait miniature. Instantly the atmosphere changed.

'Where did you get that?' asked David in a low voice, with a furious expression on his face.

Chapter Forty Five

Wednesday 30th September 2015, 12 noon

'Oh my God, what did you say?' gasped Nicola, her brown eyes wide, the hand holding her tea cup frozen in mid-air. She and Sarah had met for lunch in The Woodford Tearooms, and Sarah was telling her all about her adventures the previous afternoon.

'Well the truth of course. I bought it from Simon Maxwell-Lewis at Drayton Flea Market last month. It was awful, the three of them looking at me as though I was a criminal and had stolen it from them. I went bright red, and must have *looked* guilty!' said Sarah, again feeling her cheeks burn as she re-lived that excruciating moment when the lovely happy tea party in the sunshine-filled atmosphere had turned into a cold, dark accusatory one. 'Apparently the Barker family were very proud of their civilian and military ancestors and had kept all of those historical mementos like the portrait miniatures, medals and love letters in a trunk in one of the rooms. Once they had accepted my explanation, which fortunately they did quite quickly, they were kind enough to take me up to the second floor to show me and let me loose amongst all those Family History treasures. Oh it was heaven!' she exclaimed, beaming at the thought, the embarrassment temporarily forgotten.

'But what about the portrait miniature? How had it been separated from the rest of the collection?'

'Ah, now that is a question they couldn't answer. Not one of them had ever paid any particular attention to the contents of that trunk for over forty years, but Mr David Barker's mother had been particularly keen on preserving the family history, and it was she who had collected and catalogued everything she could find relating to the Deacon family. She was a Deacon before she married Mr Barker, one of three sisters so the family name has died out from that branch of the family, but…'

'So,' Nicola cut Sarah off before she started relating who had married whom and how many children they had, which was how these stories of Sarah's usually continued, 'if they didn't know it existed, why did they think you had stolen it?'

'Oh they knew it existed. When their own children were born David and Margaret had chosen their names from those already in the family. Within days of the birth of each of their three babies they had sat up in that room with their new-born baby and explored the contents of the trunk, searching for a name which would suit their new daughter or son.'

'Oh how sweet!' exclaimed Nicola.

'They knew about Lieutenant Commander George Deacon's portrait miniature because it was one of a pair, the other was of his wife, Victoria, and that was the name they gave their little girl. Hers was there in the trunk, I saw it, there is no way his portrait miniature should have left that room, let alone ended up for sale in a flea market!'

'So the question is,' said Nicola slowly, 'how did Simon Maxwell-Lewis get hold of it? I haven't seen much of him since the attack on the centre, he is one of

242

the dealers who chose not to come back when Cliff re-opened it. I know he and Joanna Wilde used to deal a lot together, I wonder if they still do?'

Chapter Forty Six

Sunday 4th October 2015, 7.30am

Gemma and Peter were snuggled together in his bed when her phone alarm reminded her that it was her turn to work in The Woodford Tearooms that day.

'Oh well,' Gemma sighed, 'I'd better get up and earn a living. Someone has to keep you in meat bones,' she said as she leaned over the edge of the bed to talk to Suzy the Staffie, who had her own bed in Peter's bedroom. 'Would you like a cup of tea in bed?'

'I hope you are talking to me! Yes please, in a minute.' Peter pulled her back under the covers and started to caress her purposefully.

'Oh no you don't,' Gemma laughed as she nimbly jumped out of bed, 'I have to get a move on or I'll be late, and then I'll never catch up once the first customers come through the door if it's a busy day, and I have to drop Suzy off at home on the way. I'll try not to be too late back here, Lisa is coming in at one o'clock to take over so I should be back for Sunday lunch cooked by your own fair hands. What time is Jennifer coming down?'

'Don't worry, we'll leave you some if you are late,' he grinned, clearly implying there wouldn't be anything left for her. 'You can leave Suzy here if you like, she's quite happy with me. We could explore the coast road with Jennifer and Lucy this morning, Suzy, what do you think?'

Suzy gave a Staffie chuckle and stuck her head back down on her paws.

'I think that's a 'Yes please', as long as she doesn't have to go in the sea!' laughed Gemma. 'Well if you don't mind? But I still have to get ready for work!' she said hurriedly as she saw he was preparing to make another move on her, and she skipped off to the bathroom.

Peter leant back on his pillows with a smile. Life was good. Who'd have thought that after so much emotional trauma he would have found such a wonderful, beautiful, sexy, lovely woman as Gemma. Changing his job seemed to be working out for him too, and he was enjoying working for Jackie Martin. After her initial worries about his more time-consuming approach with their clients, Jackie had started to appreciate how Peter's holistic methods suited a large number of local horse owners, and their client numbers were on the increase. Together they had run a very successful Client Evening at their Woodford clinic, designed to both raise awareness of the causes, signs and prevention of laminitis and to raise money for the Riding for the Disabled charity. So many horse owners had come up to her and said complimentary things about Peter that she knew she had made the right decision to employ him five months before.

Peter liked the town of Woodford, and was happy to spend time there on his own while waiting for Gemma to finish work. As he drove around to his various appointments he relished the surrounding Brackenshire countryside with its mix of woodland, agricultural farm land, and seaside attractions, all so beautiful that sometimes he would stop the car and get out so he could take in the view or breathe in the air for a few minutes. He looked over at Suzy, still with her head on her paws but her ears and eyes fixed on the door behind which her mistress was currently showering. Yes, next on his list was a dog, a truck dog who could accompany him on his veterinary rounds, and a companion for the times when Gemma was otherwise engaged. Not that he was comparing Gemma's company to that of a dog! He smiled again as he ran back over the last few months since he had met her, how his life had been lifted out of the troubling whirlpool he seemed to have managed to fall into with uncomfortable reminders of failed relationships and dissatisfaction with himself and his abilities.

Now he felt calm and content and exhilarated all at the same time. He loved the way Gemma approached everything in her life from parenting to running the Tearooms with her sister to choosing from a restaurant menu to planning what they would do together on a rare joint day off. She was so beautiful, with gorgeous big blue eyes and wild curly blond hair, and her body had clearly been designed purely so he could worship and adore it intimately as often as she would let him.

Was it too soon to tell her he loved her and wanted to marry her, he wondered? Possibly. They hadn't discussed any long term plans or commitments, and they had only met five months ago so maybe he was jumping the gun a bit. But why wait any longer? His children liked Gemma, he thought her children liked him, her dog did anyway. Peter shifted in the bed, sitting up a bit more as he pondered how to proceed, an idea starting to take shape.

When Gemma re-appeared, washed, dressed and holding a tray with two mugs of tea and a plate of toast with butter and marmite, she had a serious expression on her face.

'Peter,' she said, 'I've been thinking about this for a few days now, and I have a proposal to make. Don't worry if the answer is 'No', it's entirely up to you, and I'll understand if this is all too soon, but your six month lease is due for renewal in another few weeks isn't it?' He nodded. 'So, as I trust you with my dog, and she trusts you, and we get on OK together, and my kids don't hate you, would you like to give up this cottage and move in with us?'

Peter had been worried by Gemma's expression when she first walked in, but as she spoke a smile started to spread across his face. Almost all his prayers had been answered. He looked over at Suzy who was watching the toast intently, before grabbing Gemma who had guessed his intention and hurriedly put the tray down on the bedside table before he was able to reach her and pull her back into the bed with him.

'Oh yes please, I think that is a marvellous proposal. Let's celebrate!'

This time she was in full agreement with him.

Chapter Forty Seven

Friday 9th October 2015, 5.30pm

Cliff Williamson was clock-watching again, waiting for the last two customers to leave. One of them was Gemma Bartlett's new beau Peter Isaac, who kept looking at him in an odd way as though he was trying to remember something which had pushed its way to the far recesses of his mind. Cliff didn't notice because he only had one thing on his mind, he had a date with Rebecca tonight! Well, it wasn't strictly speaking a date, but she and Paul and Paul's new girlfriend (Cliff was very pleased Rebecca hadn't fallen for his charms) Louise were meeting in The Ship Inn for a drink after work, and Paul had tipped him the wink to join them.

Paul was well aware that Cliff was keen to get back with Rebecca, and even though he didn't think Rebecca had any intention of allowing Cliff back into her bed, or even her home, he thought the least he could do was help his friend out if there was any chance at all that his broken marriage could be mended. Paul had seen how much of a change had taken place in his friend's attitude towards both his wife and his children, and had marvelled at how Cliff was turning into a real family man instead of a pretend one now that he was no longer actually living with his family.

Cliff and Rebecca's break-up had worked out very well for Paul. He knew that without it he wouldn't have such a hard-working conscientious assistant in his Saleroom, and even after such a short time he couldn't imagine running the place without her. He was all for his friend working out his marriage problems, but not at his, Paul's, expense. Paul was determined not to lose Rebecca, who was now the most valued member of his workforce, but he also didn't want to stand in their way if the pair of them wanted to resume their relationship. He had seen how she had changed too, he thought she looked younger these days, and was certainly more relaxed, no longer running to a timetable of meetings and meals, and felt sure she would not want to return to her old way of life. He hoped not anyway.

Paul still couldn't believe that Cliff had deceived him all those years with his affair with the delectable Joanna Wilde, so he didn't entirely trust his old friend when he swore he wasn't seeing anyone, but he wasn't Rebecca's Guardian and as she clearly didn't want *him*, and didn't appear to be interested in anyone else, then maybe now that the pair of them were on amicable speaking terms and had even been seen out in public having a cuppa in the tearooms, Rebecca wouldn't cause a scene if Cliff 'happened' to be in The Ship Inn at the same time.

Once the customers had gone Cliff closed up the antiques centre, had a quick shower and change in his flat upstairs, and then strolled happily up the High Street to the pub where he carefully and nonchalantly walked in, executed a not very convincing double take at seeing the three of them sat together at one of the tables and offered to buy a round. Louise had been a competitive swimmer in her younger days, and she and Rebecca had been deep in conversation about Charlotte's progress when Cliff walked into the pub, so Cliff was able to slide onto the chair next to Rebecca and start up a casual conversation with Paul without causing any disruption to the flow between the two women.

Rebecca knew exactly what was going on in her husband's mind, but she wasn't interested in resuming their relationship. Although in some ways the last few months had been the worst of her life, they had also given her a freedom she had never realised she needed before, and living as a single woman with three children was lonely at times but it was nothing compared to the loneliness she had been feeling for those months between the attack on the antiques centre and the discovery of her husband's affair.

She could see Simon Maxwell-Lewis sitting in his usual place at the end of the bar, and was shocked by the furious glares he was directing at Cliff in between looking morosely into the bottom of his pint glass. Surely Cliff hadn't done anything to Simon to deserve such hatred? Although as she hadn't had a clue about his regular sex sessions with Joanna while she lived with him and shared a bed with him, she didn't make any assumptions about the man now they lived apart. She had had no contact with Simon since that day he put the final nail into the coffin of her marriage, nor had she given him much thought, but now, observing his behaviour, she wondered for the first time what his motivation had been to take that photograph, and why he had shown it to her?

Chapter Forty Eight

Sunday 18th October 2015, 12 noon

Peter, Daniel and Nathan were having a quick pint before heading back over to Gemma's house for a late Sunday lunch, which was due to be ready as soon as Lisa and Caroline had finished at the tearooms and walked up the High Street to Gemma's house.

Peter still had another two weeks' rent left on his cottage, and was due to move in 'officially' with their mother once he had handed his keys back to the agents, but to all intents and purposes he had been living with Gemma for the past fortnight.

At first, even though both boys liked Peter and enjoyed seeing their Mum light up when he was around, and they had been comfortable with him joining them for family meals, and even staying the night occasionally, once he was staying in the house on a more permanent basis both boys were uneasy with his constant presence every time they phoned or popped round. Nathan was studying at University so only came back occasionally at weekends or during the main holidays, but even then he was often out with friends or working at a part-time job, and Daniel lived in a flat in the town with his girlfriend, but they both still regarded it as their home, just for them and their Mum.

Both Peter and Gemma had tried to be sensitive to the boys' feelings, but after a few days Gemma had decided they should stop walking on eggshells and just get on with it, so for the past few weeks Gemma and Peter had been more relaxed with each other, and were now settling into life as house mates as well as lovers.

Peter had something important he wanted to discuss with the boys, so had taken the opportunity to spend some time with them away from Gemma by inviting them out for a drink, something neither boy ever refused.

'Boys, I have something I would like to ask your mother, but I won't do it unless you two are OK with it,' Peter started nervously, looking from one to the other. 'I know we have only been together for a short time, and this all may be moving a bit fast, but I feel it is right for us. I love her, and would like to ask her to marry me.' He took a gulp of his pint before carefully setting the glass down on the bar, and looked cautiously at the boys. 'Would that be alright with you?'

Nathan and Daniel had already discussed this scenario with each other, and were grinning broadly at him when he looked up.

'Go for it Peter!' said Daniel as he stepped forward and shook Peter's hand.

'We did hope your intentions were honourable, so we are pleased to hear they are,' said Nathan pompously, before laughing and also shaking Peter's hand.

'Oh!' said Peter, rather taken aback by the boys' reactions. He had been expecting a bit of resistance and had a number of back-up arguments ready, but they were both so obviously in favour of his plan he needn't have been worried about their reactions. 'Thank you, both of you, it means a lot to me. I think Suzy is also on my side, so, just your mother I need to convince now then.' He realised his heart was pounding, and he took another long drink, draining his glass. 'Another round on me please Mike!' He said triumphantly, as the enormity of what had just happened started to sink in.

When he had been rehearsing this scene in his head that morning he hadn't expected Gemma's sons to be quite so enthusiastic, and also realised that he hadn't thought very far beyond what they might say. He had already found a ring he liked in Williamson Antiques, so now both of her sons had given their permission he could buy it tomorrow, and then propose to Gemma. Or did couples choose the ring together these days? And where would they live? Would she want to live in her cottage, or buy something together? And what about the wedding, how big? How soon? Where? Who would they invite? How long an engagement should they have? The first time round it had all been so easy. He and his wife had been young, in love, and ready to buy their first house together and have children. What on earth was the protocol for second marriages in middle age?

He drained his pint, and ordered another round of drinks.

'Are you alright Peter?' asked Mike, a look of concern on his face. 'You look a bit pale.'

Chapter Forty Nine

Monday 2nd November 2015, 10.00am

PC Ian McClure was sitting at a table in Woodford Police Station with several pieces of paper spread out in front of him. He was thirty nine years old, with thick black hair and brown eyes, a big man well over six feet tall who loved his work in this part of Brackenshire which mainly consisted of dealing with unruly youngsters, quarrels in pubs due to an excess of alcohol, and traffic accidents, often all three at the same time. He was also extremely good at his job, both the locals and his colleagues respected him, it was unusual for there to be any outstanding and unresolved incidents on his crime log.

The crime committed at Williamson Antiques had been so out of the ordinary for his rural beat, and was still unsolved with no leads, it really bothered him that such a major crime could be committed in his area and he didn't know any more than he did eight months ago. He was annoyed that such apparently senseless vandalism had been carried out on an audacious scale right under his nose.

Ian had been the local police constable in Woodford for a number of years, his wife Hannah was a local girl who had been to school with Rebecca Williamson, then Rebecca Martin, and she and Rebecca were on many of the same school and youth committees and associations. According to Hannah at the time of The

Attack, Cliff Williamson had been a straightforward family and businessman, no gossip, no scandal, no black shadows surrounded him. Since the revelation of Cliff's affair with Joanna had been made public, Ian had reviewed the file but still couldn't come up with a link between the two events.

At first everyone, including Ian, had assumed it was a burglary with extra damage caused to cover up the missing item or items; then the finger of suspicion had pointed at Cliff Williamson as an insurance fraud, and even when it became clear the insurance company were taking an enormous step backwards the financial investigators thought it was just a failed attempt at making money illicitly; the stallholders were similarly viewed with suspicion, and Ian had methodically investigated every one of them, which the antiques dealers really hadn't appreciated, but no similar previous offences showed up although at least three of them had needed to sort their financial books out and bring them up to date, with the result that HMRC had received between two and seven years overdue tax payments from them.

It was the first time Williamson Antiques had come to his attention, although he knew Cliff as a local businessman and a regular at The Ship Inn. Neither Cliff nor the dealers or his employees had any history of violence or fraud in their known backgrounds; in fact they all appeared to have been law-abiding citizens contrary to the stereotype of the dodgy antiques dealers Ian had grown up with. Apart from the lax book-keeping the only thing Ian could find was an affair between two of them, and the husband of one of them being attacked in the street, and an assault on one of them in the antiques centre after the vandalism.

Finally Ian had concluded the attack had to be some sort of personal or business vendetta against Cliff, but still he had no hint of a reason why.

As Ian collated all the information, he could see that Joanna Wilde was involved in all of those events except the financial ones, as DS Patty Coxon had deduced a few months earlier, but he was sure there must be more to this, coincidences on this scale did not occur within criminal activities.

But as he studied the local crime information for a bit longer he saw that a portrait miniature belonging to a family who had employed the Woodford firm of solicitors Francis & Sharpe, and more specifically Joanna's husband James Wilde, had turned up at the local flea market which Joanna regularly visited, when the family hadn't even known it was missing. Sarah Handley's visit had resulted in the Barker family's discovery that more items were missing from Swanwick Manor, although when and how they were taken, the family couldn't explain. Ian hadn't been up there, but judging by the report of his colleague DS Patty Coxon the family only lived in a few downstairs rooms, the rest of the ground floor and all of the first and second floors had been uninhabited for several years since Mrs Barker had been reliant on a wheelchair, and even in the years before that Mr and Mrs Barker had only used a small portion of the first floor. The rooms on the second floor hadn't been inhabited for over twenty five years, although they were still home to generations of family paraphernalia stored in various cupboards and drawers and trunks.

PC Ian McClure wondered if the pieces of the jigsaw were finally starting to show themselves, if only he knew if there were one or several missing pieces. He was sure Joanna Wilde was involved, and her husband

James must be too. Maybe this had nothing to do with Cliff Williamson after all. Maybe he was unlucky to have been caught in someone else's argument.

Ian was interrupted by a call for his urgent assistance at yet another traffic accident on the local B2532. Now this was what policing in Woodford was usually all about, attending traffic accidents on the B2532.

While PC McClure was out trying to coordinate the diversions for traffic needing to use one of the main routes out of Woodford due to a tragic five car pile up which had resulted in three fatalities, DS Patty Coxon was concentrating on the Country House Thefts, as they were known, of which the thefts from Swanwick Manor had now become included. They had received a tip-off about a dealer at the Drayton Flea Market who suddenly seemed to have some good quality antique smalls on his stand, where for the last ten years he had been selling mostly furniture with just a few smalls on a card table to one side.

Although such tip-offs usually turn out to be malicious slander, the dealer, Simon Maxwell-Lewis, had already come to her attention and she was aware his selling patterns had also changed from selling his furniture through one regular local auction, to selling boxes of smalls at all four auction houses in Brackenshire in the last few weeks with no obvious change in his buying behaviour.

One of the auction houses involved, Black's Auctions, had flagged up a collection of World War I medals which had been presented to a Corporal William Deacon of the Royal Engineers, which Simon Maxwell-Lewis had put in for the militaria sale in three weeks' time. Rebecca Williamson noticed the name when she was entering their details into the sales catalogue, and after quietly checking with Sarah

257

Handley that Corporal William Deacon was related to Lieutenant Commander George Deacon of the stolen portrait miniature, she had told Paul Black who had in turn contacted PC McClure with the information. Paul was extremely unhappy about the situation, he didn't want his auction house to be used as an antiques laundering facility but he also didn't want every prospective vendor to be put off by thinking their provenances were being scrutinised too closely. His worst nightmare came true when the medals were confirmed as being on the list of missing items from Swanwick Manor, so Patty and her colleagues were almost ready to question Simon about how he came to possess them, but they wanted a bit more information before they tipped him off that they were alert to his activities. She picked up the phone to talk to PC McClure.

Chapter Fifty

Monday 9th November 2015, 10.00am

Cliff Williamson was a happy chap. His business was back on its feet, not to the extent that it had been this time last year, but the customers had returned and he had been able to increase the number of stallholders to eighteen, which included another four of the dealers who had been with him before The Attack.

He still wasn't relaxed that whatever had been started in March was now over, but he had beefed up the security system and now all the windows were fitted with both alarms and bars, and the upstairs and the downstairs spaces were covered by security cameras. The Attack still hung over him like an ever-present dark cloud, but as there didn't seem to have been any further damage to his personal or professional life he carried on re-building his present and his future with determination and enthusiasm. So when PC Ian McClure walked in with a policewoman Cliff's first thought was relief that they must have information about The Attack at last.

'Morning Cliff,' said Ian. 'This is my colleague DS Coxon. She would like a word with you. Can you come over to the Station with us for a chat?'

'Hi Ian, yes of course!' said Cliff, pleased that the police were still interested in the case and hopeful they had some news which might put an end to his fear that his antiques centre would be attacked again and all this would be taken away from him. Again. 'I'll come now. Nicola, you are OK here on your own aren't you? Des will be back soon'.

'Yes of course,' she smiled, thinking along similar lines to Cliff that the police presence could only mean good news. 'Go!'

Once they had walked the two minutes to the Police Station and were all settled down in the interview room, with Ian taking a chair set a little further back than the one Patty sat it, Patty started the interview.

'Mr Williamson, may I call you Cliff?' she asked.

'Yes, yes of course,' said Cliff, feeling a bit apprehensive about her formal tone.

'I understand that you and Mrs Joanna Wilde had an affair of a sexual nature for a number of years, until very recently,' said Patty.

Well of all the things Cliff had thought she was going to ask him, that wasn't one of them. Instantly his mind flashed to the thought that Joanna was pressing charges on Rebecca after all, and he was somehow going to have to pay.

'Yes we did. I think that is common knowledge,' he said looking pointedly at Ian.

'Were you the only person having an affair with her?' Patty asked.

The thought that Joanna might have had someone else on the go hadn't even occurred to him.

'Yes!' he exclaimed confidently, and then 'Yes' less confidently as uncertainty flashed across his face and settled there.

'And is Mrs Wilde the only person you have been having an affair with?'

'Hey what is this? Of course she is! What's going on Ian?' Cliff was seriously rattled and looked to the local policeman for reassurance.

Ian had been trying to concentrate his focus on the floor, but now he was forced to look up and meet Cliff's eyes. He had seen some of the films, and was struggling to look at Cliff without the images of him having sex with Joanna Wilde obscuring his vision. He looked at his superior officer for permission to speak, they had discussed all the various scenarios of how this interview might play out and had agreed on when and what he should say, and Patty nodded that yes, this was one of those opportunities for him to speak up.

'Cliff,' he said gently, 'look, some information has come to light and we need to know a few more details from you. Can you tell us when and where you met up with Joanna?'

'What? Why?' Cliff really didn't want to talk about this. The last few months had given him a chance to see just how shallow and ridiculous the whole thing had been, he couldn't believe he had carried on behaving in that way even throughout his courtship with Rebecca, let alone his marriage! What was he thinking? Twenty years of driving around the country for Fantasy Shagging with Joanna Wilde, he now realised, had left him with little mental, emotional, or even physical energy to fully participate in married life with Rebecca. He couldn't even remember the last time they had made love, and had an awful feeling it was years ago. Oh God, he put his head in his hands.

Patty and Ian waited patiently, Ian was glad of the temporary chance to recover his professional persona.

'Cliff, I know this must be hard' (Oooooh why did she have to choose that word!) 'for you to talk about with us,' Patty leant forward to put her hand on his arm, 'but we really would rather hear this from you than base the rest of our investigation on what we already know.'

Cliff didn't know what was going on, surely jumping around on a bed in various costumes wasn't any of the Police's business?

'What investigation? Why are you investigating my affair with Joanna Wilde?' he asked. 'Has something happened to her? Is she alright?'

Patty realised that either Cliff really was as innocent in the Wilde's fraudulent pornography scheme as he appeared, or he was a much better actor than she had given him credit for. And having seen quite a lot of his 'acting' on film she had a pretty shrewd idea which version of those two choices was sitting on the other side of the desk.

'Cliff, just tell us where and when you and Joanna met to have sex this year.'

Once Cliff started reeling off dates and places of the assignations everyone in the room felt they were on safer ground dealing with facts. As he listed the hotels, Ian ticked them off on the print out he had in the folder he was balancing on his knee. The police already had a full list of where and when the couple had met, this was a technique to ascertain how truthful their suspects were, similar to the one Sarah Handley had developed when starting conversations about family history with the relatives of the subjects in her portrait miniatures. Once Patty was satisfied Cliff was going to cooperate with them she asked him:

'Thanks, Cliff, that's great. Now, could you tell us what you did with the videos?'

This time there was no doubt that Cliff was being honest with them, if he hadn't looked so tragic he would have looked comical as a variety of expressions crossed his face in quick succession. First there was confusion, then annoyance, then curiosity, and as the full truth hit him, horror.

'What bloody video!' he almost shrieked. 'Oh God please don't tell me there is video evidence, what will Rebecca say? No no no no this can't be happening. Oh God all those bloody costumes she made me wear. Those wigs, I never liked that Viking one, it was tricky to keep on while we were, well, you know.' Both Patty and Ian nodded. The Viking series had been particularly, er, entertaining. 'She even gave me bloody lines to learn!' there was no stopping Cliff now. 'I had to brush up on my French, haven't had to speak that since GCSEs, and although Italian was quite fun to learn I never thought anyone else would hear me speak it!'

Ian thought it was interesting that Cliff seemed to be more worried about his acting abilities being on video than his sexual activities.

In a whisper he said 'please tell me, what videos?'

As Patty told him the gist of their investigation, Cliff felt his whole world collapsing again. He had thought that what he and Joanna had been doing all those years had been an entertaining and exciting distraction from their daily lives for *them*. To think that he had been exploited, that Joanna had written those storylines with camera angles and viewers in mind, to think that she had *known* that her husband would see them, that possibly thousands of people would see them, made him want to throw up. As his red face suddenly paled into a greenish-greyish colour Patty instructed Ian to walk Cliff to the Men's toilets quickly. She didn't want him throwing up in their interview room.

Well, she thought after the two men had left, it was unlikely that Cliff had financially benefited, or had even been a willing participant in the sex industry. She picked up the telephone to let her colleagues who were

ready and waiting in Newbury for the next stage of
Operation Cowboy, as they had wittily named it.

Chapter Fifty One

Tuesday 10th November 2015, 12 noon

Peter, Gemma and Suzy were walking through Brackendon Woods, all three kicking up the autumn leaves and relishing the bright if weak sun as it shone high above their heads. It was one of those beautiful November days where the air was chilly enough to mean that coats, hats and scarves were necessary, but the combined presence of the sunshine and their exertions in climbing up the footpath between the trees to the clearing at the top of the hill, meant that by the time they reached the Viewpoint with its welcome benches all three were feeling joyful, and breathless.

The benches were fashioned from wood by members of a local woodworking school, and were lovely to look at and comfy to sit in. They were arranged in a large circle facing outwards, so that anyone who had made the effort to walk up the steep hill could enjoy the far-reaching views which included the sea and the twelfth century Brackendon Castle to the South across green grassy farmland, the pretty villages to the West and East, and the more colourful and varied arable land leading to the chalky downs topped by ancient Droves to the North.

As they sat admiring the view and catching their breath, Peter produced a small box from the inside pocket of his coat. He slid off the bench and onto one knee in front of Gemma. Suzy thought this was great, and attempted to wash his face for him, which rather spoiled the romantic moment but meant that any tension he was feeling evaporated as he laughed whilst trying to push her away, all the time keeping his mouth firmly closed as he had learned that Suzy would French Kiss him given half a chance.

'Sit, Suzy, sit!' laughed Gemma. 'What on earth are you doing Peter, are you OK? Have you got cramp?'

'No, no I'm fine, wait a minute,' he said, as he retrieved the box which had fallen in the mud, and hauled himself back up to his knee, his hands now filthy too. 'OK, excuse the muck' he said, as he held the small red velvet box out to Gemma. 'This wasn't quite how I had planned it!'

He steadied himself, took a deep breath, and looked into her eyes. 'Gemma, we have only known each other for a few months, but that has been long enough for me to see how beautiful, sexy, funny, and intelligent you are, and I have never felt so happy with another person. I finally understand why people refer to their partner as their 'other half', you complete me and I love you with all my heart. I want to spend the rest of my life with you, and I hope you feel the same way about me. Will you please marry me Gemma?'

'Oh!' Gemma clasped her hands to her mouth, her eyes filling with tears. His proposal was a complete surprise to her, the thought of re-marrying had not entered her mind.

Peter shifted nervously on his knee, he could feel the damp seeping up from the ground through his trousers and suspected he would have a large muddy patch where he had been kneeling, but he stayed where he was, still holding the box with the Victorian eighteen carat gold band decorated with a one point six carat rose cut diamond up to Gemma. 'Oh Peter, that was so beautiful, yes, yes I will marry you!'

Gratefully Peter pulled himself back up onto the bench and he and Gemma sat wrapped in each others arms, both crying whilst assuring the other it was the happiest day of their lives. Eventually they pulled apart and found tissues in various pockets, wiped their eyes and blew their noses, before Gemma accepted the now very muddy jewellery box from Peter, and tried the ring on. It fitted perfectly, as it should because Peter had already sized it with another of Gemma's rings.

'Oh, this is perfect,' said Gemma has she held her hand out in front of her, allowing the ring to catch the sunlight. 'I don't want to put my gloves back on and cover it up!'

Chapter Fifty Two

Friday 13th November 2015, 6.30pm

Cliff eventually answered his phone, it had been ringing every five minutes for an hour. It was Paul.

'Coming to the pub mate? We haven't seen you all week!'

'Er, not tonight thanks Paul,' said Cliff in a croaky voice. He realised this was the first conversation he had had with anybody for days, and his voice had become sore through lack of use. He cleared his throat and tried again. 'Can't face anyone. I know you all will have seen me on video by now.'

Cliff had gone home from the police station to the flat above the antiques centre after his interview with DS Coxon and PC McClure, and hadn't come downstairs since. He had left the running of the antiques centre entirely to Nicola, Des and Barry, locking himself in his bedroom so they could still use the kitchen and toilet during working hours.

He had a lot of time to think about how appalling his behaviour had been over the past twenty years, and was still struggling to come to terms with how he had squared it with his conscience and with his self-respect. Well, he certainly didn't have any respect for himself now, and he couldn't imagine how anyone, in particular Rebecca, could have any respect for him ever again.

The one effort he had made was to Skype his children in an effort to explain and to apologise for the humiliation and embarrassment they would have to deal with once the videos became generally available. That was probably the most difficult thing he had ever had to do in his life. Although he knew the fact his face was always covered was something to be grateful for, his voice could clearly be heard and by now everyone locally would know it was him. Simon Maxwell-Lewis had made sure of that.

He spent the rest of the week unable to make the simplest decisions, from what to have for breakfast, to whether or not to answer the phone. In the end he did neither, stayed in bed, his mind alternating between racing over everything that had happened to questioning every detail of his life to blank, numb.

He couldn't bear to speak with Rebecca. He knew he would not be able to cope with the look in her eyes. In the last few months he had realised just how badly he had treated her, how he had ignored her achievements, how little of himself he had given to her, the lack of respect he had afforded to her. Cliff knew she deserved so much more than him, and he was feeling terrible about his behaviour. He couldn't imagine a time when he could be in the same room as her and apologise for what he had put her through, but he hoped he would find the courage one day.

Just not today.

'Oh come on Cliff, you can't stay holed up in your flat for ever! Come on, come and have a pint. Rebecca and Louise are here, you can sit with us, with your back to the door if you want, come on, just one drink then I promise I will leave you alone.'

'No, sorry, I really can't face Rebecca. I feel terrible for what I have done to her, and I am just not ready to see anyone else either. The thought of all the locals turning to look at me as I walk up the High Street. I certainly won't make it through the pub's door unscathed. No, all that sniggering and commenting. Sorry. I am just too ashamed, I can't do it. Thanks for thinking of me though, mate.'

'Cliff, if you don't come to the pub right now we are going to come and get you, there will be more of a scene outside in the street than a few sniggers and ribald comments inside the pub! I am telling you now, come up here and you will be amongst friends. Now get your arse in gear, we've all seen it in action so it's nothing we haven't seen before, and I expect to see you walk through that door in less than two minutes or there will be a riot in the High Street! Understand?'

Cliff grinned. Trust Paul to be brutal about it. Yes, he was right, everyone had seen the worst they could possibly see. His children and Rebecca had been up and about and walking around for the last five days, the least he could do was walk up the High Street and into the pub, where, as Paul so eloquently put it, everyone had seen it all before. He needed to start again. With everybody. He had to learn how to be Cliff Williamson, because the old Cliff was someone he didn't understand and he certainly didn't like. Despite his actions it was apparent that he still had friends, and he had family, and it was time he started to earn the love and the trust they placed with him.

But how? Cliff didn't think he had the confidence or the energy to go and wash himself and clean his teeth, let alone get dressed, leave the building, and walk up the High Street.

'Cliff!' Paul was worried about his friend, and, as this was the first time he had answered the phone all week he didn't want to lose the connection. 'Cliff, we are leaving now! Tea and sympathy will be making its way down the High Street in the next few minutes! Although the tea will probably have been spilt and any cake that was on offer will have been eaten by the time I get there mate. What would you rather, we turn up and see you in your pitiful state, or you come here with your head held high? You could always come in fancy dress, although on second thoughts probably best not to. Everybody would recognise you in costume.'

Cliff laughed, and it felt as though it was the first time he had ever properly laughed.

'OK! OK! One pint. Although I haven't eaten for a few days so a cuppa and some cake may be a better choice. Thank you, Paul. But I do have to clean up first, I have been stinking in my pit all week, I really can't come out like this. Please don't send the tea cosy mob down. I'll be in and out the shower, and in the pub in less than thirty minutes I promise, OK?'

Paul breathed a sigh of relief, he had gone to a lot of effort to organise this evening, and he needed the guest of honour to turn up. 'Alright mate, thirty minutes and not a second longer!' he warned.

Twenty-seven minutes later Cliff tried to creep into the pub, but they had a lookout on the door and everyone was ready for him. Every single one of the Regulars had come dressed up, either as a fireman, a policeman, a fisherman or one of the other characters Cliff had been coerced into playing over the years, although in contrast to his costumes they were all modestly covered. Paul was proudly wearing a painter and decorator's outfit, Mike and Sarah were standing behind the bar wearing matching sailor uniforms, Tony and his wife Lesley were wearing what looked like scarecrow costumes but Cliff guessed they were meant to be farmers, Gemma and Lisa were dressed as

271

milkmen, and even Rebecca was there, dressed up as a cowboy complete with red hairy chest and red hairy buttocks.

A big cheer went up, and soon Cliff was surrounded by jokes and laughter, with pints lining up on the bar for him and more paid for and waiting to be pulled, although Paul had told the assembled gathering about Cliff's own description of his last few days so Mike had produced a plate of sandwiches and a pot of tea, and was going to be keeping an eye on Cliff's alcohol consumption so that he wasn't ill.

Cliff was overwhelmed by the good will being extended towards him. Looking around at all his friends he realised he was lucky to have been forgiven for all the pain and misery that had been brought on several of these people as a result of his years of deceit, and was grateful for their clumsy but effective effort at Therapy.

It was too early for him to make any decisions about his future here in Woodford, but for possibly the first time in his life he was happy to be himself, and find out where that took him. He made a secret promise to them, and to himself, that from now on he would start to live for today, be considerate of the needs and feelings of those around him, and let tomorrow take care of itself.

EPILOGUE

Once Patty had given them the go-ahead the Newbury police moved quickly. James Wilde was charged with illegal earnings and failure to pay monies owed to the Inland Revenue and Her Majesty's Revenue and Customs service for the sale of the porn films, because despite his efforts to disguise the source of the films and the receipt of the money, once the police caught up with him his original film distributor gave them all the evidence they needed to proceed.

Unfortunately because Cliff's face was always disguised and because the purpose of publishing the films was not to humiliate him, the Crown Prosecution Service did not believe they could build a case under the UK's non-consensual pornography laws, but Cliff's lawyer was confident she would find a way to present a case against James to financially compensate Cliff both for the humiliation he and his family were having to deal with somehow, and if nothing else, for his share of the profits. Cliff wanted the whole thing to go away, he had the opportunity to watch the films but after the first few minutes of the first one he was so horrified at the details recorded and how clearly he could recognise himself, that he had declined to watch any more.

But most of all he was devastated that something he had believed to be an intimate entertainment between himself and Joanna had been a cold-hearted financial operation, about which she knew everything, and had colluded with her own husband to produce. His view of the last twenty years had been destroyed, Joanna and James Wilde's actions had shaken Cliff's memories and beliefs of everything to do with how he and Rebecca had met, how the business of his antiques centre had been built up, and at the heart of it all, exactly what his relationships with those closest to him really were. He could never trust anyone again, in whatever guise they came into his life. The Wildes' actions of calculating and intertwining his sexual, business and family life, while all the time Cliff believed that either he or fate was in control, shattered his self-belief.

The Police were still trying to build a case against James for the Country House Thefts as there was no evidence against him. Other than the word of Simon Maxwell-Lewis, who had a massive grudge against him, everything else was circumstantial. James Wilde knew the Law well, and had calculated every angle so that he appeared to be innocent of everything Simon accused him of. It was frustrating for the police who were determined not to give up, there must be *something* they could charge him with in relation to these thefts, and he was the mastermind behind them.

Joanna Wilde had no charges against her, despite featuring in every one of the videos her husband had been charged with selling and profiting from, there was no evidence she had either earned any money from them, or had been involved in the editing or distribution of them. Although her lifestyle demonstrated she had clearly benefited from them financially, her antiques business could account for every penny that went into and out of her bank accounts. While her husband was a legal wizard, Joanna was a clever business woman, and had covered her tracks at every turn. Despite his loathing of the woman who only a few months before he had been declaring undying love to, in his evidence for the Country House Thefts Simon Maxwell-Lewis had left Joanna's name out of every statement. This meant that, as with her husband, again the police and the CPS were extremely challenged with trying to connect her in any way to them, even though they knew she was the one who assessed and selected the antiques James discovered on his legitimate visits to the houses, and she was the one who passed them on through her links to the antiques trade. But knowing isn't enough, they needed evidence, proof, confessions. They had nothing.

Yet.

Cliff Williamson had no charges against him, he had done nothing illegal that the police were aware of. He was the victim in the sex films crimes, although without a prosecution it would be difficult for him to receive victim support through the criminal justice system, and would need to source it for himself. But at that time he was powerless to make such a big effort, and no one else, not even Rebecca, Paul, or his own parents, knew how he was feeling because he couldn't talk to any of them about it. He was paralysed with misery. His lawyer had advised him about sources of support, but Cliff was incapable of acting on her advice, he was in deep shock.

If any of the stolen antiques had been sold through his antiques centre he had no knowledge of them, and there was no proof that Joanna or Simon had sold them from Williamson Antiques. DS Patty Coxon and PC Ian McClure both thought it extremely unlikely that any of the stolen items had been sold anywhere near Brackenshire, until Simon's illegal trade routes had been cut off when James and Joanna withdrew their support from him, and they were liaising with their colleagues in Counties further North where they knew Joanna and Cliff had been meeting in the hotel rooms.

Simon Maxwell-Lewis had incriminated himself in his desperate attempt to lay the blame on James and Joanna Wilde for the sex films. Simon had the shock of his life when he had viewed Cliff and Joanna on the bed in her hotel room, not just because the Love of his Life was engaged in adultery when she wouldn't even give him a chaste kiss on the cheek, but because the Wild Times Cowboy series had been one of his favourites, ever since he discovered the Wild Times films fifteen years ago. He had no idea it was Joanna and Cliff, even though he had watched and re-watched those films over and over again.

His role in the thefts and in the assault on both James and the attack on the stock in Cliff's antiques centre was clearly spelt out as he spewed his venom about both men during the police interviews. His mixed-up feelings for Joanna, and hatred for the other two men in her life had skewed his perception of reality.

His mother was devastated.

If you enjoyed The Limner's Art and would like to know what happens next to the people in Woodford, then here is the first chapter of Book 2 in the Woodford Mystery series, by Kathy Morgan

THE BRONZE LADY

Chapter 1

Thursday 19ᵗʰ November 2015, 9.00pm

The town of Woodford is situated on a hill in the county of Brackenshire in the south west of England, and overlooks a number of villages to the west and the east, but the town was enveloped in freezing fog that November evening so nobody could see further than a few yards in front of them. The weather was even preventing the light of the half-moon from penetrating the darkness of the evening. The exterior lights of the local public house, The Ship Inn at the top of the high street, shone strongly through the gloom, providing a welcoming invitation for locals and visitors alike.

This evening was busy as usual for the landlords Mike and Sarah Handley, who had bought the freehold to the pub ten years earlier and established a comfortable environment with excellent food. By nine o'clock most of the meals had been eaten, and the drinkers were long gone, so there were probably only about a dozen customers left in the pub, scattered throughout its various rooms. The atmosphere in one corner of the bar was at odds with rest of the pub, and was more in harmony with the outside temperature because it had been distinctly chilly all evening, and even the brightly burning log fire could not permeate the heavy pressure of an unresolved disagreement between the friends who were sat around one of the tables. Paul Black and Tony Cookson were barely speaking to each other, but neither would tell the third member of their group, Cliff Williamson, what the discord was all about.

Instead they were either morosely looking into their pints, or staring off into the distance; neither one was prepared to make light-hearted chit-chat with the other. Cliff Williamson was in need of his friends at the moment after a trying few months in which he had come very close to losing his business, had destroyed his marriage and ruptured his comfortable family life. He had lost the respect of many family members, friends and work colleagues. As well as being friends, all three men worked in the local antiques trade, and so Cliff felt that Paul and Tony's support was crucial if he was to climb up to his former position of prominent local business person. In the past week he had begun to venture back out into the local community after a self-enforced period of withdrawal, and tonight he was upset that his friends, who had been such strong providers of help to him, were clearly at odds with each other and not enjoying a pleasant evening of their usual banter over a couple of pints. Cliff was keen to try to return to his familiar social life as quickly as possible, and wanted to give back some of the goodwill and support to them, so decided it was up to him to be the grown-up and make them sort out whatever the problem was between them.

'Right, come on then you two, you are not in the playground now, we all grew out of this kind of behaviour thirty or forty years ago! On the contrary you are meant to be helping me get my life back on track but neither of you has said a word all evening. What is going on?'

'Sorry mate,' said Paul, snapping out of his inner-fury. 'You are right, we should be thinking of you. We have had a disagreement over something, but it's nothing, and it's over. Isn't that right Tony?' Cliff noticed the slight pleading tone in Paul's question.

'Oh, er, yes that's right. Just a silly tiff between us; a stupid mis-understanding. Paul got the wrong idea about something, that's all. I am sure he can see things clearly now and realises the error of his ways.'

Cliff noticed Paul bristle at Tony's choice of words, and sighed. Whatever their problem was it wouldn't be resolved if Tony was going to start baiting Paul.

'Hey, this has nothing to do with me, don't you blame me for all this. I wouldn't call it silly or stupid,' Paul said with a flash of anger. 'It is looking fairly serious from my side of the table.'

'Yes, and from my side,' Tony's temper was rising too and Cliff wondered if they were going to start punching each other. Neither of his friends were inclined to resort to fisticuffs over anything, but the aggression in the air was palpable. He regretted pushing them.

'Everything OK over there lads?' Mike Handley, the landlord of The Ship Inn, called over from behind the bar. He had noticed something was amiss with the group earlier in the evening and was keeping an eye on them. He had seen the look on Paul's face and then Tony's response to it and decided to intervene by making them focus on him, rather than putting himself at risk by walking over and standing between them.

'Alright alright, calm down,' Cliff hissed at them. 'We're fine thanks Mike,' he called over, before turning back to his friends who were now sitting looking slightly shame-faced at being caught posturing like two angry cockerels. He decided to try one last time, now that they knew other people were watching them. 'Just tell me what has happened? I may be able to help.'

'No, Paul's right, it's nothing. Who wants another pint?' said Tony, convincing nobody.

281

'Oh nothing for me thanks Tony,' said Cliff as he also stood up. 'My body hasn't quite got back into the swing of long sessions in the pub. If you two aren't going to come clean about your tiff then I had better be heading for home or I'll never get up in the morning. Three pints in an evening is plenty and I can already feel the negative effects!'

'Oh, I'll walk back with you,' offered Tony. 'Somebody had better make sure you get back safely now you have turned into a lightweight.' His teasing went a little way to breaking up the tension, as they all laughed at the thought of the tall, fit, well-built Cliff Williamson being unable to hold his drink.

'Oi I'm not that bad! Anyway, I live in the opposite direction to your house, your wife will be waiting for you.'

'No, come on, the walk will do me good, and Lesley isn't expecting me home any time soon. She is working late tonight, and I made a chicken casserole earlier today for her to eat when she came in so she won't be waiting for me. In fact knowing Lesley she will be curled up on the sofa watching some drama, and not missing my 'helpful' comments about the flimsiness of the storyline at all. I'll walk down with you, and then probably make my way home from there. I have been stuck indoors all day, and think I need the exercise. Come on Williamson, get your coat, you've pulled!'

As the two men left the pub laughing, Mike Handley said quietly to Paul 'Are you alright Paul? You have been looking out of sorts all evening.'

Paul sighed and wondered how much to reveal to Mike. He knew Mike could be trusted not to betray a confidence, but after a few seconds of internal debate decided this was too risky to share. 'Yes I'm fine thanks Mike; I just have a complicated situation to sort out. Nothing for anybody else to worry about, but I have let it drag on too long. Time to put an end to this thing once and for all.'

If Paul had known then what it would take to resolve his differences with Tony, he would have confided in Mike Handley while he had the chance.

Thank you for reading *The Limner's Art*, I do hope you enjoyed it! If so please leave a review on Amazon or Goodreads, or with your favourite retailer.

For more information about me join us on the Kathy Morgan Facebook page and @KathyM2016 on twitter.

Thanks again,

Kathy

Printed in Great Britain
by Amazon